THE
UNICORN
IN THE
MIRROR

THE
UNICORN
IN THE
MIRROR

A
JOHN SINGER SARGENT/VIOLET PAGET
MYSTERY

MARY F. BURNS

ISBN: 9798636930693

Printed in the United States of America

Text Font: Garamond
Titles Font: Perpetua Titling

John Singer Sargent, c. 1880

Born January 12, 1856 to American parents living in Florence, Italy, Sargent became the most sought-after portrait painter in Europe and America from the early 1880's to his death in 1925. He produced some 900 oil paintings and 2,000 watercolors, which was his preferred medium.

Violet Paget, aka Vernon Lee, painting by Sargent, 1881

Born October 14, 1856, Violet was Welsh-English, and like the Sargent family, hers travelled throughout Europe and Great Britain, keeping company with artists, writers, intellectuals, and many socially prominent people. She was a prolific writer, and she and John Sargent were close friends from childhood—they met when they were 10 years old, in Rome. Violet died in 1935 at her villa near Florence, called Il Palmerino.

The Unicorn

On the green hill, under the thorn tree,
    the unicorn stood like a frozen wave.
Lightning played about its horn,
    its hooves danced on grass.
I stood at the hill's foot,
    watched the moon slide out of sight.
Through narrowed eyes I watched the beast:
    archetype and symbol under a dark sky.
We each knew the other's strengths and
    weaknesses, and the knowledge held us fast.
Then, for a heartbeat, poet and beast were fused,
    man-unicorn, white maned and horned.
Then each was back in his own flesh,
    having borrowed something of the other.
In silence I turned away.
The hill trembled to the beat of
    soundless hooves.

From *The Song of Taliesin*,
ancient Welsh bard and mage

"There is but one truth in art, and that is beauty; there is but one moral truth, and that is goodness; there is but one truth in the political arena, and that is justice." —*George Sand*

❧ PARIS –APRIL, 1881 ❧

The shadowy figure slipped into a doorway as the jauntily dressed young man paused for a moment at the corner, looking up and down, as if wondering whether to go home or…the soft Spring air of Paris was so appealing, so fresh, why not stay out all night? One of several churches along the *boulevard St. Germain* pealed the hour—one, two—not so very late for a young man on the town.

The shadow ground its teeth, thinking of how the young man had already spent the evening—at a café with friends his own age and older, most of them gentlemen, and artists or actors or writers as well—all of them drinking and eating, arguing their shallow ideas of Art and Beauty and Truth. Such nonsense! The shadow had watched them in growing disgust and condemnation.

The young man moved on, and the shadow silently followed.

The *Café des Deux Magots* was, of course, still open—uproariously so—lights and music spilling out the doors and windows; the patrons—mostly men, but some quite colorfully dressed women also, dancing or lounging about—and all of them drinking with abandon. The young man hesitated at the entrance, his blond curls peeking out from under a high hat, his lithe form carefully dressed in the blackest of black trousers and jacket, and the whitest of white shirts, a lavender carnation in his button hole—and then a smile broke upon his smooth face, his turquoise-blue eyes brightened! A friend called to him from inside the café, and then two young men came sauntering out to greet him and usher him in, with a glass of champagne and a kiss on the cheek.

The shadow felt the bile rise in its throat. It had seen enough. Leaving the young men and women to their questionable entertainments, the shadow moved away from the music and the lights, back into the darkness.

✠ PART ONE ✠

ʚ ONE ɞ

"WAIT, WAIT! PLEASE COMPOSE YOURSELF, my dear Emily!"
I pressed my hands firmly on Emily Sargent's own pale fingers to keep them from fluttering about so—her nervous excitement was communicating itself quite forcefully to me and, I could see, to her younger sister Violet who sat nearby, eyes wide and shining.

"Take a deep breath, now, that's it," I said, releasing her hands so I could catch up the teapot and pour some of the soothing liquid into her cup. Handing it to her, I commanded her to drink it, which she did. Emily is one of the most obliging of human beings I know, and it's often difficult—except that I truly love her as the sister I never had—to keep from making her do things just because I know she will instantly comply.

And that says a lot more about me than it does about her, I imagine.

"So, now, tell me again about this tapestry," I said, sipping at my own cup of tea. Little Violet, still in short dresses at the tender age of eleven, sat next to me on the comfortable yellow satin sofa in Mrs. Sargent's drawing room in their lodgings in the 8th *arrondissement*—John having become sufficiently famous and in demand for portraits in recent months as to be able to afford quite respectable digs for himself and his people.

"Oh," said Emily, her eyes bright at the mere thought of it. "Oh, it is the most beautiful, mysterious, astounding tapestry I have ever seen!"

"There's a Lion holding a banner!" Young Violet spoke up, her round little face eager to tell the story of these wonders. "And so many little animals! Rabbits, and foxes, and dogs…and flowers!"

Emily smiled at her little sister. "You leave out the most fantastic of all creatures, dearest—the Unicorn!" The two nodded knowingly to each other and sighed with the deepest satisfaction. Despite the thirteen years' difference in their ages, they were close friends—I felt a moment's envy, thinking of my only sibling, an older poet-brother who thought of nothing and no one but himself, his various *malaises*, and his poetry.

"Indeed!" I said, setting down my cup, and looking over the pastries on the tray to see which one I would taste next, as a fragment of verse came to mind. "*On the green hill, under the thorn tree,*" I quoted, "*The unicorn stood like a frozen wave.*"

"Where is that from?" Emily said eagerly. "What a beautiful image!"

"The Welsh bard Taliesin," I said, and gave a sly grin. "My kinsman, I'll have you know."

"Really? Truly?" Little Violet clutched my arm. "He was King Arthur's prophet and singer, was he not?"

"Well, someone's been studying her *Idylls of the King!*" I nodded approvingly.

"And is he really your ancestor?"

"According to my mother, yes," I said, realizing I was only *stretching* the truth, not actually breaking it. But no matter. "Where do you think I get *my* prophetic powers?"

"You! A prophet?" A strong male voice broke in upon our feminine tea party. I looked up to see John standing at the door of the room. He strode in, kissed Emily on the top of her head as he bent toward her from behind her chair, then straightened up and nodded companionably to me and Violet. "Then tell me, prophet, what do you think we will all be doing tonight?"

"Ah, nothing could be more clear!" I cried. I closed my eyes, put my hand to my forehead, and spoke in sepulchral tones. "We are going to the theatre, to see a play—in fact, a comedy!—produced by and featuring your great friend, *monsieur* Pailleron, *n'est-ce-pas?*" I opened my eyes and looked at him with great confidence.

"How on earth…why, yes, Vi, that's it exactly!" John looked as astonished as his sisters. I laughed and took pity on them.

"I see a set of tickets poking out of your pocket," I said, pointing to his jacket. "And, having already perused the theatre bills for this evening, I put together my knowledge of your friends and your predilections with the only play currently running that would be of interest to you, and *voila!*"

"Vi, old man, you are amazing," he said to me, and grinned as his little sister jumped off the sofa and ran to put her arms around him in gleeful gratitude.

"So," John said, lifting his sister in his arms and then pretending to stagger under her weight, "what have you all been discussing that includes a reference to prophesying?"

"Oh," said Emily, "the prophet in question is neither here nor there! What the primary subject of our conversation has been is much more unique—in short, unicorns."

John looked more than a little puzzled, but seemed also to be privately amused. He said nothing, however, and slid onto the sofa next to me, settling his sister in his lap and eyeing the pastries on the tea table in front of him.

"I was about to be informed of the appearance of this marvelous mythical beast," I told him, "when you so rudely interrupted." He grinned and reached for a lemon tart.

We both looked at Emily to continue her story.

"You know how interested I have always been in medieval tapestries," she began, and we nodded acquiescence. "And, what you may *not* know, is that I have had the good fortune to be acquainted with the director of the *Musée de Cluny*—*monsieur* Edmond Du Sommerard."

"Goodness," I said, "is Du Sommerard still there? He's been the museum's director since it was established, what was it, 1843?"

"Oh, no, dear Violet," Emily said, "That was Alexandre Du Sommerard *père!* Upon his death, the Hôtel Cluny, with all of his antique collections, was given to France for the purpose of a museum. The current director is his son, Edmond." She returned to her tale.

"*Monsieur* Du Sommerard has been involved for some time now in trying to preserve and acquire a set of tapestries that are currently in the Chateau Boussac, down in central France, you know, in Berry?" Both John and I nodded acknowledgement of familiarity with the general area. "He has told me they have a long and terribly mysterious history," Emily continued, "and he believes he is on the verge of convincing the Boussac town council to allow them to be transferred to the *Musée de Cluny* here."

"But how can you have seen them," I interrupted her, "if they are all at the Chateau Boussac?"

Emily's smile was just a bit smug. "Because *monsieur* Du Sommerard has persuaded the town council to allow one of the tapestries to come to Paris for a trial restoration and research—so that they may see how gloriously they can all be restored, and how their rightful place is here, in Paris, where all the world can enjoy them."

"And you have been to see this one?" I said, and, turning to the little girl next to me and giving her a kiss on her forehead, "and you, too, *ma chérie,* you have seen this marvel of the weavers' trade?" She nodded eagerly, but allowed her sister to answer.

"We saw it yesterday, at the *Musée,*" Emily said, her eyes shining with remembered delight. "And the *directeur* has said we can come back any time, and look at it again."

Little Violet piped up, in that perturbing way that innocent children have. "And we should so like to see *monsieur* Du Sommerard's handsome assistant, again, shouldn't we, Emily?" She turned to her sister. "What was his name?"

Emily blushed as she stammered a reply. I observed, and thought to myself, well, here is a something or a nothing for dear Emily!

"I am not sure, I don't think I recall," she was murmuring, her face pink from confusion.

"I should definitely like to see it," John interrupted hastily. "I'm always awake to finding inspiration in other expressions of art—haven't looked into tapestries much, so that might be a lark. How old does he think they are, Du Sommerard?"

"Oh, he believes they were woven some time around the year 1500," Emily said, recovering herself somewhat with the change of subject. She mused a moment. "The one we saw depicted a beautiful woman, seated, with a unicorn who had drawn near to place its front feet in her lap, whilst a Lion stood apart, watching." She paused again. "The woman held a mirror, into which the Unicorn looked to see its reflection."

"On the cusp of the Renaissance," I said, mostly to myself; then seeing that I had caught the attention of my companions, I continued. "That was a time, 1500—much like ours now—when an older way of life was passing away, and something new was stirring in the very air—medieval super-stitions and habits were beginning to give way to the siren song of science and logical thought—the individual man or woman began to think of his or her *mind* instead of a *soul*—that they might be persons in their own right, not just a serv-ant of a far away, hierarchical God."

"Goodness, Vi," said Emily, looking slightly shocked. "I hadn't the faintest notion of any such ideas when I looked at the tapestry. Perhaps you should come see it for yourself, too. I would dearly love to hear your assessment of it."

A premonition shivered its way across my heart. A uni-corn looking into a mirror, seeing its reflection—why did that image bring with it more than a touch of danger? I brushed aside the thought as an idle fancy, and re-joined the conversation.

"I would dearly love to give my assessment, Emily," I said, "and as I'm only here in Paris for a week, I say the sooner, the better! What say you to traipsing over to the *musée* this afternoon?"

Little Violet clapped her hands in delight, and Emily beamed at my enthusiasm, but spoke her dismay at my short sojourn in Paris.

"You are so much the constant traveller, Violet," she said. "Where are you off to next?"

I smiled, exulting inside myself at my pleased anticipa-tion. "I believe you may know Mary Robinson?" I said, and continued when she nodded eagerly. "She and I have taken a little cottage outside of London, for a week or so, where we will work away, writing and reading and enjoying each other's company—a kind of writing retreat to encourage the Muse for each of us." I felt a glow in my heart just thinking about it.

"Why, that sounds perfectly lovely!" Emily exclaimed. "Then we should indeed make haste to see the tapestry. And

John?" she said, looking over at her brother. "Are you free this afternoon to join us?"

John nodded a gracious *yes*, and it was settled. We were to go and see for ourselves the mythical Lady and her Unicorn.

TWO

OCTOBER 1661 – LYONS, FRANCE
At the Chateau d'Arcy

MADELEINE GAZED AT HER REFLECTION in the rippled mirror, framed in golden leaves and small polished ovals of porphyry—what she saw there did not displease her: thick coils of chestnut hair, smooth, lightly tanned skin—perhaps she should be paler, she thought, given the fashions of the court these days, but she knew she didn't really care. She reached out a hand to touch her mirrored cheek, and realized that she still wore her wedding ring, Jean's gift to her at the ceremony of their marriage, twenty-five years ago. Today, she knew, she must take it off and put it aside—for a new ring.

She rose, restless, and walked about the room—not *her* room, at home, but the one given over to her use during this time of planning and preparation, not just for her own wedding, but for her son's as well—mother and son were to marry father and daughter: two ancient, noble families merging, two generations tying the knot on the same day. Shy little Jeanne, and her own beloved François—if they were not actually in love, they would be soon, Madeleine felt sure, and it gave her comfort.

But she and Geoffroi? A *frisson* of desire set her still-slim body afire, and she closed her eyes in anticipation of the wedding night. Her husband-to-be was only a few years older than herself—strong, vibrant, powerful, a force to be reckoned with. In truth, it was more lust than love, at this point. But it was a politic match, as well. Her wealth and his influence were a potent combination—and they were both ambitious. The times were precarious for the nobility—Louis *le Roi Soleil,* though still a relatively untried youth of twenty—was testing his strength in subtle and not-so-subtle ways. Prudence was called for, and diplomacy, with a touch of audacity. Madeleine was good at all three.

She raised her hands, began twisting the heavy gold and ruby ring that adorned her finger, and gently pulling it off, she walked over to the dressing table where her casket of jewels sat, lid open, awaiting the token of her past life.

It was time to begin anew.

⟫ Three ⟪

WE STOOD ON THE COBBLED STONES in an ancient court-yard, facing a faded red wooden door under a Gothic door-way set into the rounded façade of a tower. My senses were all alert to witness the meeting of the "handsome assistant" to monsieur du Sommerard and my dear friend Emily, and I was immensely gratified that the young man himself opened the door to us, soon after we had rung the bell.

"*Bienvenue, mademoiselle* Sargent," said he, and I noted with approval that he was indeed handsome, though slightly built—fair-haired, smooth-faced with no hint of beard or moustache, with animated features and bewitching blue eyes, almost turquoise in their intensity. "I just received your note, and am delighted you have returned to the musée." His voice was low and musical, with a hint of an accent that iden-tified him as not Parisian.

"*Monsieur* Bayard," Emily said shyly. So she *did* remem-ber his name after all, I thought, but I kept my smiles to myself.

He greeted Violet Sargent as already a good friend, and then stood at attention to be introduced to myself and to John. His reaction was, while not unexpected, flattering—for John.

"*Monsieur* Sargent!" he exclaimed, reaching out a hand to shake John's—very unlike a Frenchman, I thought, but perhaps he knew that John was an American? Even so, he clicked his heels together and bowed slightly, after the handshake. "Sébastien Bayard, *à votre service.*" His smile was luminous as he gazed up at John, who, at his great height of over six feet, towered over the young man. "I have just returned from the Salon and have seen your most remarkable paintings of *madame et monsieur Pailleron*—most remarkable! But the other—Madame Subercaseaux! She is magnificent—the arrangement, the black and white of her dress, the touches of bright red—*brillante!*"

John disclaimed the praise with his usual humble demurs, and then Emily introduced me—but although the young man was polite, he was clearly overpowered by the presence of our renowned artist, and returned his attention to John forthwith. The two gentlemen conversed in rapid French, half-sentences at times, as if already well-acquainted, as we made our way inside the ancient stone building.

He walked us through a rather small entranceway, not the main door; through an archway as we passed I caught a glimpse of a somberly-dressed woman seated at a table in the vestibule, her head bent over some paperwork. The interior of the *musée* was cold despite the warm day outside, and I shivered and drew my cloak more closely about me. Our handsome young guide gestured for us to follow him up a narrow, winding staircase, whose stone steps were worn and hollowed from centuries of use. I recalled the last time I had ascended such a staircase, in company with John and Lord James Parke, all of us in hot pursuit of a thief and a murderer (a story I have previously set forth under the title of *The Spoils of Avalon*). I glanced at John, but he was too engaged in conversation with our young host to be musing over times past. I stepped back to allow little Violet to mount the stairs ahead of me, to make sure she didn't trip on the uneven steps.

We emerged through a grey stone doorway, carved with *fleur-de-lis* along the framing, into a long, high-ceilinged gallery, with mullioned windows along one side, facing north and opening onto what was probably a cloistered courtyard—I could see the tops of small trees in a square pattern. The wooden floors rippled across the expanse of the gallery in typical French herring-bone pattern, and there were several glass-topped curio tables set up in two long rows down the room. Even before *monsieur* Bayard spoke, my attention was caught by the antique items in the cabinet nearest our entry. I bent over to examine them more closely. The brilliant sunshine of the late Spring day illuminated the room by reflection from the high walls across the courtyard. I noted that there were few actual lamps in the room, so that it would be quite dim on a cloudy day, or in the Winter.

"These are some of the first *objets* that *monsieur* du Sommerard *père* collected, found buried in a field near where an old monastery had stood, but was destroyed in the Revolution," *monsieur* Bayard explained. He opened the glass case gently, but his hand hovered over the pieces, as if in warning that we were not to touch.

One statuette in particular arrested my eye—a tiny, white carving of a unicorn rising on its hind legs, pawing the air, its spiraled horn raised high in defiance or jubilation, perhaps. I turned to point it out to my little namesake.

"Look, Violet," I said, drawing her near. "Yet another unicorn, *n'est-ce pas?*"

"*Oui*," she breathed. "This is a magical place."

"We believe it was part of a chess set," the young man continued, carefully closing the glass lid once more. "Other pieces, similarly crafted from the same kind of ivory, were also found at the same time, but many were badly damaged—there is a lion, and some woodland animals, even birds and pieces of fruit. *Monsieur* du Sommerard *fils* has hopes of recovering a whole set someday."

He smiled, and led us away down the room to another door, nearly concealed in the old wood of the far wall. He touched a small panel to the right, and the door clicked and popped open, swinging away from us, inward to the next room. I looked carefully as we entered through this door— the hinges were on the inside, as I had thought, the better to conceal the door from the public room where inquisitive visitors might find it.

"A workshop!" John exclaimed, looking around curiously, his artist's senses all alive. "The light in here is marvelous!" The room had the same high ceilings as the previous one, but the windows were plain glass, allowing for a soft, indirect northern light. John went immediately to view more closely a couple of paintings, clearly being worked on and cleaned, that sat on easels near the windows. Both were rather small and dark, Flemish I thought, or German, and not of great interest to me. The rest of the workshop held scattered implements, paintbrushes, pots of congealing liquid, and piled in one corner, strange artifacts I took to be items of medieval armory and weapons—a large wooden crossbow, an ancient leather quiver filled with arrows, a collection of axe heads, *sans* handles, and a battered metal shield, embossed with stars. Slightly behind the small paintings was what appeared to be a much larger one, some five or so feet high and three feet across, but it was covered with a white sheet. John, his artist's prerogative overtaking his manners, in my view, unceremoniously threw off the covering and stood back to examine the painting.

As I drew near as well, I could see it was a religious subject, depicting a young man, naked but for a cloth around his middle, loosely tied to a tree and pierced by arrows—two in his left arm, and two more in his abdomen on the left side, as if all coming from the same direction; and the fifth arrow, as if shot from the right, embedded in his chest, just about where his lungs might be, if I remembered my secret anatomy lessons. There was a surprisingly small amount of blood, I thought, given all those arrows.

"It's very brown and rather muddy looking," I said. "And it looks somewhat unfinished." I gestured to the backgrounding for the figure, where large swatches of bare canvas abounded on the edges of the painting, and the figure's feet were mere blurs of light paint.

"Muddy!" John challenged me, and pointing to the loincloth and the legs of the painting's subject, he spoke with great excitement, and for him, at some length, about the colors. Our conversation caught the attention of Sébastien Bayard, who hurried over to us with a look of alarm.

"This is very much in the style of Titian," John was saying as Bayard drew nearer. "You can see that the paint is applied directly onto the canvas, layer upon layer, combined, mixed right there, in the midst of creation, as Titian was wont to do—as do I, and others who follow Carolus Duran's tutelage." He spoke of his *maître d'art* with solemn respect; it was a mere two years since John had left the *atelier* of the noted Parisian portraitist. He stepped back, the better to view the whole painting, and his eyes widened as he took it in.

"*Is* it Titian?" he demanded of our young host. "I could swear it is, at the least, a product of his workshop!"

Bayard nodded briefly, casting a look about him, as if to see that no one else could hear, and at the same time, he gathered up the white sheet and arranged it over the painting again, hiding it from view. "We believe, that is, *monsieur* du Sommerard believes, that if not actually the long-missing St.

Sebastian reportedly painted by Titian, it is surely a copy or an early version of it, by him or someone in his employ, following his direction."

"It is exceedingly distressing," Emily spoke up, and stepped in front of her little sister, who had drawn closer and had been curiously taking in the arrows and the trickles of blood on the sainted youth's ivory flesh. "Reading about the martyrdom of a saint is one thing, but to have it depicted so realistically…" She trailed off, suddenly uncertain, I think, that her strong opinion might be deemed impolite.

"Oh, *mademoiselle* Sargent," Bayard intervened, taking her arm and little Violet's, and leading them away. "You will be reassured to know that this saint did not, after all, die of these wounds by the arrows; no, no, no, the blessed Irene came along and healed him, and he lived to be a saint a while longer."

John and I exchanged amused glances. "We'll have to read up on the *Lives of the Saints*," I murmured, as we started to join our friends on the other side of the room, "to find out how this poor Sebastian ultimately died."

"Il a été matraqué à mort." A low voice spoke up, nearly at my elbow, causing me to start with surprise. From behind a large, tall wardrobe that stood directly next to the painting, a young woman, very slenderly built, stepped out. Her clothes were dark, amorphous in shape; blending textures and fabrics into a kind of medieval cloak and gown; her fair hair was parted in the center and fastened severely at the nape, and her pale face was smooth and, it struck me, rather blank. Her hands were hidden in her sleeves, held in front of her, like a nun or a monk. Her eyes, I noticed directly, were as strikingly blue as *monsieur* Bayard's.

"Your French is dialect, south perhaps?" I collected my scattered senses and addressed this bizarre little person. "But I believe you said, *he was bludgeoned to death?*"

She fixed first me, then John, in the stern gaze of her very blue eyes, and spoke again, this time in lightly accented English, almost as if reciting verse.

"Standing by a stairway, he accosted Diocletian; harangued him for killing Christians. Swooning at the sight, a man he thought was dead, the Emperor demanded his death yet again; on the spot, thugs with cudgels dispatched him, and threw his body in the common sewer."

Feeling greatly relieved that neither Emily nor her young sister Violet had heard this wretched tale, I opened my mouth to speak again, but was interrupted by Sébastien Bayard suddenly exclaiming and rushing over to us.

"Geneviève!" he admonished her, lightly grasping her by the shoulders. "Why are you here? You know that *monsieur* du Sommerard...." He broke off, aware of our interested looks. "Go now, go back to your meditations." The girl dropped her head, heaved a great sigh, and left the room without further demur. She seemed to disappear in a veil of smoke, but I assumed she had merely exited through yet another mysterious hidden door in the wooden panels.

Turning to us, Bayard began to apologize. "My sister," he said, with a Gallic shrug of *insouciance*. "She is a...an unusual girl," he said, "and loves to be mysterious and mystical." He then waved a hand, dismissing the interruption, and with a charming smile, led us over to where Emily and Violet stood waiting.

"No more delays!" he said. "Through this next door, you will behold one of the most wondrous of the marvels in this collection, that is, what we *hope* will be part of this collection—the Lady and the Unicorn."

FOUR

OCTOBER 1661 – LYONS, FRANCE
The Wedding at the Chateau d'Arcy

THE CHAPEL AT THE CHATEAU D'ARCY was filled with Autumn flowers—gold and rust chrysanthemums, dahlias and anemones—gathered from the castle gardens and hothouses. The small space held only immediate family, about forty people, and they had all gathered early, in their finest clothes, to be at the ready to stand and greet the two couples who were to be wed that day.

"I still don't see why Madeleine agreed to have both weddings on the same day," said a querulous old aunt, stiff in bearing despite her continuing to wear the looser styles of three decades previous. "I, for one, would not want to be upstaged by a younger bride."

Her remarks, though whispered to her attendant nephew, carried well enough in the diminutive chapel for nearly everyone to hear, including the two grooms, soon to be father-in-law and son-in-law.

"Cluck, cluck," Geoffroi de la Roche-Aynon murmured to Madeleine's son François, who stifled a grin behind a discreet cough. "Your mother is as beautiful and lithe as any young maiden, and more intelligent and canny than most of the men I know."

"She is that," François agreed fervently. He laid his hand lightly on Geoffroi's arm. "I can't tell you how much it pleases me that you appreciate her intelligence as well as her beauty. She is a unique woman."

Geoffroi nodded graciously, then cast a sideways glance at the young man. "And my *petite* Jeanne?" he said, still keeping his voice low. "Do you not find her singular as well?"

François' look of happy anticipation spoke volumes to the older man. "She is the rarest of all maidens! Pure and modest, but with a sense of humor, and curiosity, and a deep love of learning." He sighed, and smiled fully this time. "She and I understand each other."

"I am happy to hear it," was all Geoffroi had time to say, as the small organ at the top of the chapel began to peal the arrival of the brides. The waiting company stood, creating a wave of rustling satins and brocades that washed over the sacréd space.

The gossipy old aunt spoke again to her nephew. "Can you see which of them is walking first? I'll bet it's Madeleine." The aunt was short, and couldn't see the chapel entrance directly. "You must tell me, once you see!"

Her long-suffering nephew answered her patiently—she was, after all, a wealthy woman with no children—and then spoke without disguising his surprise. "Why," he said, "they are coming in side-by-side! Jeanne is at Madeleine's right hand."

"Ah, I knew it!" cried the irrepressible aunt.

The two grooms instantly separated and stepped forward to stand at the side of the woman each was escorting: Geoffroi offered his arm to his daughter, and François bowed to his mother before holding out his arm. All smiles, the four walked slowly up the aisle to the pompous strains of the organ, and upon reaching the front, paused before the communion rail.

"*Maman,*" said François, turning to his mother and taking both her hands in his, "I ask your blessing on my marriage."

"I give it gladly," said Madeleine, offering her cheek for two light kisses on either side from her son. "And I ask your blessing as well, my dearest boy." His eyes spoke his joy for her as they exchanged kisses again.

"*Ma,*" Geoffroi said to his daughter, "may you be as happy as you are good."

"*Merci,* Papa," said Jeanne, her voice trembling, her eyes moist. "I too wish you all happiness."

The two ladies then turned to each other, whispered something too low for anyone else to hear, and gracefully changed places to stand at the side of their own betrothed.

The tall, exquisitely carved doors to the grand Gallery of the Tapestries were flung open by liveried servants to welcome the wedding guests. The household of the Chateau d'Arcy had dedicated weeks to preparing food and drink, decorations and candelabra to fill the vast room with light and colour.

Long rows of linen-covered tables flanked the sides of the gallery; immense floral arrangements in between and on the tables provided a sense of intimacy for small groups of ladies and gentlemen, sipping excellent wine and tasting numerous small dishes created by Geoffroi's renowned *chefs de cuisine.*

It was rumoured that Louis XIV, the nation's young Sun King, might put in an appearance, which was more than enough to put all the ladies, and most of the gentlemen, into a flurry of spirits, equally composed of wariness and interest. Cardinal Mazarin had died the previous Spring, and the King was coming into his own sense of power and command. His wife of little over a year, Maria Theresa, was pregnant and soon to give birth. His star was rising to unequalled prominence.

Trumpets sounded a joyful trill, and the doors, which had been closed, opened again to allow the married couples to enter. Gasps of excitement and wonder accompanied their entrance, as guests gazed at the magnificent costumes worn by the brides and their grooms. Old friends recognized the theme at once, and began pointing to the tapestries on the walls of the gallery to enlighten the less-informed guests.

It was as if the tapestries had come to life: Madeleine and Jeanne were dressed precisely after the rich and gorgeous garments of the Lady in two of the eight tapestries— brocades in deep hues of red and blue made up the medieval style of gown and tunic, with long, tight sleeves, and wimples with flowing veils; on their heads were snug caps of gold and jewel-trimmed stiff cloth; ropes of gold hung around their waists, and gem-encrusted bracelets and necklaces adorned the two women.

The men were no less splendidly attired: Geoffroi's clothing mimicked the colors of the Lion of the tapestries, tawny gold tights and leather boots, a vest of golden fur with a collar that encircled his ruggedly handsome face like a mane; draped from his shoulders, as a cloak, he wore the coat of arms of the LeViste family, his distant ancestors who had commissioned the tapestries nearly 200 years previously, three gold crescents on a sash of blue against a red background.

François was the Unicorn, resplendent in all white with gold trim; he fairly shone with a light that seemed to come from within, idealistic, almost sacréd. In place of the Unicorn's single, spiraled horn, the young man carried a decorated spear, from which draped the arms of the Le Viste family as well, to honor the ancestors of the woman he had just married.

The two couples paraded slowly down the center of the room, nodding to left and right, until they reached the high table at the far end, where they turned, made a courtly bow to their guests, who by now were all on their feet clapping and calling out their congratulations, and sat themselves at the table of honor. Geoffroi signalled that the main feast was to be served.

But before he could take his seat, the trumpets blared again, and the doors were thrown open. Everyone in the room froze, sitting or standing, as the trumpets ceased and the clarion voice of the royal page rang out.

"Son Altesse Royale, Louis Quatorze!"

❦ FIVE ⌀

The Unicorn in the Mirror

WE STOOD AWED AND SILENT as we viewed the magnificent tapestry depicting the Unicorn, docile and quite tame, resting his forelegs on the lap of, I must say it, a not very attractive Lady, although sumptuously dressed. Her face had the plain, subdued look of a cloistered nun resigned to live indoors, with a melancholic expression of weariness and patience.

She held a gold-framed mirror in her lap, into which the Unicorn gazed, as if mesmerized by his own reflection, and with almost a smile, if animals can be said to smile. And I suppose that, if any animal *could* smile, it would be a mythical beast like the Unicorn.

"May we touch the tapestry?" I inquired, having come quite close to the hanging, my nose almost brushing against the silk and wool of the fabric. That near, one could not distinguish any pattern of flower or leaf or animal, but the individual knots and colours seemed, to me, irresistible, and invited a light touch of the fingers to partake, somehow, of their brilliance and their subtlety.

Bayard hesitated, which I took as permission, and lightly brushed my fingers across the woven surface, communing, I thought fancifully, with the hands that had twisted and placed the knots some four hundred years ago. Then I stepped back to join my friends who still stood at a more respectful distance, gazing for all they were worth.

"You see how the edges are frayed and eaten away," Bayard pointed out for us.

"Rats," said little Violet helpfully, looking solemn. "Probably using the bits for their nest."

The thought made me shudder, and I moved a step further away. But John leaned forward, taking in the considerable damage done to the decorative band of dark blue that had clearly served as a "frame" for the subject of the tapestry.

"Are you thinking to restore the surrounding band to its original size?" he asked, turning to Bayard, but continued without waiting for a reply. "And do you know how large a frame it constituted?"

"I can answer that, Sébastien," said a new voice in the room. We turned as one, and saw what I could only assume was *monsieur* du Sommerard himself, having just entered through a side door. He was an older gentleman, probably in his early sixties, but well-preserved and rather regal in his mien, with longish, dark hair, a greying beard, and a general air of discreet fashion. I recalled that the *musée* had actually been his family home—or one of them—before his father had given it, and most of his private collections of antiquities—to the state. I wondered how he felt, now, being the "director" where he would have been the master of it all, but for his father's generous will.

"*Mesdames, messieurs,*" the director bowed to us all from a short distance before he advanced further into the room. Following close behind him was the soberly-dressed woman I had glimpsed as we passed by the main entrance hall. She was a plain-faced, respectable looking woman, dressed in dark clothing, her brown hair in an unfashionable style (even in my estimation, who rarely notice such things), drawn back rather severely from her face. She held herself with an air of prim resignation. The director seemed to assume that he needed no introduction, as he began speaking without giving Bayard an opportunity to present us to him.

"I see you have returned quite promptly to view our lovely Lady again," he said, addressing Emily who, with a greater attention to the proprieties than the director, immediately pronounced my name and John's in introduction.

"Of course, the famous American artist," he said, with an air of supercilious interest. I thought his tone quite odious, and I was delighted when John laughed aloud, and bowing slightly to the director, replied, with some cheek.

"*Merci* for the 'famous' part, *monsieur* du Sommerard, but at home, in America," he said, "I'm referred to as 'that French artist', don't you know?"

Du Sommerard stiffened slightly, clearly affronted, and only inclined his head in response. I was waiting for him to introduce the woman who accompanied him; I saw her eyes flicker toward him, but he seemed oblivious to her presence. Young Bayard was more polite. "This is *mademoiselle* Berthold," he said, but without further explanation, and we all bowed and nodded accordingly. A deep flush had succeeded the woman's formerly pale complexion.

Du Sommerard returned to John's original question.

"From the general design of the other tapestries, still residing at Chateau Boussac," he explained, "we believe the border was originally about twelve inches deep, although they vary somewhat based on the size of the whole tapestry."

I took upon myself the role of conciliator, for some reason—possibly to keep Emily from embarrassment in front of the young assistant—and continued the conversation, focusing on the tapestry.

"It is my understanding, sir," I said, "that the *musée* is very close to convincing the town fathers of Boussac that all the tapestries should be brought here, for preservation and display for all the world to see—a very just and laudable objective, to be sure."

"You are absolutely correct, *mademoiselle* Paget," he said, his feathers smoothed at my tone. "And we are at a very critical juncture in our negotiations." His voice dropped to a lower, conspiratorial tone. "I have it on good authority that the Baron Rothschild has made an offer for the tapestries himself, to carry them away to his estate, no doubt, where no one but his friends will see them."

We all shook our heads at the idea. "That must not be allowed to happen, *monsieur!*" Emily interposed. She looked at me and John. "Is there not something we can do? Get up a subscription or, or something?"

"Do not worry, *mademoiselle* Sargent," the director said, smiling with no little appearance of smug self-importance. "I have many influential friends in high places, and we will not allow these treasures to be spirited out of France."

I refrained from replying as my impish spirit wished, and instead turned our attention to the tapestry again.

"Whose is the coat of arms on the banners?" I asked, and looked at Emily. "You, my dear Emily, are noted for your knowledge of aristocratic families, both in France and England. Can you identify it?"

Emily blushed as all eyes fastened on her. "I'm afraid I cannot," she said. "It is a very simple design, and the crescent, I believe, possibly indicates a connection with the Crusades?" Her tentative statement drew an approving look from du Sommerard.

"Excellent, *mademoiselle*," he said. "That indeed, is one possibility, but I am obliged to admit that no one, either in Boussac or here in Paris, has uncovered the mystery of this coat of arms—as yet!" He turned to his assistant and, gazing with frank admiration at the young man, spoke in an almost caressing tone. "Sébastien, perhaps you would like to speak more to this issue?"

Bayard began the tale obligingly. "The Chateau Boussac, where the tapestries currently reside, is not, we believe, their original location. The last of the family de Carbonniere, a *mademoiselle* Pauline, now deceased, sold the chateau to the town of Boussac in 1837, who have leased it out as a residence since then, to various people. We have it from some documents from the de Carbonniere estate that the tapestries came to the chateau in the mid-1660's, possibly from somewhere near Lyons." He gazed up at the Lady and the Unicorn. "The style of these works of art is very much in accord with other tapestries, created around 1500, in the workshops of Lyons. But the coat of arms remains a mystery."

John too was regarding the tapestry, looking deep in thought. "Why is the Unicorn resting in the lap of the maiden, and what is the significance of its looking in the mirror?"

Sébastien glanced at his employer, who nodded his permission for the assistant to speak again. "The legend of the Unicorn states that only a virgin, pure of heart and body, can subdue the wild and magical beast, who tamely sits with his front hooves in her lap." He paused for a moment, reaching a hand up to touch the edge of the tapestry. "As for the symbolism of the mirror, educated guesses are all we have at this point."

"Such as," I intervened, "the old 'Vanity of Vanities' trope?—that was popular in *Le Moyen Age*. Perhaps Narcissus falling in love with his own image?" I mused a moment longer, and as my companions kept silent, I continued. "Or, in more modern terms, a reflection of the inner self? A mirror is a kind of window, in a symbolic sense, through which, or *in* which, we see ourselves reflected without a veil, we see ourselves through our own eyes—into the very soul, as it were."

Emily looked at me in surprise. "I thought you didn't believe in the soul, Violet?" she said teasingly. "Only the mind, and the life of the mind!"

I answered her more seriously than even I expected to. "I wouldn't care to deny the existence of a spiritual...*entity,* shall we say...that is part and parcel of the human animal. Psyche is, after all, the goddess of the mind and the spirit, the light and the dark, but mostly, that which is hidden within."

"The Lady looks so very melancholy," said little Violet suddenly. She turned to Sébastien Bayard. "Why is she so sad?"

"I do not know, little one," he answered her. "Perhaps because—according to the legend—she was persuaded to entice the Unicorn from its wild forest and become a tame captive." He shook himself as if seeing a dark vision, and smiled ruefully. "There are versions of the legend that indicate the maiden tricked the Unicorn into surrendering to her, whereupon the King's men hunted him and killed him."

"Killed him! Oh, no!" The little girl turned beseeching eyes to the assistant. "Surely they wouldn't have killed him!"

"Ah, but fear not, child," interposed du Sommerard, in a kindly tone, "for, like the Christ, the Unicorn was restored to life by the magic of his single horn which, dipped in his own blood, gave life back to the creature."

John gave a sudden impatient gesture, and I, knowing him well, imagined that he felt he'd had enough of magic and legends and Christian allegories. He turned abruptly to Sébastien.

"I say, might I have another look at that Titian," he said, taking the younger man by the arm.

"What's this? The Titian?" The museum director looked angrily at his assistant. "What have you been telling *monsieur* Sargent, Sébastien?"

"Why, nothing, that is, I—he guessed—," the young man stumbled to explain, but John interrupted.

"I am quite a student of Titian, sir," John said, "and of course I couldn't help but be struck with the similarity of style, as well as the subject matter." He looked curiously at du Sommerard. "What is your own estimation of the painting?"

Du Sommerard responded testily. "That there is a small possibility of it being a Titian, but more likely it is by a student of his workshop!" He glared at poor Sébastien, but then seemed to make an effort to recover his good manners. "We are deciding whether to ask experts to come and examine the painting, but I personally am convinced there is nothing to it." He turned to the woman, Berthold, who had accompanied him.

"I'm sure our guests would appreciate a glass of tea before they depart," he said to her, and then turned back to us. "I apologize, but my presence is required elsewhere, or I would accompany you and converse further." He bowed in our general direction, and with one more sharp look at Sébastien—who seemed to know exactly what it meant—he left the room as he had come, quietly and quickly.

There were a few moments of awkward silence. I took it upon myself to speak for all of us.

"*Merci beaucoup, mademoiselle* Berthold," I said quietly. "It is not within our power to stay for tea, although we are grateful for the offer." She nodded once, curtly, and left the room without a word.

"Nonetheless," John said softly, as Sébastien gestured with his hand for us to walk back to the door, "I'd like to take another look as we pass by."

"Certainly," said Sébastien, although he looked rather unhappy at the prospect.

Sébastien seemed to recover somewhat of his spirits as he escorted us back through the workshop—where John spent several minutes closely inspecting the painting of the martyred saint—and then through the gallery of antiquities in the glass-topped cabinets. Just as we were about to descend the spiral staircase, John turned to Sébastien and delighted us all by asking if the young man would like to join our party at the theatre that evening. He blushed and stammered most becomingly, and it ended with his grateful acceptance of the offer. But then a look of consternation crossed his smooth brow.

"Ah, but Geneviève!" he said, and shook his head. "*Désolé, monsieur* Sargent, but I cannot leave my sister alone at home at night."

"Then she must come with you to the theatre, I insist," John said kindly. "We have plenty of room in the box."

Sébastien smiled with pleasure at this generosity, and promised to bring his sister with him.

Emily quietly glowed with her own delight, but I thought there was something more in John's wishing to further the acquaintance—whether for her sake or for his own, I could not decide.

SIX

OCTOBER 1661 – LYONS, FRANCE
Le Roi Soleil at Chateau d'Arcy

MADELEINE AND GEOFFROI EXCHANGED GLANCES as the King processed further into the grand gallery, rippled waves of curtseys and bows advancing before him. It was always "rumoured" that royalty would show up at the weddings of the nobility, but it rarely actually occurred. Why had Louis chosen to grace their celebration?

The faint line of worry on Geoffroi's brow was mirrored in Madeleine's tightened lips—he had had a role, albeit small, in the *Fronde* of the Princes, a nobles' rebellion against Mazarin (and therefore, the King), which ended without much bloodshed but a great deal of humiliation for the noble class some eight years ago. Madeleine's late husband had also been involved, to an even lesser extent, their ancient feudal lands in Boussac being well out of the way of the reach of political squabbles. It had become apparent over the years since then, much to everyone's relief, that the King held no grudges—but still….

The wedding couples hastened to move from their high table to greet the King on the gallery floor; Madeleine had enough presence of mind to throw an alarmed look at the castle's *châtelaine,* an intelligent and industrious woman, Griselde, who nodded her instant understanding. A chair worthy of the King was already being set in the center of the high table, with all the appropriate plates, linens, cutlery and glasses, as if it had been there from the start.

"Your Majesty," Geoffroi said, bowing low with a graceful flourish of one arm, while Madeleine, lightly touching his other arm, curtsied deeply. "The honor of your visit to us is beyond description, and we are forever in your debt." The King nodded graciously, and Geoffroi continued. "May I present my newly wedded wife, Madeleine des Grillets de la Roche-Aynon."

The young King, now in his twenty-third year, extended his hands to both of them, grasping them in the friendliest manner, with a lively smile on his face.

"We offer our most sincere congratulations on this occasion," he said, then catching sight of the younger newlyweds, turned to them with his hands held out.

"And this must be the daughter and son," he said, "who, following the excellent example of their respective parents, have also joined together these eminent families."

"*Oui,* your majesty," Madeleine responded. "My son, François and his bride Jeanne." The King favored the young bride with a lingering kiss on the back of her hand, and Geoffroi, with an effort, kept himself from frowning as he saw the King's thoughtful assessment of his daughter's charms, heightened as they were by her modest blushes and wedding day excitement. *Grâce à Dieu,* he thought, the days of the feudal *droit du seigneur* are well behind us. Louis, young as he was, was infamous for his amorous adventures, although his marriage seemed to have settled him, at least during this first year.

"Your majesty," Geoffroi said, again bowing and waving the King to be seated at the center of the high table.

Madeleine, relieved that the place was set and waiting for their guest, saw with a sideways glance that room had been made at various tables for the King's retinue of courtiers as well; she knew that all the servants and lackeys who accompanied the King would be taken care of in the kitchens, stables and their own servants' quarters. Thank heavens, she thought, Chateau d'Arcy knows how to provide hospitality for royals.

She turned her attention to the progress of Louis to the table, and saw that he had taken hold of Jeanne's hand, and was leading her to sit next to him, on his right, while François, looking pale but otherwise under control, sat to his bride's right hand. With a quick look at her husband, Madeleine made her way to sit on the other side of the King, acting, as she presumed Geoffroi wished, as a shield between the two men, and also placed to provide a diversion from the King's too close attention to her new daughter-in-law.

The feast began, and the wedding guests settled down into chatting and drinking, with frequent glances directed to the high table to discern any inkling of drama or trouble—food for gossip later on.

"May I ask if Her Royal Majesty was well when you left Paris, sir?" Jeanne put the question shyly but clearly to the King, and Madeleine, though she could not see his face, did notice that his shoulders tightened and his chin lifted. Little Jeanne was not so naïve, perhaps. She leaned forward ever so slightly, though discreetly refrained from catching her daughter-in-law's eye. The King's response was telling.

"Maria Theresa has been so surrounded by nurses and doctors, midwives and priests," he said, sounding a touch rueful, but mostly amused, "that I have scarcely exchanged three words with her these past five months."

"But I hope and pray to our Blessed Mother that her health, and that of the child, is all that could be wished for," Jeanne said sincerely.

"Thank you, my dear," Louis said, his tone softened. "I'm sure your prayers find a direct path to the Holy Virgin Mother's ear, and she will watch over my wife and heir."

Madeleine surmised that Jeanne's innate goodness would only be making her more attractive to the young King, and was glad when a servant arrived to offer the King a dish of pheasant, stepping in between him and the young bride. She seized the opportunity to engage him to herself.

"We are most honored indeed, your Majesty," she began, "that you have graced our household with your presence, especially at this time of the year." She composed her face to innocence, so that he would not suspect sarcasm. "Late October in this valley can be so dreary and cold. I dare not assume that this small wedding affair of us is all that drew you out into the provinces just now."

Louis turned to her, a thoughtful look on his face. "It is indeed an insalubrious season for travel," he said, watching her. "But a monarch has a duty to be among his people, and have his presence and attention felt by all." He paused, taking up his wine glass, though not drinking. "The warmth of your hospitality will soon cure any chill I may have felt."

There was a subtle warning here, Madeleine felt sure; she made her way carefully with her next words.

"Thank you, Majesty," she said, looking down humbly. "All your subjects feel, as do we, that we owe you so very much, for your personal interest and care for us, and the way you are guiding *la belle France* into a new age of high culture, philosophy, the arts!—we are awe-struck by the beauty and stability you are bringing to us, to all your people."

She raised her eyes to his again, trying not to betray her rapidly beating heart; again, his intelligent eyes assessed her. Then he smiled, nodded his acknowledgement of her compliment, and took a long draught from his wine glass.

Everyone had been waiting for their King to take up a fork and begin eating it was the custom—and he suddenly, it seemed, became aware that he had food on his plate. He speared a piece of pheasant with the two-pronged fork and tasted it, nodding his approval. With a feeling of relief, Madeleine also picked up her fork and ate, and soon the clink and clash of silver at all the tables sparred with the increased noise of laughter and conversation.

But Geoffroi was anxious, having heard this exchange with his wife, and while approving of her abilities, also noted the King's continual attentions to Jeanne, and François' unsettled looks. Something must be done, and quickly. Between two of the seemingly innumerable courses, Geoffroi nodded a signal to his son-in-law, and the two rose together, bowed to the King, and made their way out by a near door, as if to use the necessary room.

The two men stepped aside into an alcove hidden behind a large screen. "You must go tonight, with Jeanne, straight to Boussac," the older man said in a whisper.

François nodded. "I completely agree, but won't it…won't the King find it insulting? What will you say?"

Geoffroi smiled grimly. "Your mother and I will manage something between the two of us, do not worry. Just go as soon as possible—perhaps Jeanne is feeling the need to retire soon?" he hinted. François nodded again.

"You go back to the table now," the older man directed. "I will see to it that whatever you need will be ready for you in two hours—a carriage will be at the far end of the stables,

our most trusted servants will do everything—leave through
the outside door that is near where your room is—Jeanne
knows the way."

A few more exchanged whispers settled it, and François
returned to the table while Geoffroi made haste to find his
steward and give directions. He was back in the gallery before ten minutes had passed. A glance and a reassuring nod
to Madeleine set her heart at ease, and as she continued to
engage the King in conversation, Geoffroi saw his daughter
lean toward her husband, who whispered in her ear for a few
moments. Shortly afterward—and Geoffroi marvelled at
this instance of deception in his daughter—Jeanne half-rose
from her seat, as white as snow and promptly fell back in a
faint into her husband's arms.

Immediately servants ran to assist her and François,
supporting her as she came out of the faint, and assisting her,
accompanied by her maid, he remembered to turn to the
King, bow, and apologize for their hasty departure. The
King waved a hand to dismiss them, an inscrutable look on
his handsome face. He turned sharply to face Madeleine,
who herself had risen to assist her daughter-in-law if needed,
but who now sat down again at the behest of the King.

"Madame," he said, taking a bottle of wine from a waiting servant, and pouring it himself into her glass. "The new
young bride is, perhaps, anxious about the coming night?"
He poured himself some wine, and held up the glass as for a
toast, but it was only for the two of them. He looked at her
appraisingly, with appreciation. "You, perhaps, might understand her fears, but you yourself are already experienced in
the delights of the marriage bed, *oui?*"

Madeleine felt a shiver of fear race through her, then it turned to anger, and cold calculation. *If this is what it takes*, she thought. She leaned in slightly.

"*Oui*, your Majesty," she said softly.

҂ Seven ҂

Friday Night – 6 May 1881 – Paris
À La Comédie Française

WE WERE INDEED A FULL BOX for the theatre performance that evening, our party having expanded to include not only John's mother and two sisters (his father preferring the quiet of his study), and my own self, but also the Bayards *soeur et frère*, and one of John's very best friends, Carroll Beckwith, an artist and studio-mate, also an American, whom I had met before. We awaited the non-Sargent contingent of guests in the lobby of the immense and ornate theatre—Carroll arrived promptly, and after a very short time, an attractive young woman, dressed in a reasonably fashionable gown and trim hat, approached us and spoke to John.

"*Monsieur* Sargent," she said, and as she spoke, her interesting voice made me realize that she was Geneviève Bayard—utterly transformed from the medieval apparition we had seen earlier that day. "I am so sorry to say that Sébastien has been detained, but that he will do his best to come as soon as he can, and join us at the interval."

"I hope it is not illness or some trouble that keeps him from joining our party," John said, genuinely concerned.

"Oh, no, *monsieur*," Geneviève said, a slightly vexed look crossing her face. "It is the *musée,* and du Sommerard, that keep him running at all hours." She lifted her shoulders in an expressive shrug. "But he feels he must be responsive, because of the Lady."

I was about to inquire further into this enigmatic remark, when the black-cloaked footman appeared in the hall, striking the tones that announced the play would begin in a few moments. Our group hastened up the staircase and through the door to the box seats, attended by more footmen, found our situation, and quickly distributed ourselves amongst the chairs—Mrs. Sargent and little Violet in the front two on the left, with Emily across the aisle space in a seat on the right. There was an empty seat next to her, which I judiciously forbore to occupy, with the objective of having young Sébastien sitting there before too long. I chose the row behind her, and turned to invite Geneviève Bayard to sit next to me, which she did, quite gracefully.

John and his friend loitered at the back of the box, finishing their cigarettes, and (I hoped) ordering something refreshing from the attendant, to be brought to our box at the first interval. Within moments, the orchestra struck up a lively tune, the gas lights (yes! such an innovation!) were lowered somewhat, and the curtain rose.

I soon found my attention wavering from the comic scene on the stage below—it was too old a tale, a young wife and an aged husband, a secret lover, a foolish housemaid, and a case of mistaken identity—I knew how it would end. My senses and my mind were engaged by the young woman sitting next to me, not only because she was clearly nervous and ill-at-ease (probably worried about her brother), but because I was also intrigued by the two quite distinct, almost opposite, modes of dress in which I had thus far seen her. I wished very much to engage her in conversation, and luckily, the loud laughs of the audience and the continual shouts and screams from the stage provided a screen for the low-voiced conversation I wished to hold with Geneviève.

"I hope you will forgive my lack of proper greeting in the lobby just now," I said, thinking that an apology would be a good way to start. "But I hardly recognized you from this morning."

Geneviève smiled, a sincere and good-humoured smile, I thought approvingly. "My brother is very indulgent with me, and allows me to live out a little fantasy whenever I come to visit the *musée*."

"Of being a medieval nun?" I asked, doubtful.

"Oh, not quite a nun," she said. "A medieval woman, to be sure, most of whom dressed the same way the nuns did—it's what women wore in those days."

"Only the nuns never changed from that habit," I said, and watched her from the corner of my eye. She caught the pun instantly, and almost giggled, putting a hand to her lips to cover the sound.

"I never would have taken you for a punster, *Mademoiselle* Paget," she whispered.

"Please," I said, liking her more and more, "please do call me Violet."

She lifted her hand to take my own in hers. "And I am Geneviève, my dear Violet." We shook hands firmly.

We turned our attention to the stage again at a sudden burst of laughter and the sound of a horse neighing. There was actually a real, live horse on the stage, prancing about and pawing the air so vigorously I feared for the bonnets and headresses of the actors nearby.

Settling into the next scene, I couldn't help but notice that my companion continued to show signs of restlessness. She glanced frequently at the door, watching for it to be opened, I presumed, and present her with her brother. Her knitted brows betrayed a growing anxiety that tensed her otherwise smooth features.

"Do not worry," I leaned over and whispered, "I am sure your brother is just waiting for the interval to enter the box, rather than interrupt us, don't you think?"

She nodded acceptance of the idea, but I could see it hadn't helped allay her worry.

The curtain fell on the first act, and the bustle of people moving about and talking filled the house. I was gratified to see that the attendant had already brought in some wine in an ice bucket and a plate of appetizing little somethings; a second table held glasses, plates, napkins and cutlery. The attendant bowed his way out, and closed the door.

"Splendid, John!" I cried, rising from my seat at the same time as Geneviève rose. Little Violet, Emily and Mrs. Sargent also turned round and smiled at the welcome refreshment. We gathered in the back of the box, where John duly introduced *mademoiselle* Bayard to his friend Carroll Beckwith.

"Mr. Beckwith is a professor of art in New York City," Emily added, leaning forward into the group clustered around the refreshment table. "And he is a wonderful portraitist when he's not teaching."

"My dear Miss Emily," said Beckwith, emphasizing his usually barely noticeable Missouri drawl, "I greatly appreciate your compliment." He gazed solemnly into his glass of champagne for a moment. "I must admit, the duties of a professor of art tend to hinder the actual creation of said art, on the part of the professor."

"Nonsense!" John said, cuffing his friend lightly on the shoulder. "I saw your studio when I was there last year, and you're creating some brilliant portraits, Carroll, you know you are."

"Not like what I've seen from you at the Salon today," Beckwith rejoined, shaking his head. "You never cease to amaze me—and yet, I expect you will surpass yourself time and again."

Geneviève, although I could see she had previously been distracted, turned her attention to this conversation. "My brother is a great admirer of yours, *monsieur* Sargent," she said, accepting a glass of champagne from him at the same time. "We were both at the Salon yesterday, and I believe he went again this morning, just to view your works once again."

John acknowledged the compliment with a shy nod, and, being the kind soul I know him to be, immediately caught Miss Bayard's underlying worry. "Do not be anxious about your brother, *mademoiselle* Bayard," he said. "You know how men get when it comes to their work—we lose all track of time when we are caught up in the moment."

Geneviève nodded, but did not seem convinced.

"Perhaps," I said, addressing her, "if he does not appear by the second interval, we could arrange to have a note sent to your home—if he is very late, he may have decided to simply forgo the play altogether."

Geneviève smiled, a little sadly. "Our *home* is far from here," she said. "We are in lodgings, while we—while Sébastien assists *monsieur* du Sommerard with the tapestry."

"Oh, is that so?" I said, curious about this unusual sibling pair. "Why, if I may ask, is his assistance of such great help to du Sommerard?"

The young woman looked as if she had rather not answer this question, but just for a moment; then, shrugging, she replied, "Sébastien and I are from Nohant, which is a small town not too far from the Chateau Boussac, where the tapestries have resided for some hundreds of years." She stopped at this point to take a sip of champagne, and although she seemed reluctant to continue, I maintained a look of expectant interest, holding my tongue in order to encourage her to loosen hers. John, too, was listening in; I noted that Beckwith had turned to the other ladies in our party and was regaling Emily and Mrs. Sargent with some tale of New York.

"Our revered parents, both of whom died several years ago," Geneviève continued, "were great friends to Aurore Dupin, Baroness Dudevant—and she was like a grand-aunt to me and my brother when we were growing up."

My eyebrows shot up in surprise. "Aurore Dupin? You mean, George Sand? The author?" I puzzled over this a moment. "And how is she connected to the tapestries?"

"Ah, it is a long story," said Geneviève, "and as it appears that the play will begin shortly, I will only say, that she was instrumental in resurrecting the tapestries and saving them from destruction—long before I was born, of course."

Through the long second and third acts, I mused upon the interesting connections that my new acquaintance had revealed. I was, of course, familiar with the works of George Sand—who was not?—and I recalled that the rather infa-

mous writer had died not very long ago, about five years perhaps. I searched my memory for anything I knew about her,
and dredged up some scandals about her many lovers—
Chopin and Liszt among them, it would appear she favored
musicians—and also the fact that she frequently wore men's
clothing and smoked a pipe! Fascinating.

When the second interval arrived, and Sébastien did not
appear, Geneviève could barely keep her seat for anxiety.

"I must leave," she insisted. "I must go back to our
lodgings and make sure my brother is well. What if something has happened to him, if he has taken ill, or…." Her
distress was so extreme that I turned immediately to John.

"We must take Miss Bayard home," I said in a low
voice. "You and I, John, let us do this for her, she clearly
isn't in any frame of mind to stay here now."

"Of course," John said. He whispered a few words to
Carroll, then to his mother, arranging for his friend to see
that his mother and sisters were safely taken to their apartment. I gathered up my things as I relayed the plan to Miss
Bayard, who was grateful, though terse, in her expressions
of obligation.

In a few moments, we were walking down the staircase
and out the door. The cool Spring air of Paris was refreshing
after the heat and closeness of the theatre. A line of cabs
waiting for the audience to turn out made it easy to be on
our way with the utmost expedience.

After giving the direction to the driver, John sat back in
the seat across from us as the horse lurched into action on
the cobblestone street. He leaned forward and placed one
hand on top of Miss Bayard's. "I'm sure we'll find that everything is all right," he assured her, though a glance at me,
even in the dim light from the streetlamps we were passing,

showed me he didn't feel all that sure himself. I too was experiencing an increasing dread, although I could not have explained why.

We rode the rest of the way in silence, pulling up before long in front of a three-story building that immediately showed itself, to me   used as I was to staying in such places when my family's funds were at a lower ebb than usual—as a *pension*, in short, a boarding house. There was a light on in the front lower room.

Geneviève made ready to leave us. "I cannot thank you enough for your courtesy, *monsieur* Sargent, and I ask your forgiveness for making you, and Miss Paget, miss the end of the play."

"Do not mention it further, I beg you, we are only too happy to be of service," John replied, and opening the door to the cab, he alighted, then waited to accompany her to the door.

"Vi," he said to me, "I'm sure all will be well, and I'll return in a moment."

I watched eagerly as the two walked up the steps, rang the bell, and then stepped inside when the door was opened. I caught only a glimpse of a thin, upright, little *concierge* who appeared to look John up and down with great suspicion, and then closed the door firmly. After an endless five minutes, the door opened again, and John walked out, with Geneviève on his arm, and the door closed behind them. My heart sank—this did not bode well.

I heard John give the driver the address of the *Musée de Cluny* as he assisted Geneviève into the cab. I took her hand in mine after she seated herself, and she grasped it as a lifeline.

"Oh, *mademoiselle* Paget," she gasped. "He is not there, and has not been there all evening."

I didn't know what to say, and the dread I felt kept me from offering soothing platitudes. We sat in suspenseful silence during the short trip to the *musée*, which loomed dark and ominous in the night sky as we approached.

"I have a key," murmured Geneviève, somehow answering the question I had in mind without my having spoken aloud. I nodded, and pressed her hand in sympathy.

After instructing the driver to wait for us, John led the way through the darkened courtyard, illuminated by streetlamps on the other side of the ancient stone walls. When we approached the same door through which we had entered earlier in the day—it seemed so long ago now—he lit a match so that Geneviève could see the lock for the key. Her hands were steady, although she seemed to me to be about to faint, her breath was so shallow and labored. What was it she feared so mightily? Would we not simply find her brother working at his desk at some tedious assignment from du Sommerard?

Luckily, a gas lantern was at hand just inside the door and, lighting it quickly, we started up the winding stone staircase. The utter darkness beyond our light seemed almost palpable, and we stepped carefully. The door at the top of the staircase was slightly ajar, and it creaked noisily as John pushed it open further.

The long gallery of *vitrines* was as I had pictured it mentally earlier that day—very dark, with reflected light from the windows glinting off the glass of the cabinets. Hurrying down the main aisle, we could see, at the far end of the room, a slim crack of light outlining part of the hidden door into the workshop.

"Ah!" Geneviève exclaimed, relief clear in her voice. "Sébastien must be there, still at work!" We hastened to the doorway, pressing on the spring to open it, and walked inside.

An oppressive silence met us. There were two lamps lighted, near the center of the workshop, which gave adequate light to see most of the room easily. A quick survey showed there was no one there, but as we progressed further into the space, John cried out.

"The Titian! It's gone!" Indeed, the easel on which it had been placed was not only empty, it was broken in pieces and lay on the floor.

"Sébastien!" cried Geneviève, running now to the far end of the workshop, to the door that led to the room with the Lady and Unicorn tapestry. I called to her, running to catch up.

"Wait! Geneviève, wait!"

But she had reached the door and, flinging it open, almost tumbled inside. I was right behind her with a lantern, which I had grasped on my way. I held it high, and turned to hand it to John, who was fast behind me. He held it higher, and as we stepped into the room, we saw revealed to us, in the wavering light, the figure of Sébastien, laid out upon the large wooden worktable, tied with ropes, and with arrows piercing his body through his clothing at several points.

Geneviève gave a great shriek and fainted on the spot, falling back into my arms. I struggled to hold her so she would not fall and harm herself, and was able to lower her to the floor. "He may still be alive!" I cried out.

John stood aghast for a moment longer, then leaped into action. I saw him approach the pitiful figure, and place his hand gently on the young man's neck, feeling for a pulse of life.

"Oh, God, Vi," he said, his voice harsh, "he's as cold as ice."

With a great effort, my rational self overcame the horror and fear that had coursed through me. "Don't touch anything else," I said to John. "We must summon the police."

EIGHT

OCTOBER 1661 – LYONS, FRANCE
Events at Chateau d'Arcy

MADELEINE WAS NOT CALLED TO THE KING'S BED that night—or any night. She knew not what blessed reflection of reason or religion may have turned Louis from what had appeared to be his lustful objective, but she was grateful to the point of weeping. She had not mentioned anything to Geoffroi, but had given herself to him without delay as soon as they retired to their marriage bed, thinking only that he would have her first, should the King interfere sometime in the night. She fell asleep at last, commending herself and her fate to the protection of the saints.

But morning broke, late as the time of year decreed it, and she was curled up inside her husband's arms, sleeping, when the maidservant crept in to build up the fire and draw back the hangings at the window to let in the daylight. Madeleine's first thought was to lie in bed, drowsing and making love all day, then her eyes opened wide, and she sat up with a small cry.

The King was still in residence—she had better be up and looking about her, in order to manage the rest of the day, and every day, that His Majesty might deign to stay with them at Chateau d'Arcy.

She shook Geoffroi, at first gently, then more vigorously as he showed little sign of waking. "My love, awake, arise!" she whispered in his ear, and then gave a little squeal as he suddenly encircled her in a strong grip and rolled her over on the soft mattress, engaging her in a deep kiss.

"*Non, non, mon cher,*" she murmured against his lips, desiring nothing more than to say yes and surrender. He fell back, resigned. "*Oui,*" he said, "the dratted King awaits." With a giggle and a kiss to his forehead, Madeleine unwound the bedclothes from around herself and pulled aside the heavy velvet curtains that enclosed them in their bed.

"Jeannette! Where are you?" she called for her maid, and was soon in her own dressing apartment, preparing for whatever the day might hold.

It was even more eventful than she could have imagined.

The housekeeper had clearly been up for hours by the time Madeleine came downstairs to consult with her in the kitchen, which was a bustling hive of fragrant activity—cooking, baking, warming wine and preparing trays of food to deliver to the various bedrooms.

"Madame," Griselde greeted her with a slight curtsey, looking only a bit harried by the pace of the preparations. "His Majesty has not yet sent for his breakfast, but I have consulted with his man, and have everything ready for him, whatever he may ask for."

Madeleine smiled her relief and thanks, and then leaned forward and embraced the woman briefly, much to their mutual surprise. "*Merci,* Griselde," she whispered. "You are a life saver. No one matters as much as the King, *comprenez-vous?*"

"*Oui, Madame,*" the good woman whispered back. "*Je comprends tout à fait.*"

The King had arrived with a rather small entourage, for him, only about forty people, comprising his personal servants, some twenty or so armed cavaliers, a couple of priests, and a few courtiers, all men, who seemed strangely docile—this last opinion Madeleine heard from Geoffroi, who knew most of the courtiers fairly well, and who was curious as to their subdued behavior; formerly, these men had been bold and almost unruly when travelling about in a cadre, with or without the King.

"Perhaps Louis, and Maria Therese, are exerting a civilized influence at the court," Madeleine suggested to him. He nodded thoughtfully, and said how that might be so. They were now seated in the breakfast room, where Madeleine had directed everyone should be served with large platters of food set down upon the tables, or on sideboards, and people were encouraged to help themselves. They were an easy, friendly group of people, including the courtiers, and the room was lively with chat and laughter. No one had even noticed, she murmured to her husband, that the younger newlyweds were absent. He smiled and whispered that he wished they could be the same.

Madeleine hadn't even imagined that the King would join the party at breakfast—it was well-known he rarely appeared at table until luncheon, especially when he travelled, presumably being immersed in matters of state, volumes of correspondence, and directing policy, in his morning hours. Great was her surprise, and everyone's, then, when the doors swung open and Louis appeared, simply dressed in a riding habit and soft boots, and waited while the company rose and bowed or curtseyed to their King.

"Please," he said, waving a hand, "be as you were, I am just another hungry man looking for breakfast." No one moved or said anything, and he smiled indulgently. "I beg of you, please comport yourselves as if I weren't here." Of course no one took him seriously, but the courtiers, being perhaps more used to his ways, sat down again and encouraged others to do the same. Geoffroi had risen and approached the King to guide him to an appropriate seat.

"Ah," said Louis, "I see your good wife is *au courant* as to the latest ways of dining," referring to the dishes set out upon the tables. "I approve—for breakfast only, though, don't you think?" He sat next to Madeleine, directing the question to her with a smile.

"*Naturellement,* your Majesty," she said calmly. "You have a superb instinct for what helps people to be sociable and comfortable, without dispensing with the proper order and convention." She lightly touched her lips with a napkin. "It would never do to serve so informally at luncheon or dinner."

"I am delighted we agree," Louis said, and helped himself to a magnificent arrangement of sliced fruit. "I would very much enjoy having another look at the tapestries in the gallery," he continued. "I wasn't able to see them very well last night, but I have always heard that they are some of the best of their kind." His gaze took in Geoffroi as well as Madeleine.

"Of course, sire," Geoffroi answered. "The Lady and the Unicorn tapestries have a long history in my family, and are much revered by the people hereabouts—we open the Gallery at Christmas time so that people may view them and enjoy their beauty."

"But that is such a wonderful, generous gesture on your part!" the King rejoined, looking pleased. "One of the deepest desires I have is to share the culture, beauty and art of our beloved country—ancient and modern—with all my people. I am encouraged by this practice, that our nobles will yet become the vanguard of a new civilization of education and humanities, where *la belle France* will lead the way."

The King had spoken loudly enough for several people to hear, and one of the courtiers raised his glass to commend the sovereign's words.

"*Louis et la belle France!*" The toast was repeated, and glasses clinked all around the room.

In the leisurely time that followed breakfast, Geoffroi and Madeleine accompanied the King to the gallery to view the tapestries. He asked many intelligent questions about them, both their manufacture and the symbolism of the subjects, showing himself to be well-versed in the legends about the mythical Unicorn.

"Your daughter, having been raised here in the sight of these tapestries daily," said the King, addressed Geoffroi, "must be intimately acquainted with the stories and, perhaps, influenced by them?" Madeleine felt her pulse quicken, as if they were moving onto dangerous ground, although the King had made no reference to Jeanne or François the whole morning. Maybe, she hoped, he assumed they were exercising the rights of the young and newly-wed, and taking their time before joining the rest of the company. But not to appear, when their King was in residence, could easily be taken as insulting and disrespectful. *Please, please don't let him ask where they are,* she begged her saints. Geoffroi, she noticed, did not seem alerted to the same feelings she was experiencing—perhaps she was over-reacting?

"My daughter has loved these beauties since her earliest years," Geoffroi was saying easily, and he smiled at the memory. "Many a time have I wandered this hall with her, listening to her imaginings and re-tellings of what each tapestry could mean, inventing fantastic stories about the little animals, and how they would band together to defeat the Lion or ride away on the Unicorn, with the Lady cheering them on!" Too late, he caught his breath—the tale was far too close to the nobles' uprising against Mazarin and the King not even a decade ago. The King pursed his lips, and gazed thoughtfully at his host, and subject.

"You have raised her to be an independent spirit, then?" the King asked quietly. Geoffroi answered just as quietly.

"My little Jeanne has been educated to know her own mind, but to temper her imagination with her duty to God and to her sovereign," he said simply. "She believes in beauty, goodness, justice, and mercy."

The King acknowledged this statement with a gracious nod of his head. Madeleine felt a moment's relief, then froze again at Louis' next words.

"And where are the young newly-weds?" he asked. "Still abed?" He smiled, but was clearly waiting for an answer.

Just then—Madeleine was later to thank all the saints she had ever prayed to—the far door flung open and a royal messenger approached at a run, flung himself on one knee before the King, and breathlessly beseeched permission to speak.

"What is it, Mercury?" Louis spoke, his voice sharp with apprehension. "The Queen?"

"*Oui*, Majesty," the young man gasped out. "The birth is near, if not already accomplished. I left the palace before dawn."

The King turned to Geoffroi, but there was no need to speak; his host was a man of action.

"I will see to your Majesty's carriage and horses immediately," Geoffroi said, and strode from the room. A look at Madeleine as he left communicated all.

"Our household is at your disposal, Majesty," she said. "I will have the servants assist you in every way——."

She broke off as the King laid his hand on her arm, gripping it firmly. For a moment, she thought, he looked like any young man facing the prospect of becoming a father, and fearful for his wife and child.

"Will you pray for them, Madame, and for me?" he asked softly.

Touched to her heart, Madeleine nodded, tears springing to her eyes. They stood together a moment longer, and she found the courage to speak. "Do not worry, Majesty, your queen is young and strong, and she has physicians enough to tend to her, she and the child are in good hands, praise God."

"*Merci, Madame,*" the King said, then squaring his shoulders, he walked quickly from the room, calling for his attendants. Madeleine breathed a long sigh of exquisite relief and gratitude, and then nearly ran to find Griselde and put into motion all that was needed to hasten the King's departure.

At the end of a very long and busy day, Madeleine fell into bed at the side of her husband, too tired to do more than caress his cheek. The King had departed, on horseback, within an hour of receiving the news, with the courtiers and his chevaliers, leaving the rest of his entourage to pack up everything and make the long trip by wagon and carriage, later in the day. Madeleine had overseen the preparation of provisions for their journey, and in addition, had the satisfaction of bidding any remaining wedding guests farewell; most were within riding distance of Chateau d'Arcy, and were eager to return to their homes with tales of the young King and the wedding entertainment.

"My dear wife," Geoffroi murmured to her, lying on his back with his eyes closed. "What may I do to thank you for the magnificent way everything—including and most especially Louis himself—was managed? You saved us all time and again."

Madeleine shivered with tired delight. "My dear husband, it is to your credit that your household is already so well managed that it can perform such wonders that even a King would have no complaints!"

He turned to her, enfolding her in his arms. "Truly, though," he said, "is there not something I can give you that will cheer your heart and strengthen you after all this mighty effort?" He kissed her forehead tenderly.

"There is one thing," she said softly. "I would dearly love to journey to Boussac, as soon as we may—I miss it so!" She didn't add that it was François she missed most, even after only one day. "I want to be sure that Jeanne and François have everything they need, and that they are happy there. If I could be there soon, then I will be satisfied, and content to return here as mistress of Chateau d'Arcy."

"Then we shall do it," Geoffroi said. "I hope you do not mind, but I promised Jeanne, as her bride gift, that I would bring to her two of the tapestries—her favourites—

when she was settled at Boussac. Upon my death, they will all be hers."

Madeleine's response was immediate. "Do not speak of death!" she cried, crossing herself, then smiled. "But the tapestries are yours to do as you will with them, and such a reminder of her happy childhood here will go far to make her happy in Boussac." She kissed him back, hungrily. "I've been thinking about re-decorating that old gallery anyway, my love." She squealed in delight as he grabbed her by the shoulders and kissed her.

✠ PART TWO ✠

⚡ ONE ⚡

SATURDAY – 7 MAY 1881 – PARIS
An Unexpected Visitor

AFTER SEVERAL TEDIOUS HOURS SPENT convincing the representatives of the *Sûreté* that we were not murderers, John and I were allowed to depart, taking poor Geneviève with us. She was subdued to the point of insensibility, and although I was reluctant to leave her alone, I was heartened by the sour little concierge's reception of her boarder—she actually put her arms around the young woman, exclaiming over her and helping her up the stairs, all the while shooting angry looks at me and John, as if it were our fault.

"Poor thing," John said. "What an unspeakable event, and to see it with her own eyes!" He passed a shaky hand over his face, and leaned back into the carriage as we drove away. A quick glance at me prompted him to lean forward and speak again. "And you, too, Vi," he said, kindly taking my hand and pressing it. "No one should have to see such things."

I nodded my head in silent agreement. Truly, I was shocked at the grisly sight of Sébastien tied to the wooden table, his body carefully laid out in imitation of the saint whose name he bore, and the arrows—those horrid arrows!

Something ticked in my brain, pulling me away from the dreadful sight into a more detached observation.

"There was no blood," I said, after a moment, and I saw John cock his head slightly, appraising.

"You're right," he agreed. He, too, seemed eager to put the appalling vision far from his mind, and focus on facts. Our eyes met as the carriage rumbled onwards, our faces lighted by the streetlamps as we passed them by.

"That's not what killed him," we said in unison.

"The arrows were…shot into him *after* he was dead," I followed up, feeling an overwhelming, if irrational, sense of relief that poor, handsome Sébastien hadn't died in such a ghastly way. But strange, very strange, that arrows should be so handy to the murderer's task! Surely they weren't just lying about the room—or would he have brought them with him? It was unaccountable. Something stirred in my memory, but did not emerge—I would have to wait.

"But then, what—how did he die?" John pursued.

I shook my head. "One presumes the police will determine that, if they have any sense at all, when the body is autopsied."

We were silent together for a moment. But once started, my mind raced through all my impressions of the body, the room, the fixtures. What else could I recollect?

"What, if anything, struck you about the room?" I asked John, reluctant to speak my own thoughts first.

His brow furrowed slightly. I gazed for a moment out the window of the cab, and noticed we were crossing the dark, swiftly flowing river now, under the gaze of the great cathedral, and would soon be at my *pension,* where John intended to drop me and then continue to his own flat. The night sky was beginning to fade, and it amazed me to see that the light was creeping up behind the buildings to the East. I turned back from the window as John spoke again.

"Other than that the Titian—if it is a Titian—was missing? And the easel it had rested on was broken?"

I nodded. As John remained silent, I prompted him.

"The tapestry?"

He looked puzzled, then slowly started to nod. "Yes, it was…somewhat askew?" He frowned.

"Yes," I said eagerly. "It looked like someone had tried to take it down from where it was hanging, but I rather imagine that would take more than one person to do it successfully, don't you?"

John agreed, and we both fell silent, thinking.

I gave a deep sigh. "What with poor Geneviève fainting, and having to summon the *Sûreté* to the scene," I said, "I'm afraid my usual powers of observation have somewhat failed me."

John smiled sympathetically. "I am very certain that, given a little time, you will more thoroughly remember all manner of things which you observed at the time, and have hidden away to be brought out later, under calmer circumstances."

I nodded my head appreciatively. "Thank you, John," I said. "I have known that to happen before, so I will be encouraged." Then I shrugged. "Not that my, or anyone's, observations are likely to be called for—the police will do their usual bungling, indifferent job—and our statements will be dismissed as irrelevant." I pursed my lips in scorn. "Death by misadventure, or by persons unknown."

"If we aren't outright arrested for the murder ourselves," John added wryly, and I knew he was thinking of when that had actually happened in Venice, when he had spent a very long day with the *Carabinieri,* defending himself from outrageous accusations.

"Well," I smiled, following up his allusion, "at least the French police are a little more organized than the Italians. I saw that there was actually a medical examiner among the officials who arrived." I mused on an idea. "Perhaps there might be some way to get more information…." I broke off at the disapproving look John directed toward me. "What? I only want to know what happened!" He shook his head, and refrained from any open admonishment, as the carriage stopped at the door of my *pension.*

"Heavens!" I said, looking at the front door, which was opening as I gazed, to reveal the anxious face of my landlady. "What will *madame* Millefleurs think I've been up to?" (Her actual name was Rochambaud, but she always wore dresses and shawls saturated with tiny flowers and birds, hence the *sobriquet.*) I always stayed *chez elle* when in Paris, and the truth is, she was very acquainted with my odd ways.

"I doubt she'll think anything at all, Vi," John said. "You have her wrapped around your finger, you know." He stepped out of the carriage and held his hand out to help me alight, then led me the few steps to the door. *Madame* Millefleurs, looking relieved, swung the door wide and ushered me in, giving only one curious—and rather interested—nod at John, whom she had met before, and who was laughing as he climbed back in the cab.

"*Mademoiselle* Paget," murmured my landlady, "if I did not know you better, I would think there was something almost scandalous about you having been out all night."

"Nothing more scandalous than murder," I said in reply, and because she was used to my fanciful wit, she merely laughed and allowed me to pass through the hallway to my room without further questioning.

After a few hours' refreshing sleep, I was sitting at my desk in the comfortable corner room late the next morning, writing down my thoughts about the unaccountable events of the previous night, when a gentle tap on the door interrupted my thoughts. It was Eloise, one of the *pension's* staff, a young woman who helped out in the kitchen and with serving at the boarders' repasts.

"*Mademoiselle* Paget," she said, bobbing in a slight curtsey as I opened the door, "you 'ave a gentleman visitor." She was practicing her English, which was getting quite good. She was an intelligent girl, and I often relied on her to procure morning buns and coffee for me when I rose too late for the *petit déjeuner* served at the *pension*.

"At this hour!" I said, glancing at the clock on the mantle—it had just struck eleven a few moments ago. "It must be *monsieur* Sargent, *non?*"

But Eloise shook her head, and held out a card for me to take. Surprised, I took the card, expecting it to be some detective from the *Sûreté*, come to harass me further, but my surprise was inordinately heightened when I saw the name.

"Charles Wilkinson!" I couldn't help but say the name aloud, and smiled broadly in wonder and, I admit, a secret delight. I looked up to see Eloise watching me with great interest. "Please tell him, my dear, that I will be down presently."

She curtsied again. " 'e is in the *librarie*, *mademoiselle*," she said—the "library" in this *pension* being a rather large

closet of a room with a bookcase filled with French ro-
mances and moldy English novels—but still, there were two
comfortable chairs near a large window that looked out into
the flowery courtyard. I nodded my acquiescence and turned
back into the room to make myself presentable for this unexpected guest.

I hurried to smoothe my frizzed hair and shake out my
crumpled skirts. Charles Wilkinson! The last time I saw him
was in Venice, more than a year and a half ago, when our
paths collided—literally—and then merged as we worked
together to solve the mystery of a servant girl's death by
drowning (as I have shared in a previous story, *The Love for
Three Oranges*). I took a deep breath, opened the door, and
walked slowly down the stairs with what I hoped was a
charming *insouciance*. My rapidly beating heart told me I was
anything but calm. The door to the library was open, and I
crossed the threshold with a smile.

"Mr. Wilkinson, what a pleasant surprise!" I said, holding out my hand for him to shake; we held hands rather
longer than is customary, and then parted with an increase
in embarrassment, on both sides, I perceived. I invited him
to sit, and then seated myself.

"And to what do I owe this visit from the 'consular
consultant' to Europe and Great Britain?" I said, trying for
a light tone. His position and activities for a nascent international policing force seemed to suit him, as he looked as
chipper and handsome as he had in Venice, only perhaps a
little greyer about the temples, which added to his distin-
guished looks.

"My dear Miss Paget," he said, looking slightly reproachful. "When last we met, you were addressing me as
'Charles'—cannot you do the same now?"

I laughed, and felt myself blushing. "Only if you call me by my first name as well," I said, then hurried on to cover my response to his words, as a sudden thought occurred. "You're here about the murder—are you not?" Then again, as my mind was focussed now, I hazarded a guess, mindful of his profession. "No, it's about the missing Titian, isn't it?" I looked at him with some keenness.

He threw up his hands in defeat. "You have guessed it on the spot," he said, smiling. "I should have been disappointed, you know, if you showed yourself any less sharp than in our former dealings with each other."

I smiled in return, and then looked to the open door to see Eloise standing there with a tray of coffee and croissants, hesitating at the threshold. I nodded for her to enter, and she placed the tray on the table between our two chairs.

"Merci, ma petite," I said. *"Nous nous servirons nous-mêmes."*

"Oui, mademoiselle," she said, and left the room quietly—but not closing the door entirely. It was only proper. I poured us each a cup of coffee—Charles took his black, mine had both cream and sugar—and settled back to hear his explanation.

"We have been tracking a network of art thieves," he began, taking a sip of coffee, then replacing it on the tray where it grew cold as he continued to speak, though not very coherently. "Having been alerted by…our sources…that there was a painting by Titian at *monsieur* du Sommerard's museum, that we felt would be of some interest to the person we are investigating—we had planned to set up a trap—but we were too late," he said, shaking his head.

"You have been to the *musée?*" I interrupted. "Did you see—" I broke off, not wanting to name the horror again.

He nodded, grimacing. "I was called there early this morning, apparently just after you and John left." He smiled slightly. "Imagine my surprise when the detective in charge mentioned your name, and John's—as possible suspects!"

I rolled my eyes—*most unladylike,* I could hear my mother saying. "I should imagine they'll give up that idea sooner rather than later, now that you've become involved?"

"One would hope," he said, more seriously than I expected. I stayed silent, waiting for him to continue.

"It seems logical," he said, "to assume that poor *monsieur* Bayard was, most unfortunately, in the wrong place at the wrong time, and surprised the thief—or thieves—as they arrived to take possession of the Titian."

"But the manner of his death—the staging of it," I couldn't help but interrupt, "in imitation of the subject of Titian's painting, that St. Sebastian—why would ordinary art thieves go to such dramatic lengths? And besides," I pursued, as Charles seemed about to reply, "our poor Sébastien was not killed by any arrows piercing him." I looked sternly at my detective friend. "Do you know yet exactly how he *did* die?"

Charles sighed deeply, and then rose from the chair to close the library door firmly. I steeled myself to hear the sordid details, but nonetheless I felt a thrill of anticipation.

"First," he said, sitting down, "this is no ordinary art thief—there *is* something fiendish in his *modus operandi*—he has done this before, left a victim arrayed and presented like the painting that was taken."

"You say 'he'," I said. "You are convinced it is one person?"

He shrugged. "A mastermind, if you like, who directs others at times, but yes, essentially, just one person." He took up his coffee cup, glanced at the cooled liquid and put it down again. "Second, my dear Violet, you—as usual—are quite correct about his death. The arrows were applied, as it were, *post-mortem*. In actual fact, they did not even pierce his flesh, just his clothing; they were merely laid in place, to look like the painting." He paused. "*Monsieur* Bayard was strangled, not with some kind of cord or thick string, but with bare hands."

I was silent for several moments, taking this in, and grieving that so young and personable a man as Sébastien should lose his life so dreadfully, and his poor sister! Left on her own to console herself as she might.

"And the tapestry?" I said, shaking myself from my reverie.

Charles looked puzzled. "Tapestry?"

"Yes," I said with impatient asperity. "The Lady and the Unicorn looking in the mirror. You didn't notice that it was askew where it was hanging?"

He shook his head, but caught on quickly. "You saw it earlier in the day. Yes," he added, seeing my surprised look, "I know you were there, with John and his sisters. So it looked different from when you had seen it earlier?"

I nodded. "Both John and I noted it, and thought perhaps it looked as if someone had tried to unhook it from the ceiling, but failed—or perhaps was interrupted."

He shrugged again, clearly thinking it of little importance. "It's possible the thief thought it of some value, and attempted to remove it, but the Titian was the real prize—and the staging of Bayard's death makes it incontestable that the man we are after was the one involved."

"But it isn't actually confirmed that it *is* a missing Titian, is it?" I insisted.

Charles threw me a sharp, closed look. "Why do you say that?"

"It's what *monsieur* du Sommerard said," I replied, thinking back. "And he was quite upset to learn that Sébastien had spoken of it to me and John."

We both sat deep in thought for a few moments.

"I'm going to need your assistance with this, Violet," he said at last. "Yours and John's, if you are both willing."

I nodded, almost absent-mindedly. My mind was churning—I thought he was too off-hand in dismissing the importance of the Lady and the Unicorn. Something itched at the back of my mind, and I was determined to find out what it was.

"In particular," Charles continued, and I pulled my attention back from speculation, "I would like to interview the sister, Geneviève, I believe her name is?" He looked at me with a half-apologetic smile, behind which I could easily see his flattering confidence in me. "I am hoping, you see, that you will accompany me—she may feel more comfortable if there is another lady present. She was unable to tell my colleagues very much last night, understandably."

"I am happy to oblige you in this," I said, adding with a wry smile, "I have a few questions of my own for the young lady." I did not say it, but I had the feeling she had a great deal of information to impart, but for some reason was keeping silent. "Shall we go presently?"

At his nod of agreement, I rose from the chair, and I recalled that he had mentioned needing John's help as well.

"Shall we stop at John's apartment on our way?" I asked, then paused. "Assuming, that is, that you have a carriage at your disposal? It's not far out of our way to where Geneviève is staying."

"Absolutely," he said, rising also and taking my hand in his. "I can't tell you how delighted I am to have us—the three of us—working together again." He bestowed a brief kiss on the back of my hand and, disengaging, I sped from the room to hide my blushes and get ready to "work."

I wondered, briefly, as I dressed for going out, whether the international organization that employed Charles Wilkinson would ever consider engaging a female agent—for pay?

What an amusing idea!

Two

July 1738 – Boussac, France
Great Expectations at Chateau Boussac

THE MID-SUMMER HEAT HUNG UPON THE LAND like a wet linen sheet, stifling any wayward breeze and paralyzing even the bees into drowsy inaction. *I shall go mad,* thought Louise de Rilhac de Carbonnières, mistress of Chateau Boussac, *if I'm imprisoned in this wretched place much longer.*

Her only hope of diversion—and possible escape—was pinned to the long-delayed royal visit. Louis XV had almost miraculously succeeded to the throne by virtue of the deaths of all three nearer heirs to his great-grandfather, Louis the Sun King; at age thirteen, he had been crowned and proclaimed King, but nonetheless, fifteen years on, he ruled under the strict guidance, softened by the politic flattery, of Cardinal Fleury, who used the King's lazy, pleasure-loving nature to his own great advantage.

Which left the young King with a fair amount of time on his hands.

Louise strolled languidly through the dark, almost cool halls of the chateau—even the ponderously thick stone seemed turned to charcoals by the relentless sun. It was nearing sundown, very late in the day at this time of year, but as she turned from the hall into the long gallery, with its north-fronting, long windows, the faint waft of cooler air brushed her cheeks. She wasn't given much to self-reflection, though it was all the rage these days, she had come to learn, at Versailles especially. Her much older husband, insisted on reading to her in the evenings from that detestable *philosophe* Montesquieu, and for the sake of marital harmony, she attempted to appear interested in her self-improvement; she much preferred the sardonic Voltaire—his jabs at the Church found a place in her heart for the resentment she held there tightly. Men dressed up in medieval robes, telling everyone not to do the things that they themselves did, secretly—except that everyone knew about it. She tossed her head at the thought.

She wandered over to stand in front of her favorite place in this gallery that held the eight colorful tapestries—the largest of them all, of the Lady crowned and queenly, holding a tall rod of power, with the Lion and the Unicorn kneeling to either side of her. Regal, self-contained, wise—all the virtues that Louise wanted to see in herself, and sometimes thought she did—if only she could be given the chance to prove herself—if only she could be a queen—or at least, influence a King.

Her great-grandmother, Madeleine des Grillets de Rilhac de la Roche-Aynon, to give her all her patronymics, had been a favorite of the Sun King, and if the family legends could be relied on, had been influential at his court. It was she who had sent the tapestries here, from Lyon, a wedding gift for her son and his wife. More than that, there was little enough known about the origins of either the tapestries themselves, or the stately, powerful woman depicted in them.

A small smile softened her lips for a moment. Rumour had it—and Boussac was not so far from Versailles when it came to rumours—that the Queen, after bringing ten royal children into the world in as many years (Louise shuddered at the thought), had bidden the King from her bed. Her life was given over to pious meditation and prayer, surrounded by plainly-dressed handmaidens and quiet servants. She had done her duty, apparently, and felt justified in laying aside sensual pleasures to feed her spiritual needs. But the King was a young man, not yet thirty, and approaching the prime of life; it followed he would be seeking a mistress. Louise herself was young and vibrant—and in dire need of a man's attentions.

Was now the time to become the woman behind the throne? A sudden gust of wind set the tapestries to waving in the gallery, and Louise saw that storm clouds had gathered to the north all of a sudden, and the sky was darkening quickly. At the same moment, her steward Émile strode quickly through the far door, stopped for a brief bow, and spoke, his tones measured (as always) but, she could tell, trembling with some inner excitement.

"We have word, *madame*, from the foresters, that the King's entourage is nearing Boussac." He glanced away for a moment at the fast-forming storm, and his brow wrinkled. "They are resting at Nohant, and will be here within a few hours."

Louise was jolted into action; she felt alive again. She asked questions in quick succession. "And my husband? Where is he? Does he know? Is the household prepared?"

Émile answered her promptly, as they both began to walk out of the gallery—there would be much to be done.

"The master is resting, in his chambers, and asked not to be disturbed, for any reason."

Louise halted abruptly, and felt a hot flush rising up her neck; she knew what that meant, that 'resting', and for a moment a wave of rage engulfed her. She had married her cousin Georges to keep the Chateau in the family, and because he seemed civilized and easy to manage, but his physical predilections and desires were another matter entirely. Émile was studiously looking away, and turned to straighten a wayward cloth on a nearby table; it gave her the time she needed to bring herself under control. He sensed it quickly, and spoke again.

"The household, *madame*, is in good order, and given what I have been told about the numbers of the retinue— they are small, fewer than twenty—I am quite confident that we have all the necessary resources to make our royal guest comfortable."

"Good, very good, Émile, thank you," she said, turning on her smile that had always been called brilliant. "You know I trust you as no one else in this household."

Émile bowed as he held open a hallway door for his mistress. "You do me great honor, *madame*." She sailed past him toward the dining room, her mind already moving on.

"Do we have *any* ice left at all?" she said. "The King *does* love iced wine in Summer."

⅋ THREE ⅋

SATURDAY – 7 MAY 1881 – PARIS
About the Art Thief

THE SATURDAY MARKETS WERE TEEMING with buyers and
sellers as our carriage wound its way through the uneven
streets of the rather disreputable *Marais*, en route to the elegant apartment John used as both home and studio. I hadn't
thought of it before, but now realized with some distress that
we might encounter Emily, and little Violet, who perhaps
were just learning this morning of the death of their friend.
I chewed on my lip in consternation (another bad habit, according to my mother), and was startled out of my deep
thoughts when Charles spoke.

"Violet, please tell me what you are thinking," he said,
in very considerate tones. "I fear you are distressed beyond
what you may have acknowledged, even to yourself, about
this terrible event."

"Oh," I said, giving myself a little shake, and attempting
a smile. "It is not for myself that I am deep in reverie, but
for another, who had found…who perhaps had thought…"
I stumbled over my words, not wanting to expose poor
Emily's feelings. "Someone, in short, who was very fond of
Sébastien Bayard, and who will be most unhappy when she
hears of his death."

Charles was nothing if not discreet, and merely patted my hand in a comforting way.

"Tell me more about this art thief of yours," I said, willing myself to focus on our *case*. The word itself, I admit, gave me a little thrill. "What else has he stolen? You mentioned there was another murder as well?"

Charles, who was sitting across from me in the carriage, leaned forward, his measured voice belying the tension his body betrayed. "I have only joined this case recently," he said, "some six months ago, and this time, we felt we were very close to catching him. But my colleagues have been tracking this man for at least two years—and our research indicates that he may have been active for many more than that."

"Do you think he knows you are on his trail?" I said.

Charles shrugged. "Given that he seemed to be taking his leisure last night, what with setting up the…" he paused, seemingly aware he wasn't really talking to colleagues, "the death scene, I rather imagine he felt confident he would not be interrupted."

I nodded in agreement, and waited for him to say more.

"We call him The Revenant," Charles said, checking my response before continuing.

"The Ghost," I said, nodding. "Is that because he appears and disappears at will, going through walls and that sort of thing?"

"Yes, I'm afraid so," he sighed. "We have tracked him, in the last two years, from Florence to Vienna, to Brussels and now here, in Paris."

"What other works of art has he stolen? I assume they have not been recovered." I took a moment to glance out the window, saw that we were still some streets away from John's abode, and turned again to Charles.

"Not yet," he said, with some asperity. "In Florence, he made off with a smallish sort of square painting, about so big"—he held his hands about fifteen inches apart—"that was attributed to da Vinci, an unfinished portrait of a young woman. It was in private hands. That was about eighteen months ago."

The carriage gave a sudden lurch, almost throwing us both to the floor; Charles rapped his cane on the roof, and was answered by a torrent of French curses and excuses. After a moment, we drove on.

"In Vienna, and this was an earlier one, nearly three years ago, there was a somewhat larger canvas, maybe two feet by three, this time a Botticelli sketch, or rather, a draft for a larger painting, one of the seasonal things he did, Spring, I believe."

"Again in private hands?" I ventured, and was pleased when he nodded.

"The third piece was actually a small clay figure, the model, it is believed, for the young David by Donatello; the final sculpture is, of course, at the Uffizi in Florence, but this small figure was…"

"In private hands," I finished his sentence. He looked perplexed for a moment, then thoughtful.

"Even though the Titian was at the Musée de Cluny," I said, thinking it through as I spoke, "it was still not something on public display. We need to find out how it came to be in du Sommerard's possession in the first place." I pondered this a moment, wishing I had brought some kind of notebook and pen to write down my thoughts.

"I believe the *Sûreté* detectives are looking into that," my friend murmured. We were silent for a few moments.

"Something else strikes me about the Revenant and his choice of art," I said, smiling a little at the name.

"That they're all Italian artists?" Charles said.

"Yes, that's one thing," I replied. "But even more, each of the works was somehow unfinished, or not the final work of art—a draft or a model, or, simply not finished." I mused on this, but couldn't put my finger on what that might mean.

"What are you thinking, Violet?"

I shook my head. "I'm not sure, but there is *that* about the theme of incompleteness that may tell us something about the character—and motives—of our thief." I looked at him and smiled ruefully. "But come, tell me which of these instances also had a dead body involved."

Charles looked cautiously at me. "You are certain you want to know?"

"How else can I help you if I don't have all the facts?"

He nodded briefly. "I actually don't have all the facts for that incident," he admitted. "Just what my colleagues referred to in passing, that a previous theft scene—the one in Florence—included the body of a middle-aged man, dressed in women's clothing. The cause of death was not mentioned," he added, looking troubled. "I may have assumed it was murder." He glanced up at me, his brilliant blue eyes fastening on mine. "I shall find that out, it may be important." He hesitated a moment, then added, "I hope you will understand if I request that you do not reveal anything I have just said about the art thief we are seeking, especially to Miss Bayard."

I looked at him in astonishment. "Surely you don't think *she* has anything to do with that?" He shook his head, but I did not take that as a substantial negative. "Of course," I said, recovering myself. "Of course I shall do as you request."

The carriage lurched to a halt and, looking out, I saw we had arrived at John's apartment.

"Shall I tell the driver to wait?" Charles asked.

"Yes," I said. "I'm hoping we won't be long at all, we will just collect John and be on our way to see Miss Bayard." My dread of encountering Emily returned, and I hoped, feeling cowardly, that we would find her indisposed and unavailable.

We were ushered into the dining room, where the remains of a largely uneaten morning repast lay scattered on the table. Emily was seated at one end, alone in the room, and upon our entry, she immediately jumped up and ran to me, throwing her arms about me and bursting into tears.

"Oh, Violet," she sobbed into my shoulder. "How terribly, terribly awful, I can't imagine…" Further words were impossible, and I did all I could by patting her back and murmuring comforting sounds as I held her. After a moment, she drew back, looking forlorn and apologetic, and then horrified as she became aware of Mr. Wilkinson in the room.

"Oh!" she said, applying her handkerchief to her tearstrewn cheeks. "I am so dreadfully sorry, Vi, I didn't see…you will excuse me, sir," she said, composing herself with a great effort.

"Dear Emily, do not distress yourself about him," I said. "This is Charles Wilkinson, you will recall I told you about him? The person in Venice to whom we owed your brother's release from the *Carabinieri?* He is involved in helping the *Sûreté* solve this horrendous crime."

With another great effort, Emily acknowledged the gentleman and invited us to sit.

"My dear," I said, declining her offer by continuing to stand. "We are here only to collect John, whose help we need. We are going to Miss Bayard's *pension* to…discuss this sad event with her."

Emily looked up at me wearily, and shook her head. "John is not at home, he went out about an hour ago. He didn't say where." She smiled sadly. "He was greatly discomposed, I must say, more than I have ever seen him." She put her face in her hands and began to weep again. I felt helpless in the extreme, and was wondering what on earth I could do to assuage her feelings, when luckily Mrs. Sargent entered the room, quickly assessed the situation, and took charge.

"My dear Violet," she said, barely glancing at Mr. Wilkinson, "you must excuse our poor Emily, she is feeling quite poorly. Come, my girl," she said, addressing her daughter and laying a gentle hand on her shoulder. "Why don't you have a good lie down, and in a little while, we'll have some fresh tea?" Emily rose, unresisting, and let her mother escort her from the room. Mrs. Sargent spoke to me as they passed by.

"Violet, if you are here for John, he is not in the house," she said. "I will come back if you want some tea."

"No, thank you very much," I said. "Emily told us about John, so we'll just be on our way and catch up with him later."

"As you like, my dear," she said, and left the room.

I glanced at my detective friend. "I'm sorry that I didn't adhere to the usual politenesses of introductions," I said, knowing of course that he didn't really mind.

"Not at all," he said. "I'm sorry your friend—John's sister?—is so unhappy." He looked grim. "We shall find who did this murder, and he *shall* be punished."

Moments later, we were back in the carriage, both of us silent and thoughtful. In fifteen minutes, we pulled up in front of Geneviève's *pension*, and soon were ushered into the little drawing room, where we were surprised to see not just Geneviève, but John as well, sitting next to her and holding her hand; and a third person, a man unknown to us, who jumped up on our coming in, looking nervous and unsettled.

"Vi!" John exclaimed, rising in haste and coming over to kiss my cheek. He looked drawn and pale, as if he hadn't slept all night. He glanced at my companion, then looked again more closely. "Charles! Why, I never!" He shook hands heartily with our former conspirator from Venice, a smile briefly brightening his face. A sudden look of comprehension flashed in his eyes. "You are here, in Paris, about this dreadful event?"

"Yes, John," the agent said, keeping his voice low. "There is much for us to talk about."

John nodded, and turning to Geneviève who, I had discerned, was looking at the scene with little interest, introduced Charles to her. John seemed to be overlooking the third person in the room with them, but Geneviève roused herself briefly from her lassitude to do the honors.

"Please allow me to introduce an old friend of mine, and Sébastien's," her voice breaking slightly, "*monsieur* François DesRosiers, of Boussac."

"Carbonnières," the man said, apparently correcting his friend. "François Louis de Carbonnières." Geneviève had spoken in French, which said to me her friend did not speak English, or at least, not well. She looked over at him, with what I fancied was a mixture of concern and irritation, and watched as he bowed in greeting. I took it upon myself to offer our condolences for Sébastien's death.

"*Bonjour, monsieur,*" I said, with grave politeness. "*Permettez-moi de vous offrir nos condoléances pour la mort de votre ami.*"

He bowed again, and without saying another word, seated himself on a straight-backed chair near the window, offering his former, more comfortable seat to me with a small gesture. He was a compact and slender man, a little older than the rest of us, perhaps in his mid-thirties, with abundant brown, wavy hair, beardless but with a small moustache with upturned edges, and dressed very well with—it seemed to me—a studied carelessness. His brown eyes were intelligent but lacking humour. He was attractive in a conventional sense, I suppose, but somehow unremarkable—except for the puzzle of his name. How could Geneviève not know his correct name?

We all sat down in a decided state of awkwardness, no one quite knowing what to say. Suddenly *monsieur* de Carbonnières rose, went to Geneviève and whispered something to her, at which she nodded faintly, then he stepped back, bowed to her and then again in the general direction of the rest of the company, and departed.

After a few moments, there seemed a clearing of the tension that had filled the room, and I took the lead with our investigation.

"My very dear *mademoiselle* Bayard—Geneviève," I said, turning to her. "I fear that time is of the essence, and we have some questions for you."

Four

July 1738 – Boussac, France
A Dangerous Kiss

THE EXPECTED ARRIVAL OF THE KING brought such a change to the silent halls of the towering fortress of Boussac that Louise felt her heart lift in gratitude for the hope and delight it engendered in her. Georges, her husband, had been apprised of the impending visit in time for him to don appropriate dress and make an appearance in the main receiving room well before the entourage entered at the gates.

"*Madame,*" he said courteously, bowing to her. He was a good-looking man, some twenty years older than she, but still slim and vigorous, with thick brown hair that he had cropped short to accommodate the tightly rolled, powdered wig that was in fashion. Louise, suppressing her anger, which at other times would goad her to intemperate speech, succeeded in appearing with her husband all that was gracious and cheerful; her hand rested lightly on his arm as he escorted her outside, to stand at the top of the magnificent staircase which rose from the courtyard stones. She was not sorry to be obliged to separate from him then, as her voluminous ruffled and draped *pannier* more than filled the space between and around them.

The principal servants of the upper household began to line the courtyard, ready to bow and assist the visitors with every need. It seemed as if everyone's breath was held in excited anticipation, and no one spoke.

The rhythm of steadily beating hooves announced the approach of the King's entourage, with himself foremost on a large black stallion. They had travelled simply and swiftly, without the usual painted carriages full of splendidly dressed courtiers—more a hunting party of friends and companions, dressed in leather boots, linen shirts and light capes—than a self-indulgent, pampered young monarch on tour with half his court. Louise had seen the latter on other occasions, and much preferred the former—the King would be so much more approachable without all the fawning, quarreling, contentious personages who made up his court at Versailles.

She and Georges descended the staircase to meet their King as he was handing the reins of his horse to the head ostler, looking about him in apparent appreciation of the ancient fortress, still strong since before the time of the Crusades.

"Your most excellent Majesty," Georges intoned, bowing deeply, with Louise in a gracious curtsey at this side.

"*Mes sujets et mes amis,*" the King said affably, holding out his beringed hand for them to touch with their lips, after which he lightly caressed Louise's cheek with the back of his hand, an amused twinkle in his eye. She couldn't help it— she blushed, *comme une petite fille!* she thought to herself—but then she noted that the King seemed to find her blushes even more appealing, as the appraising look softened his fine features and dark eyes.

"You have only increased in beauty and grace since we last met, my dear Louise," he said. Then he turned abruptly and signalled to his entourage, at which they all dismounted and came forward to be presented.

The party quickly sorted themselves, with horses led off by grooms, and servants showing the men's attendants to their masters' quarters. The King's men numbered ten, three of whom were known to Louise and her husband; the others were unknown but all were made welcome. A spattering of rain from the fast-moving clouds hurried the group into the chateau, and any conventions of formality seemed to disperse with the friendly and companionable attitude of the King towards his men and his hosts. Very soon, as the King spoke his preference for cooling drink and a comfortable situation, they were seated in the *petit salon* used by the family, where the northern aspect invited soft breezes through the tall, open doors and windows—the rain had swept through the gardens quickly, leaving the air refreshed and the trees and flowers sparkling.

Louise was the only lady present, and she bloomed and shone brightly from all the attention, which was courteous and courtly. She had exchanged her wide, pannier-encircled skirts for a less formal gown that showed her youthful shapeliness. After a while, she became aware of the interested glances that passed between some of the younger men and the servant maids who were in and out of the room, bringing refreshments and renewing the wine and cognac. There would be some hustling and whispering in the hallways tonight, she was sure. After a little more time—and much wine and spirits—the laughter and conversation in the room grew louder, and she overheard some coarse expressions from the men who sat furthest from her and the King.

Her attention was drawn to Louis, who had just risen from his sofa and was gesturing to the assembled company to keep their seats; he walked over to stand before her.

"Madame," he said, then smiling softly, "Louise, my dear, although this is my first visit to Boussac, I have heard much about the beauty of its gallery of tapestries." He held out his hand, in which she placed hers, and assisted her to rise. "I would be delighted if you would escort me there and tell me all about them."

"Your Majesty," Louise said, curtseying slightly and inclining her head in submission. She stole a quick glance at her husband, whose face was inscrutable and bland as he watched her pass by with the King; then he turned back to the attractive young courtier with whom he was conversing. She noticed Émile as she left, standing alert to any needs of the guests, and felt a grateful satisfaction that all would go well under his watchful and correct management.

"I fear my men may be too boisterous for you, Louise," the King said, holding her hand on his arm with his own pressing hers gently. "We have ridden a long way, and the comforts of your household"—he paused as a young and buxom maid passed by, trying to curtsey while holding a platter of fruits and nuts without coming to grief—"are inviting them to relax and be, perhaps, more informal than strict propriety allows."

"Not at all, majesty," she assured him, although she couldn't help a glance at him that showed him a glimpse of her true opinion—amused and tolerant, aware of the breaches of etiquette but choosing to allow them. "With you to guide them, sir, their behaviour cannot help but be without reproach."

Louis threw his head back and laughed out loud, squeezing her hand as he did so. *"Touché!"* he said. "I love a woman with a sense of humour." He drew her nearer to himself, and her softer gown allowed her to feel the pleasant warmth of his thigh against hers. He reached a hand out to touch her cheek, looking a very well-communicated question quite directly into her eyes.

Louise felt a stirring in her body, a deep firing of desire and longing that quite took her by surprise, and, she feared, showed only too openly in her eyes as she gazed back at Louis. Her marriage to her cousin, some three years before, had only prompted the most ceremonious couplings at first, rousing nothing so much as confusion and distaste in her, and after a year or two of embarrassing and increasingly cold encounters, her failure to produce any children at all, to say nothing of a male heir, effected the cessation of their marital relations for which she was deeply grateful.

Servants in the great hall were standing ready to open doors at their approach, bowing low as the King and their lady passed by. They entered the tapestry gallery, and Louise signalled to the footman to depart and close the door behind him, leaving her alone with the King.

He moved a few steps along the gallery ahead of her, having gracefully disengaged her hand from his arm, and looked keenly up at the tapestries.

"The legendary Unicorn and the royal Lion," he said, coming to a stop to peer more closely at the woven images. "The myth and the fact, the ideal and the real, isn't that how you would see these?" He waved a hand to include all seven tapestries hanging in the room. The softened light of the late Summer evening filtered through the long windows, creating a warm glow that glinted off the gilded chairs, bronze candlesticks and the golden threads intertwined in the tapestries.

"Yes, majesty," said Louise, moving to stand beside him. "Also, the spiritual and the earthly," she said. "The Unicorn has long been seen as a symbol of the Christ, pure and gifted with healing touch, while the Lion is the sign of worldly power and might."

Louis smiled, and sauntered on to the next tapestry, then stood back a little and surveyed all of them. He appeared thoughtful. "Why do you suppose," he said, "that there is only a woman in these tapestries, with the Lion and Unicorn for companions? Why are there no men? But ah, I see," he interrupted before Louise could answer, "there is another person, but a woman, too, probably a servant, yes?" Louise nodded, and spoke.

"Your majesty is no doubt familiar with the legend that claims only a virgin can attract and tame the wild Unicorn—again, a symbol of the Virgin Mother and the incarnation of Our Lord in her womb."

Louis nodded, then looked amused and about to say something, but he pursed his lips and assumed a listening attitude. "Go on," he said. Louise wondered at his interest, and although she felt a definitely exciting undercurrent of an altogether different subject behind his words, she answered calmly.

"I have studied these tapestries all my life," she said, and then, catching the King's raised eyebrow, she smiled and added, "Young as I am, majesty, I have lived a solitary life here at Boussac, and these tapestries are the most interesting elements of this place, so I have devoted many hours to looking at them and endeavouring to determine what they mean."

"Do tell me," he said, drawing near her. They were both looking up at the tapestry that depicted the Lady binding a delicate wreath of flowers, with her maidservant standing by holding a golden platter of flowers to be used in the wreath. The Lion and the Unicorn flanked the pair of women on either side, holding a divided standard and a flag, respectively, and gazing at the Lady with reverence.

Louise took a deep breath; the King was standing slightly behind her, and had moved close enough to press against her; she could feel his warm breath on the back of her neck. It made her dizzy.

"I believe these tapestries tell a story about the Lady as she journeys through her life, both physical and spiritual," Louise said, trying to master the rising desire that the King's close presence inflamed in her. "In this one, she looks younger than any other image, so I think of it as the 'first' in order. Also," she added, catching her breath in a little gasp as she felt the King's lips on her neck, "the making of wreaths is typically an activity of young, unwed girls."

"And the Unicorn? The Lion?" murmured the King, as he continued to caress her warming skin.

"Pythagoras tells us," Louise continued, not without an effort, "that the ancient mysteries of numbers relate that the 'one' of things stands for the spiritual, and the 'two' for the physical and spiritual together." She gasped again as the King's arms went round her waist, clasping her to him.

"Please go on," he said. "I do so love to mix philosophy with sensuality." His fingertips brushed against her breasts lightly, and she felt a stab of desire ripple through her.

"The Unicorn's flag is whole and undivided, as it is completely spiritual," she managed to say. "While the Lion's standard, split into two"—was all she could say as the King deftly turned her around and into his arms. He finished her sentence.

"Represents the royal attributes as both physical and spiritual, the earthly"—he began kissing her neck and bosom, continuing to murmur—"and the divine." He looked at her and grinned. *"Comme le roi, non?"*

"Oui, majesty," Louise could barely breathe, and when the King leaned in to kiss her lips, at first gently, then with increasing urgency, she nearly fainted with the heady sensation.

Gasping for air, she drew away momentarily, and they looked at each other for a long moment. *This is dangerous, to kiss a King.* Then she gave way entirely, and drawing him to her, kissed him fiercely, not ashamed to reveal her deep hunger—and then there was no going back.

⟑ FIVE ⟑

SATURDAY – 7 MAY 1881 – PARIS
Secrets and Untold Stories

"WHAT IS IT YOU WOULD LIKE TO KNOW?" Geneviève said in a soft voice, looking sadly at me and Mr. Wilkinson. It grieved me to be questioning her, but the manner of her brother's death seemed to me a crime of unresolved passion—strangulation with one's own hands is so very *personal* a way to commit murder—and *that* suggested perhaps a more than familiar relationship between the murderer and his victim. Geneviève might have, I conjectured, even all unwittingly, some important information about her brother that could help reveal his killer.

Charles and I had settled it beforehand that I could pursue this line of questioning, whereas he would take the lead in regard to the theft of the Titian.

I glanced at Charles, who gave a very subtle sign for me to continue; he seemed to fade into the background, sitting a little outside the circle formed by me, John and Geneviève. John had resumed his seat next to her, turned toward her, and I leaned forward to make the space more intimate. It occurred to me that the ability to become unremarkable—invisible, even—would be quite an asset for someone whose work was centered on unobtrusive surveillance. It made me doubt that I would ever be fitted for such a position. I brought my straying mind back to the task at hand. How to begin? I thought about that dreadful moment when the three of us had discovered poor Sébastien's body.

"My dear Geneviève," I said, "I hope that what I can tell you now will give you *some* relief, about the manner of your brother's death." She looked at me, puzzlement and apprehension in her demeanour. I hurried on. "As dreadful as we at first thought, the arrows"—I hesitated—"the arrows were not the cause of his death; they were simply laid upon him, touching only his clothing, so he would not have felt their sting."

I saw her eyes filling with tears, and she grasped at John's hand tightly. "Go on," she whispered.

I ventured another glance at Charles, who I saw was looking intently at Miss Bayard, so I continued. "The police have determined that poor Sébastien was strangled"—I got no further, as Geneviève gasped and her eyes rolled back—she fainted dead away, falling against John, who quickly put his arms around her to keep her from falling off the sofa. I fumbled in my reticule for salts and, rising, uncapped the tiny bottle and waved it under her nose. With a very ladylike sneeze (I could never have achieved such a genteel sound, I am sure), she regained herself and sat up, looking about her in a confused way.

"But what…how…what does that mean?" She managed to speak, and carefully disengaging herself from John's embrace, looked at him, and then me, fearfully. "I don't understand."

I saw that John was just as shocked as Miss Bayard; his face was white as linen, especially against the darkness of his beard and mustache. I chided myself severely; I had utterly forgotten that John was not privy to the information I had lately learned from Charles, about the manner of Sébastien's death.

"I'm so sorry, John," I said, laying a hand on his arm, "and Geneviève," I said, turning to her, "it grieves me to be the one to inform you both of this matter."

"But what, indeed, does it mean, Vi?" John asked, then turned to Charles to repeat his question. "What are we to make of such a death? And of such a presentation of poor Sébastien's body—what kind of twisted mind would do such a macabre thing?"

Charles maintained his silence, so I sat back down and tried to formulate an answer to this troubling question.

"It is possible," I said, trying for an even, objective tone, "that the manner of his death indicates that there may have been a sort of, well, relationship between Sébastien and…and the person who did this." My words died out in the stillness of the room as their meaning sunk in. To my consternation, I saw John change color—as flushed now as he was white before—and his expression become closed and austere. Geneviève looked only more bewildered.

"Do you mean to say, Miss Paget," she said, "that it is possible that someone whom Sébastien knew—an acquaintance, or a colleague—" she broke off, but continued to look at me, the question open on her face.

I nodded. "Or a friend…," I hesitated. "Or perhaps someone even closer."

Geneviève was startled. "Sébastien has no lover, that is, not as far as I know," she said, looking troubled.

I let that go for a moment. "May I ask, how long have you been in Paris, Geneviève, you and Sébastien?"

"Why do you ask?" she said, looking wary for the first time since we had begun. I did not answer, having learned that an awkward silence is often a spur to keep someone talking. She spoke again.

"We—that is, Sébastien travelled here first, at *monsieur* du Sommerard's request—he accompanied the Lady here from Boussac," she said. I thought it interesting that she referred to the tapestry in that manner. She continued, "When it became apparent that he would be here much longer than expected, I decided to join him."

She glanced at me, then John. She seemed to have forgotten altogether that Charles was in the room. "We are not used to being apart," she said, and I saw the tears well up in her eyes, but she remain composed.

"And when did Sébastien arrive here?" I pressed gently.

She closed her eyes a moment, then opened them. "He left Boussac some time in February, at the beginning of Lent," she said. "I followed him in April, just after Easter."

"So the tapestry has been here since then, too, since February?" I said. I thought her way of marking time by religious holy days and seasons unusual, even quaint. But then, I follow no religious observances whatsoever, so that sort of thing always strikes me as vaguely medieval.

She nodded, and was stopped from talking further by a cough which caught at her throat and seemed to be choking her. John leapt up and poured some of the now-cooled tea into a cup, and handed it to her; she drank, and the cough subsided.

"Are you aware of any acquaintances or friendships that your brother may have formed while he was here in Paris for those two months without you?" I asked.

She shook her head. "His letters to me were very frequent, nearly every day, and I remember nothing in them about any particular person—that is, no one that he mentioned more than any one else," she said, and thought silently for a moment. "Of course, he wrote of du Sommerard, and the staff at the *musée,* and maybe some places he visited in the city, but—nothing that I can recall, I'm sorry." There was something about her response, however, that made me think she was concealing something.

I was wondering if it would be too much of an impertinence to ask her to see Sébastien's letters, when to my surprise John spoke up. "Dear Geneviève," he said, taking her hand gently, "if you by chance have any of his letters here with you, it is very possible that some mention of a new acquaintance or perhaps some club or restaurant that he visited may have escaped your attention. Would you allow me to look them over to see if any such thing can be found?" He looked so seriously and so intensely at her that she seemed mesmerized. "I give you my word, I shall be most discreet. But it so very important that we try all avenues of information, don't you think?"

She nodded her acquiescence, and rising, though a bit unsteadily, she said she would retrieve any letters she had from her room. I could see that a few minutes' reprieve from our presence and our questions would be a great relief to her.

When Geneviève had left the room, closing the door behind her, I turned immediately to John. I didn't need to speak, as he saw my question in my face. He had risen from the sofa, and was walking to and fro in great agitation, though much suppressed. Finally, he came to a stop and addressed me and Charles together.

"I had not—there was no time or opportunity before this—I must tell you now, that I have been acquainted with

Sébastien Bayard for some time now, in short, since his arrival in Paris in February." He passed a shaking hand over his face and exerted strenuous control over his clearly ravaging emotions. "I could not say this before his sister, not knowing…if she…" He broke off, then spoke haltingly. "It is possible that some of the…company…that he was keeping…it could be useful to ask them, to find out if any one knows anything."

Charles and I exchanged astonished looks, and I felt a sinking in my heart at the possible import of John's words.

We heard Geneviève descending the staircase with soft steps, and I only had time to tell John we would speak of it later, when the door opened and she re-entered the room, a small bundle of letters, tied by a ribbon, in one hand. She gave them to John without a word, then sat down again heavily, as if exhausted by her errand.

"I shall take infinite care of these," John assured the poor young woman, who only nodded, "and return them to you as soon as possible." He had regained control of his emotions, but I could see his inner turmoil still affected him strongly.

"Miss Bayard," Charles spoke for the first time, and all of us turned our eyes to him. "Can you tell me anything about the Titian painting at the *musée?*"

She looked puzzled. "I am not sure what you mean, *monsieur.*"

Charles kept his eyes steadily on hers. "Do you know when, or how, the Titian—I should say rather, the supposed Titian—came into the possession of *monsieur* du Sommerard?"

She shook her head. "It was there when I arrived in April, just where you saw it yesterday," she said, looking first at John, then at me. I marvelled at her words—was it only yesterday that we had gathered at the *musée,* to see Emily's wondrous Lady and Unicorn? Weeks seemed to have passed since the previous morning.

"Did your brother tell you anything about it? Or du Sommerard?"

She thought a moment. "I believe we both remarked about it, given it was my brother's *nom sacré,*" she said slowly. She had used the old French term for her brother's given name. "He did tell me, when I first arrived, that the painting was being thoroughly examined to determine if it was actually a Titian."

"Did *he* think it was actually by Titian?" Charles pressed.

She shook her head again, and smiled sadly. "My brother is not an art expert, *monsieur,*" she said. "He had hopes of becoming more knowledgeable…" Her voice faded away, perhaps realizing how those hopes were now extinguished.

"And du Sommerard?" Charles continued. "Did he ever speak of it to you?"

"*Non, monsieur,* he did not," she said, a little too quickly, I thought. "He and I—we did not speak much—we did not, we were not," she stumbled a little, out of delicacy perhaps? "We did not get along." She looked up, a shade of defiance on her face. "I thought he did not treat my brother very well."

Charles was silent but attentive, and it made her speak again. She shrugged, a very Gallic, dismissive movement.

"He did not pay Sébastien what I thought was a just wage, for his efforts and time," she said. "And more than that, I felt something more, between them, a kind of imbalance of the wrong kind of power, perhaps—as if du Sommerard was pressuring my brother somehow." She looked very sad. "It was a feeling that grew over time, as I did not often see them together, and I did not say anything to Sébastien—I thought perhaps I was imagining it—I was very protective of him, you see, as he was of me."

I could see she had reached the end of her strength, and interposed to put an end to the questioning for now.

"You have been more than helpful, Geneviève," I said firmly, ignoring Charles' slight start of surprise. I rose quickly. "We will leave you now, to rest as you can—as you should."

The two gentlemen rose as well, and as the door was opened just then by the concierge, come to rescue her grieving boarder, I assumed from the reproachful look on her face, we all took our leave. John bent and whispered something to Geneviève, to which she nodded and pressed his hand gratefully, and we made our way through the hall and out the front door.

The sun was shining in the most appalling and heartless way; the birds were singing and flitting among the trees; passersby laughed and chatted, oblivious of our sore hearts and puzzled brains. The coachman dismounted to open the carriage door, and I turned to John as we stood on the sidewalk at the kerb. He clutched the bundle of letters in his right hand.

"John," I said, laying my hand on his arm, "you will peruse these letters carefully, I know, but before that, we need to know more about what you meant—your acquaintance with Sébastien?"

Charles nodded, affirming my request. "Perhaps," he said, "we would be more private if we discussed this at my office?"

I felt John stiffen, and in my heart, Charles' suggestion had the sound of an official inquiry, but I shook off the thought, and reminded myself that Charles was our friend, and could be trusted.

"Yes," I said quietly, "I think that would be best."

John looked so completely miserable, I almost changed my mind, but he held out his hand to help me into the carriage, and climbed in behind me without a word.

SIX

NOVEMBER 1738 – CHATEAU BOUSSAC, FRANCE
A Wondrous Turn of Events

WINTER CAME EARLY THAT YEAR, and rain lashed the battlements of Boussac without mercy. Following the King's visit in the Summer, Louise had lived in the hope of a letter—a summons—to the court at Versailles, so that she might be spirited away on the wings of desire, and power, to the freedom for which she so longed. She had desperately wanted to change her circumstances, and thereby change her fate.

But it was not to be.

An altogether different kind of circumstance now surrounded her, closed her in, and foretold a very altered future, one that she thought she had been denied—she was with child.

The life she carried inside her was the son or daughter of the King of France, this she knew for certain—he was the only man other than her husband with whom she had ever lain, and she and Georges had parted ways long before Louis appeared. But what did that mean? She tortured herself with this question unceasingly, once she had determined that she was actually pregnant—what should she do? Inform Louis? Would he even want to acknowledge this child? She mused on the possibilities. He had only one son, his eldest, the Dauphin; a second boy had died five years ago, at the tender age of three. There were daughters, of course, eight of them!—but daughters were not heirs, useful for marriages of alliance only.

But would he spurn her, assume it was another man's, as if she were some harlot passed around the court? In the very short time she and Louis had spent together, during that week in July, he did not seem to her a cynical or dishonest man—despite his penchant for adultery (which was understandable, given his circumstances), he was modest and unassuming, eager to please and to be liked.

She had little if any fear of what Georges might think, or do. Although both of them would know it was not his begotten child, the very fact of having a child born to Boussac would be a benefit, a shield, an unlooked-for gift from God—no, Georges would not quibble over its paternity, in fact, given that he could count as well as the next man, he might be amused to think he would be raising a royal bastard.

There was power in that, a certain kind of power, subtle, to be used subtly—bastards had been known to gain kingdoms and even thrones before this—and Louise grew calmer in the face of this possibility. It helped her determine one thing, at least—she must find a way to induce the King to acknowledge the child as his own, not openly, perhaps, but in some certain, provable way, should it ever become necessary or desirable to bring forth proof.

She stood at the window of her bedroom, and looked out at the wind lashing the trees and bushes below in the drenched and forlorn garden. She would need a strong, clever ally for this battle, one whose well-being was as caught up in the event as hers, and the child's. She drew a deep breath, and mentally prepared herself to make the first move—she must tell Georges.

"I was wondering when you were going to tell me," Georges said, looking down at her with a faint smile. He stood at the fireplace, one arm resting on the mantle, while she sat on a small, comfortable sofa in the warmest room in the chateau, an extension of the conservatory, where charcoal fires were kept banked and glowing throughout the Winter, to keep the fragile plants alive and growing. It was late evening, and dark, after dinner, and although he had been clearly surprised by her request to speak with him privately for a little, he acquiesced with some grace and, she could see, curiosity.

"You know?" Louise was annoyed at his perceptiveness.

"I'm not blind, my dear," her husband said, downing the remainder of his glass of brandy in one gulp. "Pregnant women have a certain look, you know, sleek and rosy and dreamy," he said, then laughed. "Once they've gotten over the dry heaves and the queasiness."

She grimaced; it had indeed been the case with her. "You seem to know a lot about it," she said grumpily.

"Oh yes," he continued, enjoying himself immensely. "I noticed what you ate—or wouldn't eat—as far back as"—he looked up as if consulting a chart—"early in September, have I got that right?" He set down his glass and walked the few steps to stand directly before her, looking down from his great height. There was no amusement in his face now.

"So," he said, "my dear wife, do you want to tell me who is your lover—the father of this child—or do you want to make me guess?"

Louise looked up at him in distaste, and felt a moment's flicker of fear. Was he going to take this badly, like some peasant husband enraged at another male sniffing around his mate? The thought gave her the strength to show contempt for such low behaviour, and she looked up at him coolly.

"Well, it's not you," she said, defiance helping to make her voice unquavering, although her heart was pounding.

Georges looked intensely at her for a long moment, then threw back his head, laughing uproariously.

"*Touché!*" he cried, and unceremoniously sat down next to her on the little sofa. "I always have admired your spirit, dear Louise," he said. He looked at her almost kindly, and took her hand. "I admit, I have been rather a bad bargain for you, haven't I? You really deserved a better husband."

She looked at him, cautious and waiting for a trick.

He played with the rings on her fingers for a few moments.

"Nonetheless," he said. "We are husband and wife, and now we shall be mother and father." Louise marvelled as she saw his countenance soften at the thought.

"It will be all right," he said, and gave a great sigh. "Have you told him? Have you told…the King?" He looked at her keenly; she felt she was being regarded as an equal, as almost, perhaps, a partner. "What is your plan?"

Louise's thumping heart began to subside, and she felt it easier to breathe than she had in several weeks. She leaned back with a sigh, and then began to outline her ideas to her husband, about this remarkable child who was upending their lives, and perhaps, directing their fate.

❧

"He told you this himself, did he?" Georges mused thought-fully about what his wife had just related to him.

"Yes," Louise said. "I had only heard the rumours that the Queen bid the King away from her bed, but he told me that her doctors had insisted her life would be in danger if she had another child—especially after this latest miscarriage last Spring."

"Well, well," said Georges. He smiled just a bit. "Do you think, and I realize this is a delicate question, Louise," he said. "Do you think you are, perhaps, his first *liaison* out-side of his marriage?"

Louise considered this. "It's possible," she said, "you recall how much they were devoted to each other in their first years together." She thought again. "And he did say that he was much offended and hurt by her refusing to lay with him, this past year." She looked up at her husband. "Why do you ask? Do you think it is of some importance?"

"Oh, I think it's just that a man has a certain, what shall I say, fond affection for his first mistress, you know, that can lead him to be rather sentimental about her—that is, if she doesn't present him with any trouble or demands."

"So you think it may be to our advantage if such is the case with me?" Louise asked cautiously, feeling her way through such an extraordinary conversation—with her own husband, about her infidelity, with the King! She could hardly believe it herself.

"Yes," he said. He had risen from the sofa and was now walking about the room, having refilled his brandy glass, sip-ping at it absent-mindedly. "As long as we don't play this with a heavy hand, I think we—and this child—*our* child—will benefit greatly. You see," he continued eagerly, "if we present it to the King as shall we say, an *heir-in-reserve*, with the solemn promise not to ever make it public unless he chooses, he may perhaps be induced to make a private declaration."

"But that is assuming a great deal," Louise objected. "That is assuming the child will be a boy."

Georges nodded, but did not seem concerned. "I have every faith in you, my dear," he said. "One so strong and vital as you will bring forth nothing but males."

"Silly man," Louise retorted, though without acrimony, as she struggled to rise from the sofa, which was low. Three months of pregnancy had increased her weight considerably, although she had been able—she thought—to hide it under voluminous skirts. Georges immediately stepped forward to assist her, and she was caught off guard by his tender manner.

"*Merci, Georges,*" she said, feeling a bit awkward. They stood face to face for a moment, and she felt even more mixed emotions when he bent forward and kissed her forehead.

"Be well, my dear Louise," he said. "I truly look forward to having a child to raise with you."

℞ SEVEN ℘

SATURDAY – 7 MAY 1881 – PARIS
L'Ordre de la Licorne

WE WERE SEATED IN WHAT I COULD ONLY TERM a cold and dreary cell of a room in the *Sûreté*. The floor was wood, darkened by boots and coal dust and substances I didn't want to dwell upon too closely. Charles sat on one side of an old table, scarred with scratches and fissures, with one leg shorter than the others, so it rocked in an ungainly manner whenever one of us shifted positions, our elbows on the table for balance. John and I sat next to each other, across from Charles, facing a set of windows above shoulder height, through which cloudy sunlight sifted across our faces, but left Charles' face in shadow.

I shivered at the implications of this interrogatory atmosphere, this dank and gloomy place of menace and incarceration. Was John once more to be subjected to the indignity of being thought a suspect? I trembled at what I had heard my old friend say, that he had known Sébastien Bayard for some months, and had not revealed it upon "meeting" him yesterday, presumably for the first time. What could it portend?

And yet, I should have had more faith in Charles as a friend and a colleague, however irregularly sorted—for soon the door opened and a subordinate came in with a tray that he set on the table before us, revealing a most welcome bounty—hot coffee, cream and sugar, and an abundance of pastries, croissants among them, along with butter, jam and slices of smoked ham.

"Forgive me for this detestable room we're in," Charles said, gesturing to us to help ourselves to the food. "The *Sûreté* looks rather askance at myself and others in my position—we are considered interlopers and gentlemen-*amateurs*, flitting here and there chasing ghosts." He looked around with a sigh, then poured himself a cup of coffee. "At least the food here is as good as at any café, I'll say that for the chaps who keep this place."

"Indeed," I said, sipping my coffee with cream, and taking a bite of a *pain au chocolat*. Heavenly! John drank his coffee absent-mindedly, I thought, and said nothing. He seemed even unaware of our surroundings, so deep in thought was he. After a few minutes' further silence, however, wherein we fortified ourselves with the strong and fragrant brew, John took the lead.

"I'm sure you're puzzled about what I have said, and concerned that there may be something sinister or dire in the circumstances of my short acquaintance with Sébastien Bayard," he said, looking up briefly first at Charles, then longer at me. I shook my head involuntarily, and opened my mouth to speak, but Charles spoke first.

"John," he said, "I have absolutely no reason to suspect anything sinister about your acquaintance with Bayard, and certainly there is nothing in the world that would cause me to harbor any notion of wrongdoing on your part." He leaned forward and placed his hand for a moment on the artist's arm. "We have been through enough for me to know—and trust—your character as an upright and honorable man, no matter what it is you may feel you need to tell us now."

I gazed surreptitiously at Charles Wilkinson, searching his face for the meaning behind his words—what had he discerned that I had yet to learn? It made me uncomfortable, thinking that I was to discover, perhaps, something about my dear friend that was previously unknown to me—but that I should have, somehow, had the perspicacity to perceive.

John smiled, a little grim, at Charles, then shook his head, squared his shoulders, and prepared to speak. I set down my coffee cup and steeled myself to not betray any emotion at what I might hear, but rather to listen attentively without judgement—a task more often honored in the breach than the realisation for me.

"There is a…society, shall we call it, a society of gentlemen whose approach to life—whose path in life, perhaps—is off the beaten track, what might be seen as *bohemian,* and yet, which is a path of beauty, and love, and a deep connection to the Ideal, the Unique." He paused, drank his coffee, and continued after a silence. It was nearly the longest, most complete sentence I had ever heard John speak.

"*L'Ordre de la Licorne,*" he said, and moved his hand briefly, as if to say *that says it all.* But we waited in silence for him to speak again.

"There is a particular restaurant where the Order gathers, from time to time," he continued, looking into his cup, then up at us briefly. "I'd rather not say more, if it is not needed." His smile was tremulous. "Confidence—trust—is paramount for the members of the Order, and I have given my word, as have we all, not to betray that trust."

Charles nodded, keeping silent, and a slight twitch of his fingers in my direction indicated to me that he wished me to do the same. I bit down on my lip to keep my questions inside, for the time being.

"Sébastien was introduced to the group by a friend of mine, who vouched for his character—he is not, at this point—that is, he *was* not"—John's voice broke slightly with the jolting memory of Sébastien's death—"he was not a member, just a guest, but a most charming and welcome one." He took a deep breath, looked again into his now empty cup, and set it down firmly.

"I saw him there on three or four occasions, I think," John said. "He was very interested in art, and those of us of the Order who were artists became well acquainted with him, as he visited our studios and came to our exhibitions."

Charles interrupted, quietly. "So you saw him outside of the Order's meeting place?"

John nodded. "I had asked him to join me and some friends for dinner twice or so, and he readily fell in with the group—he was quite perceptive about the visual arts, and had a delightful way of creating a narrative about a painting, almost as if he were writing a story about what he saw, or intuited, about the subject." He mused a moment, a sad smile on his face. "He was very often spot on in regard to the emotions and atmosphere of a given painting—especially portraits"—here he gave me a knowing look—"which he analyzed very intimately and with a depth surprising in such a young man. Rather like you, Vi."

I could no longer hold my tongue. "But this all sounds quite friendly and collegial," I said. "What makes you think that some person, or persons, in this company would be likely to take against poor Sébastien so intensely that he would murder him—and in such a theatrical way?"

John grimaced at my forthright words, but I held my ground, looking at him directly and expecting an answer. Charles leaned forward with greater interest.

"Odd that you should use the word 'theatrical'," John said. "The one person who showed a certain *animus* toward

Sébastien was a young actor, determined to be a great tragedian, but who we determined was not a suitable candidate for membership in *L'Ordre de la Licorne*, and was therefore denied entrance."

"What was it that made him not suitable?" I asked.

John shrugged. "He had an intemperate nature, fell into arguments quickly—in short, he was an angry, unsettled person—though when not angry, extremely likeable and entertaining—much as becomes an actor." He thought a moment. "He had a way of disregarding all rules, or rather, dismissing them as not applicable to such as he. The members came to the consensus that he drew too much attention to himself."

"And that would not be a good thing for the Order," Charles said calmly. "As he is not a member," he continued, "can you tell me his name?"

John looked exceedingly unhappy at this request. "I'm not sure I can do that," he said. He raised a hand as Charles began to speak again. "Perhaps there is another way to— investigate—this man?" He looked away, then back again. "Perhaps I can seek him out, and…and…try to find out about his activities, his whereabouts last night?"

Charles nodded slowly; I could see the reluctance in his face to allow this. "I understand your desire for discretion," he said, then seemed to make up his mind. "Very well," he said. "I'll give you two days to find and talk to this man," he said, sounding more official than previously. "After that, well, we shall have to proceed on different grounds."

"But why," I broke in, "did this actor have ill feeling toward Sébastien, by all accounts the most charming of men, and the least likely to give insult or occasion for dislike?"

I saw John and Charles exchange a look at my question, and was surprised when Charles obliged me with an answer.

"I believe that for some persons, whose self-image is both fragile and powerful, often the case with actors, the experience of rejection is a frightfully strong spur to vengeance." He glanced at John, who nodded his head.

"Rejection!" I repeated, my mind in a spin. "Being rejected as a member of *L'Ordre de la Licorne*, you mean?" But before either of my friends could respond, a light broke into my muddle. "Ah," I said quickly. "Something more personal than that, then."

We three sat silently for some moments, but I was the first to rouse us up.

"We have two days, then," I said, rising from the table. I didn't want my silence or inaction be interpreted to mean I was distressed by the illumination I had just experienced about *L'Ordre de la Licorne.* "Oh, yes, John," I said, forcing a cheerful tone, "you don't think you are going to be allowed to do this all on your own, do you?" He returned my sally with a weak smile, and I saw Charles shake his head.

I walked about the room for a moment, thinking.

"I believe I shall visit Miss Bayard again," I said. "I am sure there is more to be gleaned from her. You, John, as you said, should follow up on that person of interest from *la Licorne.*" He nodded, and I noticed that Charles was looking at me mock-expectantly, as if waiting for his assignment. I smiled at him.

"And you, Mr. Wilkinson, will, I believe, be most productively employed by interviewing *monsieur* du Sommerard, will you not?"

"Even so, Miss Paget, even so," he said agreeably, and also rose from the table. He looked at John, and smiled encouragingly. "We have our marching orders, John, it seems," he said. "Please be careful," he added, and glanced at me, his look suddenly somber, almost severe.

"Both of you," he said. "This is not a game."

Eight

MAY 1739 – Paris, France
An Audience with the King

THEY HAD DECIDED TO WAIT, INDEED, until the birth of the child—their son, whom they named François Georges Louis de Rilhac de Carbonnières—before relaying any news to the King. They had debated for months whether a personal visit were to be preferred over merely sending a trusted messenger with a letter, which would of course, be liable to being read by anyone and therefore defeat their objective of secrecy and discretion. In the end, it was decided the family of three would spend some months in Paris, and determine a way and a time to meet privately with the King.

Little François had been born toward the end of Lent; Easter was early that year, so after the holy days had passed, and the child had been baptized, *la famille de Carbonnières* set out to take up temporary residence in Paris, close enough to Versailles to be available for an audience, and in splendid enough surroundings to make it suitable to invite the King to visit them—a possibility, they thought, given his occasional but very kind letters to Louise since their encounter the previous Summer. The de Rilhac family, anciently of

Boussac, still held title to an *hôtel* in the Marais *arrondissement* of Paris, with Louise as the current owner, so to this small but finely proportioned mansion, she and Georges and their son now travelled, having sent servants, furniture, clothing and other *accoutrements* before them to ensure a comfortable residence.

A fresh and sunny day oversaw their arrival in the transitioning City of Paris, with large public squares and magnificent buildings commissioned and planned by Louis XIV, the present King's grandfather. But the change from open country to city quarters, narrow dark streets, and the bawling of sellers of every kind of product imaginable shook Louise's senses until she felt stunned by the noise, the smells, and the overwhelming numbers of people bustling to and fro. They were welcomed at the door of their mansion by the trusted Émile and other servants—Louise was grateful to hand baby François to his nursemaid and seek a hot bath and a rest for her aching back. Her husband took himself off to his own quarters, led by his valet, probably, she thought, for much the same relief as she herself desired. They would meet at dinner.

"We have received a response from the King," Georges said quietly when they were seated at the dining table. The servants had placed the dishes and wine on the table, and had withdrawn, leaving the two alone.

"*Non!* Already?" Louise tried to suppress her startled feelings—Hope? Fear? It was hard to tell. She reached for her glass of wine instead of the platter of fish, her appetite having suddenly disappeared.

Georges, on the other hand, helped himself calmly to the fish, and then the tiny red potatoes and carrots in a white china bowl, and began to eat.

"His Majesty is pleased to come visit us here," Georges continued.

Louise concentrated her thoughts on this news; she looked over at Georges, and spoke almost in a whisper. "Coming *here*…" She thought rapidly. "Do you think he suspects?" she said. "About the child?"

Georges shot her a bemused glance. "I sincerely doubt that there is very little that occurs throughout the kingdom that is unknown to the King—especially where it concerns his own *activities."* He stressed the last word with a lift of his well-shaped eyebrow.

Louise set down her glass abruptly, spilling a few drops. "Do you mean…a spy? In our household?"

Her husband shrugged. "Why do you think I have been behaving myself so well this past ten months?"

"I…I don't know that I thought anything at all," Louise said. "Your behaviour is your own concern, not mine." She took a long swallow of wine, then reached for the decanter to refill her glass, not adding any water this time. The soothing liquid both calmed her and inflamed her inquietude.

"You're saying," she said at last, "that someone in our household informs the King of our…our…"—she struggled to contain her sense of outrage—"our actions, our conversations, our *lives* every day?" She looked incredulously at her husband. "Do you have any idea who it is?"

Georges shook his head, then shrugged again. "Perhaps I do," he said. "But it doesn't really matter—there would always be someone, you see, and frankly, in this matter, it will probably work to our advantage."

"What on earth do you mean?" Louise cried, then took hold of herself and lowered her voice when she spoke again. "How can it be to our advantage to have a spy relaying every word, every action, every idea in our heads to His Majesty?"

Georges looked at her levelly. "Have you, or I, said or done anything treasonous? Or even disrespectful to our sovereign? Are we plotting a coup? Spreading evil gossip throughout the court about the King in any way?" He smiled at her. "Of course we have not," he said before she could answer. "And I am convinced that the King looks upon us as trustworthy and loyal subjects—with the added benefit of raising a spare *Dauphin* far from the intrigues of the court."

Louise thought carefully about what her husband had said, then nodded slowly. "It is true," she said, "that the letters—and the presents—we have had from Louis have been very kind and generous." She thought to herself that she should re-read those letters for more explicit hints of the King's knowledge and intentions.

"Which doesn't necessarily mean very much," Georges waved a hand, "coming from any monarch, but Louis, I think, is a sentimental and actually rather good-hearted man, despite the ill influences around him at court." He looked at her again, smiling more broadly this time. "I hadn't had time to tell you, but I received the other day a letter of recommendation—rather out of the blue—for a child's nurse who is looking for a position in Boussac, yes little out-of-the-way Boussac! She comes with the very best of references, and apparently is willing to work for an amazingly reasonable fee." He returned his attention to his dinner. "I think we can infer why and from whom she was sent to us."

Louise took in all this information with a sense of wonder mixed with trepidation. She felt her appetite returning.

"And when is His Majesty gracing us with his presence?" she said, reaching for the fish platter.

"Tomorrow morning, fairly early," Georges said, grinning at her look of surprise. "I think it's wise of him to get in and out of the palace before most of the court is even awake."

"Good heavens!" she cried. "There's barely enough time to prepare!" She made as if to rise from her chair and begin immediately, but Georges laid a gentle hand on her arm to keep her seated.

"Émile already knows," he said. "Rest easy, Émile will take care of everything."

The May sunlight had just begun to creep across the rooftops and gild the towers of Notre Dame, and the mist on the river was still clinging to the dark surface of the water as the King's carriage rolled up to the door of Hôtel de Rilhac in the Marais. Watching from an upper window, Louise noted that the carriage was plain, with no coat of arms or gilding, and was drawn by only two horses, with a single coachman. But the man who alighted was definitely Louis, and before she could close the curtain, he looked up and saw her at the window—she was elated when his face broke into a friendly smile, and she smiled back. She turned into the room and rushed downstairs to greet him herself at the landing on the first floor. What she hadn't seen were the small cadre of horsemen who were stationed before and behind the carriage at either end of the street, keeping a careful watch over their sovereign.

Émile was already escorting the King up the stairway from the street door, and had taken the King's cloak. Georges and Louise arrived at the foyer at the same moment, Georges having come from the library on the same floor. They bowed low, and as they straightened up, the King held out both his hands to them.

"My dear friends and loyal subjects," Louis said, smiling graciously, taking each one by the hand. "It is good to see you both here, in Paris."

"Majesty," Georges spoke first. "We are overwhelmed at your kindness and generosity, especially in your taking the trouble to visit us here in our home."

"Not at all," said Louis. "I like to be out and about in the early Spring mornings, so refreshing." He looked about him at the well-appointed foyer, its cream-colored walls and gleaming parquet floors reflecting the strengthening sun from a skylight high above, and from windows at either end of a long hallway. Paintings of the French countryside were hung at even intervals between pilasters painted a pale blue. "This is a lovely little house," he said. "Seems very comfortable."

"Merci, mon roi," said Louise, curtseying. "It has been in my family for many generations." She gestured toward an open door in the hall. "May we offer you some refreshment?"

The King inclined his head in acquiescence, and Georges led the way to the small breakfast room. Once inside, however, with the door closed and no servants around, the King spoke before they even seated themselves.

"We are most desolate," he began, speaking with the royal pronoun, which struck an official note in the conversation. "Most desolate," he repeated, "that we cannot remain very long in your company. And, if we may speak plainly, may the child be brought here, in my presence?"

Louise grew cold with a sudden fear, and glanced at Georges, whose serene countenance gave her a little burst of courage. She curtsied to the King. "*Bien sûr, Majesté*," she said, and hurriedly left the room.

Swiftly she climbed the stairs to the nursery. Opening the door quietly, she nodded to the nursemaid who was sitting in a chair by the window, knitting; she motioned to the nurse to remain seated, and went herself to the crib that held her beloved François. The baby was awake, cooing softly to himself as he gazed happily around him. His eyes lighted up when he saw his mother's face, and Louise's heart bounded.

She gathered him up in a soft blanket, tucking it securely around him, and held him for a moment, breathless at the sheer wonder of this little life she had brought forth—a prince! The son of the King, however irregularly conceived. Murmuring a prayer, she carried François back down the stairs and into the breakfast room, where she found Louis and Georges standing by the open windows that faced the inner courtyard, admiring the trees newly in leaf and the numerous birds that flew and darted among their nests.

"Ah!" Louis cried as Louise entered the room, and he approached her quickly with soft steps. He glanced at the bundle in her arms, and she was pleased to see a softened look cross his narrow face. "May I?" he said, holding out his arms. She very carefully placed the baby in his waiting arms, and stepped back a bit, holding her breath. No mother ever thinks any man can hold a baby the right way—but Louis showed himself adept at handling an infant.

"*François Georges Louis, comment-vas-tu?*" Louis murmured.

Louise was startled, and shot a quick glance at her husband—they had not mentioned the name of their child in their message to the King. *So the spy is real,* Louise thought, but found she was less perturbed about it than previously. Perhaps Georges was right, and it was not something they had to worry about. She shrugged inwardly. It was certainly not something they could do anything about, in any case.

Louis looked intently at Louise, then at Georges.

"Monsieur—Georges," he said, simply and with great dignity. "You have a most beautiful and healthy son here, do you not?"

Georges knew what was being asked of him, and he bowed his head to the King, and said, "Majesty, this boy will always have my complete love and protection all his life, and every advantage of education and religious principles that we can provide."

The King nodded, satisfied, and turned to Louise. "And you, *madame*, dear Louise, you are happy with this blessing of a son?"

Louise could barely speak, her throat tight with unshed tears. She nodded, and managed to murmur. *"Il est ma vie, Majesté."*

Louis gently handed François back to his mother, then he unfastened a small brooch from his lapel—a royal signet, with an engraving of a Unicorn and a Lion, dotted with rubies and sapphires, and surrounded with gold—and he pressed it into Louise's hand.

"In case it should ever become needed," he said. "But *le bon Dieu* will hopefully not ask that of us."

Georges and Louise, speechless at this awful moment, bowed again to the King, and when they looked up, he was striding out the door. Georges put his arms around his wife and son, and moments later they heard the house door clang shut, and the discreet carriage clattering away across the cobblestones.

PART THREE

ॐ ONE ॐ

SATURDAY – 7 MAY 1881 – PARIS
History and A Surprise

THE THREE OF US WENT OUR SEPARATE WAYS, John and Charles setting out on foot in opposite directions, and I gratefully seated in the carriage, the driver of which Charles had directed to take me back to Miss Bayard's *pension*. We had agreed to meet at John's apartment for a late supper, and share the results of our further investigations.

As the carriage crawled through the busy streets, I thought intently about what John had said—and what he had not said. What was one to make of this *bohemian order* of which he had spoken? I admit frankly that, old as I was at that time (the grand age of four and twenty), I had a rather imperfect understanding of the variety of relationships in which men and women could entangle themselves—but one hears things, you know—and I was not unacquainted with the concept of the "Greek friendship" as it pertained to men. John Addington Symonds, after all, had just published an outrageous book of poetry extolling *l'amour de l'impossible*— which Oscar Wilde was said to have read and approved.

I felt myself getting into a quandary: what need had I to know anything about John's personal life? And yet, he had laid it on the table, so to speak, that *some part* of that personal

life was pertinent to our murder inquiry. I recalled, with further mystification, that there had been rumours about John
possibly being engaged to a mutual friend, Charlotte Louise
Burckhardt, just this past Winter, but as yet nothing had
come of it. I shook my head in frustration. John would pursue his own angle on this murder, I told myself, in his own
way and within his own circle of friends, and would reveal
or not whatever was appropriate—beyond that, I should not
go, nor even venture to speculate. I had my own track to
follow—Miss Bayard—and to her I firmly turned my attention, as I discerned that the carriage was mere streets away
from her *pension.* I had better organize my thoughts.

The driver very obligingly dismounted to help me out
of the carriage; I thanked him sincerely and told him I would
have no further need of his services. After a few moments'
wait at the door of the *pension,* I was admitted by the scowling
concierge to the small drawing room I had seen only hours
earlier that same day—I marvelled how time seems to both
dilate and constrict, alternately flying past and creeping
along, leaving one in a ridiculously dizzy state, and unsure of
the actual day and time. *It is Saturday afternoon,* I reminded
myself, and just last night we were at the play, and afterwards, found poor Sébastien's body.

Geneviève soon appeared, pale and listless, but looking
as if she had perhaps found some rest in the hours since I
had visited her. A maid followed shortly, with coffee and a
few biscuits—it not being quite the hour for tea, as well as,
being a French household, tea not being quite the thing for
its ordinary boarders. I was grateful for the sharp tang of the
coffee, smothered as it was by the heavy cream I poured into
the cup.

"My dear," I began, not without some trepidation; I feared her habit of fainting might carry her off with only me to attend her. "Everything possible is being done to discover the person who committed this horrendous crime," I said, deciding to gloss over the complications of Charles' *revenant* art-thief. "I have returned to you to see if there are, perhaps, other things you may have recalled that could help identify anyone who might have done this." I could see immediately she was readying to issue a quick denial, so I continued in another vein.

"Perhaps, though, you could tell me a little bit about yourself and your brother," I said, "and how you came to be connected to that wonderful tapestry of the Lady and the Unicorn." I took a sip of my coffee. "I recall you said something about George Sand last evening, at the play, that was most intriguing—how she saved the tapestry from destruction?" I hoped that this prompt would invite her to be more open, and it appeared to be the right note to strike.

"*Madame la Baronesse, oui,*" she said softly, with a sad smile. "She would be so distressed to hear about Sébastien." She took up her cup of coffee but did not drink. "My parents were very good friends with the Baronesse," she said, "and we lived quite close by, so were in and out of each other's houses all the time. Of course, the Baronesse was absent from Nohant a great deal," she smiled at the thought, and lifted her chin to indicate the great city outside the windows. "She spent many years of her life in Paris, and travelling about with her lovers, of course." This was said very simply, as a matter of course, and I had indeed read accounts of the many, and famous, lovers, this remarkable woman attracted to herself—Liszt and Chopin among them.

"But in her older years," Geneviève continued, "she settled at Nohant, where she had raised her daughter Solange and her son Maurice—they were some years older than I and Sébastien—but we all entertained each other, with music and drawing and walks around the countryside. Nohant is a very small village," she said, as if in explanation.

"It sounds quite charming," I said encouragingly.

"*They* were charming," she said, "and Madame la Baronesse was the most wonderful, imaginative, playful woman I've ever met!" Her eyes held a brief spark as she remembered. "She would write little plays for us all to perform, with special parts for each of us, and we would be allowed to dress up in all manner of beautiful dresses and suits, coats and hats—Baronesse had several wardrobes full of wonderful clothes!" Her face took on warmth and color as she recounted clearly happy days. "I was often a fairy-tale princess, and my"—she stumbled here, looked distressed, and finished with what I could only think was a different ending to her thought than she had originally been about to say—"and Sébastien loved playing the *chevalier* on a gallant steed."

I nodded, shifting forward a little on the sofa in order to pour myself more coffee. Geneviève had still not taken a sip of her own coffee, so it felt awkward to offer her more. We sat in silence for a few moments.

"The tapestry," I said, leaning back again. "What can you tell me about it?"

She looked into her cup, noticed the coffee had gone cold, and put it back on the tray. "Tapestries, plural," she said. "there are six of them, although I believe there used to be more."

"Du Sommerard said they were woven around the year fifteen hundred or so?"

Geneviève nodded. "They are very old," she said, and grimaced slightly. "And two of them are in very, very bad condition—the Chateau Boussac is older even than the tapestries," she continued. "It was first built in the ninth century, as a fortress, and was added to through the years, to the present day. It is a cold and damp place, for the most part," she said, with a little shiver, "and the rats got to them, too, of course, even while Lady Pauline was still in residence."

"Lady Pauline?" I queried.

"The last of the de Carbonnières," she said.

The name stirred my memory. "Wasn't that the surname of the gentleman who was visiting you this morning?" I asked.

Geneviève looked slightly irritated, then sighed and answered. "*Oui.* François desRosiers—he styles himself a de Carbonnières." She waved a hand as at a foolish nonsense. "He has this idea...*ce n'est rien.*"

It means nothing—I wondered about that, and put it aside for the moment.

"And how did George Sand—the Baronesse—come to visit at the Chateau Boussac?"

She was silent at first, then roused herself. "Madame la Baronesse often went to stay there, after Lady Pauline left."

I thought this odd. "Why did she stay there? Especially if the owner no longer lived there?"

Geneviève shrugged. "This was some years before I was born, in the late thirties or so—Lady Pauline told the town fathers of Boussac she would sell them the chateau—and everything she left in it, including the tapestries—as long as she could visit them when she wished; the town took it over and at first rented it out, and someone, I forget his name, but a friend of La Baronesse, leased it for a time, and she often visited him there. That is how she discovered the existence of the tapestries—they fired her marvelous imagination, and she set to work to save them from further destruction."

I considered this; it was an interesting story, probably repeated, in some ways, in every country chateau that had fallen into disrepair and solitude since the Great Revolution of 1789, which had displaced—or executed—so many of the French nobility.

"And how did you—or was it only Sébastien—come to be the caretakers of this particular tapestry, the one that *monsieur* du Sommerard has at his *musée?*"

This time Geneviève answered quite promptly. "Sébastien and I often accompanied La Baronesse, from the time we were ten or so, and her children too, on her later visits to Boussac, where she would meet with the town fathers, inspect the tapestries, and tell us stories about what they were and what they meant. My...Sébastien took a great interest in the art of weaving, and educated himself about the masters of tapestry, at Bayonne and Arles, and was particularly knowledgeable about the legend of the Unicorn and its symbolism. When *monsieur* du Sommerard came to visit, some fifteen years ago, he was impressed with my brother's expertise, although he was only about sixteen years of age at the time."

She tossed her head a little, out of a fond pride, it seemed to me, and admiration for her brother's zeal and knowledge. "Du Sommerard and Sébastien kept up a correspondence, and when the town fathers finally agreed to send the one tapestry—The Lady—here, to Paris, for restoration, Sébastien was asked to come with her." She gave a deep sigh. "La Baronesse would have been so proud of him," she said, and looked up at me. "You probably know, famous as she was, that she died only six years ago."

"Yes," I murmured sympathetically. "It is my misfortune that I never met her, although I have read so many of her books." I mused a moment over all that Geneviève had told me. "So, Sébastien was about, twenty-nine years of age?" As she nodded, I continued, "He seemed so very, very young to me, I would have guessed some years closer to twenty."

She smiled, tears beginning to well in her beautiful eyes—so startling a blue, so like Sébastien's. "Perhaps, then, you would be surprised to know that I am the same age?"

I *was* surprised, I admit. She seemed to me even younger than twenty. I blinked then, and blurted out, "You are twins?" Somehow it compounded the tragedy of Sébastien's death enormously. "I'm so, so sorry, my dear Geneviève," I said, adjusting my relation to her in my own mind—she was older than me by four years.

"*Merci,*" she said simply, and sighed again, her tears beginning to fall. "I do not know how I can continue to exist without…without my other half." She touched her handkerchief quietly to her streaming eyes and I—although it is not my usual way—rose from my seat and sat next to her, taking her hand and pressing it in sympathetic silence.

I took my leave soon after, perceiving that the poor woman was exhausted, and made my way—on foot this time, Charles' carriage no longer at my disposal—back over the *Pont-Notre Dame*, across the isle and onto *rue St. Jacques*. I had much to think about as I wandered, but soon determined that the one place I needed to see again was the *Musée de Cluny*—definitely to look at the tapestry again, and perhaps speak with du Sommerard. If I was lucky, I would find

Charles there interviewing him—I quickened my steps, turned onto *boulevard St. Germain*, and reached the ancient gates of the *musée* just as Charles Wilkinson was striding up the boulevard to the same destination.

"Charles!" I cried out to him, startling him from an apparent reverie. I grinned. "What took you so long?"

He grinned back, somewhat ruefully, but did not answer my question. "Why am I not surprised to see you here?" He took my hand and bowed over it gallantly. "I assume you're to join me for my interview with *monsieur* du Sommerard?"

"Indeed I am," I said confidently. "Shall we go in?"

He shook his head again, smiling, and opened the gate.

Two

10 May 1774 – Boussac, France
The King and the King's Son

"*LE ROI EST MORT! VIVE LE ROI!*" The word had gone out from Versailles in the early hours of the tenth of May, and a relay messenger on horseback reached Boussac late in the evening. Louis XV, the Beloved, *le Bien-Aimé*, was dead, in the fifty-ninth year of his long reign.

"Praise be to God, the King's grandson is there to take his place," François said. He and his mother, Louise de Rilhac de Carbonnières, stood together at one of the floor-to-ceiling windows in the Gallery of Tapestries, gazing out across the lawn and gardens, a riot of colors and myriad shades of green as a verdant Spring took hold.

His mother said nothing, merely stared blankly at the scene laid before them. Nothing showed in her face, but François, now thirty-five years old, had long learned to read this enigmatic woman even when she did not speak. Her stiff arms, crossed over her chest, told him something was troubling her.

"*Qu'est-ce que c'est, maman? Qu'est-ce qui vous dérange?*" Some instinct led him to keep silent after these questions, and he fought to suppress a rising sense of excitement—he felt something dramatic was on the horizon.

Louise drew in a long, shaky breath, put her hand on her son's arm, and turned away from the window. Still silent, she began walking toward the wall of tapestries, which despite their age and faded appearance, always fascinated both mother and son—years of examining them, dreaming about the stories they depicted, and learning the names of the plants and animals scattered across the backgrounds had fixed the Lady and her two stalwart defenders, the Lion and the Unicorn, firmly in both their imaginations and hearts.

"He was your father." Louise spoke just above a whisper, but every syllable thrilled through François' consciousness like lightning in his blood. Disparate pieces of his life began to fall into place, to make sense at last—his mother's silences whenever there was talk of the King among their guests; his father's kindly but distant love; his own features, so like his mother's but not at all like his father's; and his own sense of being somehow different—somehow *more* than others, although at times he felt he was so much *less* than everyone else. The blood that flowed so vibrantly through him at these thoughts—it was royal blood, the most royal of all, in a line stretching back to ancient times. He felt it. He felt he had known it all his life.

The heady sensation this knowledge gave him caused the floor beneath his feet to pitch and swirl, and he felt the steadying hand of his mother grip his arm a little tighter. The two of them stood staring up at the gorgeous tapestry that depicted the Lady holding the standard with the crescents flying across it, flanked by the adoring Lion and Unicorn, who gazed up at her serene and queenly countenance.

"*Le Lion et la Licorne*," his mother whispered. "And you, my son, are both of them together—the strength of the royal Lion, and the transcendent nature of the Unicorn."

François came to himself abruptly. "A royal bastard," he said, although the words did not taste of bitterness. "Unknown. Unacknowledged." He turned to look at his mother, and said the final word that had come to him. "Unwanted."

A fierceness suffused his mother's face. "*Non!* Never that, not by me, not by *him*, not even by…my husband. *Oui,*" she said, taking in his look of surprise. "Your papa—the one who helped me raise you—knew it all, and understood, and promised to faithfully fulfill his duty to a child who might one day"—but here she broke off, unwilling to finish the thought.

"That day has come and gone," François said softly. "We have a new King now." He paused. "My nephew."

Louise sighed, suddenly spent of her usual nervous energy. Her son led her to a small sofa across from the tapestries, and they sat down together. She searched his eyes, and reaching up, touched his cheek tenderly.

"Should I have told you sooner, *mon fils?*" she said. "I thought I would tell you, just after your fa—after your *papa* died—you were just fourteen then, Lord, is it twenty years ago now?"

"Twenty-one," he said, automatically, then smiled slightly. "You know me and numbers, *maman*," he said, twirling his hand around his head. "They are always there in my mind."

"Like your true father," Louise said, almost wistfully. "He had a curious, mathematical mind—he should have been an engineer!" She laughed, remembering the young

King and his projects. She grasped her son's hand in both of hers.

"Ask me anything," she said. "*Vraiment,* I will tell you whatever you wish to know."

François shook his head and smiled. "Not right now, *chère maman,* but perhaps some other day." His smile faded. "But there is one thing." He was looking at her earnestly, and his look sent an arrow of sorrow to her heart. "Am I acknowledged, in any way? Is there some…proof?"

Louise bowed her head, looking down to gain some time. She hadn't expected he would ask that question so soon; this had all come upon her too fast. But she had known this moment would come some day—why hadn't she prepared the right answer? *Bien,* she thought, not without a sigh of relief, it is in *le bon Dieu's* hands now—it is my duty to tell the truth. She began, haltingly.

"Ten years ago, when the *Dauphin* died—so tragically—I thought then of telling you, in case—but Louis himself was still so hearty—and then the *Dauphin* had sired three healthy boys with that Polish princess—such a woman—so it seemed cruel to tell you what might make you long for—what would not be, in all likelihood."

A deep silence grew between the mother and son. She knew she hadn't answered his questions, and he was waiting.

"Our beloved King knew you were his son," Louise said firmly. "He visited us—Georges and me—when we went to Paris just after you were baptized." Her voice broke for just a moment. "He held you in his arms, and he whispered something to you, and he called you beautiful." Tears blurred her vision as she remembered that tender moment. She cleared her throat, and shook off the tears, and spoke again. "Your papa was actually quite comfortable with the arrangement, and you know he loved you very much." She glanced at her son, who had turned away his head, and she continued. "And then, when the *Dauphin* died, I wanted very much to write to him, to the King, but it could not be done with any delicacy."

Her son nodded, as if he understood, and after a moment turned to her, his eyes bright with the shine of tears. "He showed tenderness to me, and he knew I was his son," he said softly. "That must be enough for me, then."

Louise caught her breath, but tried to maintain an unchanged demeanour. He was not going to press for more! Perhaps she needn't tell him everything, not just yet—about the brooch, and the letters—and that last letter, upon the death of the Dauphin. Maybe she had time to breathe, and think again.

"Does anyone else know? I mean, in our family?"

Louise cleared her mind and brought her attention back to her son. She shook her head and answered carefully. "*Non,* no one alive here anymore knows anything of all this." She paused, and François rose from the sofa and extended his hand to help her rise.

"What will you do, *mon fils?*" Louise asked gently. Looking into his face, she had the feeling that he had matured—indeed, aged—in the last few minutes. What weight had she placed on her beloved son? But relief was at hand in his confident reply.

"I shall go on with my life," he said, smiling. "I will marry Marguerite as planned next month, and I'll settle down and have a house full of grandchildren for you in a few years."

⚡ THREE ⚡

SATURDAY – 7 MAY 1881 – PARIS
In which we question M. du Sommerard

A SUDDEN THOUGHT, GRUESOME ENOUGH, STRUCK ME as we began to enter the *Musée de Cluny*. "Have you had the results of the autopsy, Charles?" I asked.

He shook his head, frowning. "Apparently last night was particularly busy in regard to murderous activities in the city. The medical examiner has not yet had time to examine the body, beyond the preliminary look at the scene." He glanced up at the silver and grey stone walls of the *musée* and grimaced.

"I suppose," I said, "that given it was clear the cause of death was strangulation, there didn't seem to be much reason for hurrying?"

Charles sighed. "You are probably right, but nonetheless, one never knows quite all the facts until the examiner has really done his work."

This caught my attention, and I stopped him under the archway of the main door with the touch of my hand on his arm. "Do you expect something different, or something additional, to be found out from the autopsy, Charles?"

"No," he said slowly, "I can't say that I do, but I have learned the hard way not to be too sure of anything until one knows it all."

"Well, *bonne chance* with that, is all I can say," I said with a smile. "One rarely has the good fortune to know everything."

We entered the main door to the *musée*, not the smaller tower door with the spiral staircase that we had used the day before on our visit to Sébastien and the tapestry. We were greeted by *mademoiselle* Berthold, who was seated at her table in the vestibule; without looking up, she began to say that the *musée* was closed for the day due to "unfortunate circumstances," but Charles interrupted her to give his name and business. She seemed to stiffen at his words, as if affronted, but she instantly rose and invited us to follow her, presumably to du Sommerard's office. She did not appear to recognize me—or else she was ignoring me deliberately.

She announced Charles' name as we were ushered into a large, well-appointed room where du Sommerard sat, rather gloomily, judging from his hunched shoulders, in a large leather chair turned to face the window into the courtyard. He had swung around in our direction when the woman tapped on the open door, looking annoyed, then confused, then wary—all three emotions playing over his features in rapid succession—as he rose to greet us.

"Have you found who committed this atrocity?" he demanded, all belligerence and bristling superiority. He and Claire Berthold exchanged mutually irritated glances, and he gestured for her to leave the room and close the door.

If Charles felt annoyed, he showed nothing in his features or voice, whereas I was immediately incensed. However, I schooled myself to remarkable restraint, and merely replied in a cool voice, "Your zeal for justice is admirable, *monsieur* du Sommerard," I said, noting Charles' stifled smile as he approached the *musée* director. "But as it is less than four-and-twenty hours since the murder was discovered, I would postulate that it might be a trifle early to expect an arrest."

I sat down in one of the two chairs facing his desk, without being invited, and was pleased to see du Sommerard quickly attempt to recover his manners.

"Miss Paget," he said, gesturing with one hand to invite me to sit, and extending the other to Charles, whom he greeted with suspicion. "Mr. Wilkinson."

Charles nodded, and the two gentlemen sat down.

"*Monsieur* du Sommerard," Charles began, leaning back in his chair slightly. "Our investigation into this tragic event is inevitably linked to the now missing Titian—the possible Titian—painting of the Martyrdom of St. Sebastian." He was watching the man narrowly, as was I. The director's glance flickered to me.

"May I ask why Miss Paget is here?" he said.

Fair enough, I thought, but I kept silent and let Charles offer an answer.

"Miss Paget is helping my agency with our inquiries," he said smoothly, and left it at that.

Du Sommerard sniffed. "It was your agency who approached me about the Titian," he said.

"That is true," Charles conceded. "I have learned from my colleagues that they had gotten word of the Titian being transferred to you for inspection, some months ago, by a certain private party here in Paris?"

I glanced at Charles, this being news to me, of course; but why was he being so discreet about this "private party"?

"*Oui*," said du Sommerard. "The party in question inherited the painting—that is what he told me—and wanted it appraised for its provenance and value."

Charles took up the obvious point. "Do you have any reason to believe that the painting came to this person by some other route than inheritance?"

Du Sommerard shook his head vehemently. "*Non, monsieur,* I took him at his word, which, I'm sure you will agree, is unimpeachable."

Charles nodded. I was itching to ask some questions of my own, but thought it the wiser course to have Charles pursue his line of inquiry first—I wanted to see where he was going.

"Once the painting was in your possession," he said, "did you ever put it on public display? Talk about it or show it to people, other than your staff?"

"Not at all," du Sommerard answered testily. "It was a private matter; the painting was in the workshop, never in the public rooms."

"Which of your staff members were aware of its possible importance, and the owner who sent it here?"

Du Sommerard looked thoughtful, and also a little shifty, I thought. "Claire Berthold, whom you met just now," he said, inclining his head toward the outer room. "As the manager of visitors to the *musée*, and deputy supervisor of our collections, she is aware of all the details of this matter." He picked up a pencil on his desk and played with it absentmindedly. "Poor Sébastien knew of it, of course, but he did not know who sent it here." He paused. "No one else."

"And when my agent approached you about the possibility of laying a trap for this art thief we are following," Charles continued. "Who knew about that?"

"*Mademoiselle* Berthold and myself," the director answered firmly. "No one else."

"What did the agent tell you about the art thief?"

Du Sommerard raised a brow, as if surprised. "Tell me? Not much," he said, and shrugged. "Just some things about where he had struck before, and the objects or paintings he had taken." He looked down at the pencil in his hands, then put it aside abruptly. He seemed suddenly irritated. I decided it was a good moment to jump in.

"*Monsieur* du Sommerard," I said, leaning forward in my chair. "You said that the Titian was in the workshop, therefore no members of the public could see it, and yet I and my friends were led there by Sébastien Bayard yesterday; we saw the painting and spoke at length about it." I watched his face as it began to grow alarmingly red, and I continued. "Of course, neither I nor my companions are under suspicion for either the theft or the murder, but is it not possible that Sébastien—or someone else on your staff—invited other people into the workshop?"

"He should not have done that!" The man nearly shouted the words. "He knew that I did not wish anyone to see the Titian!"

"In truth," I said, pleased to have incensed him, "Sébastien brought us there to view the tapestry of the Lady and the Unicorn, and to do him justice, he tried not to talk about the Titian once my friend John Sargent had noticed it."

Silence descended upon the room as the director regained his control, then I spoke again.

"How valuable is the tapestry?" I asked. "It seemed to me, last night, as if someone had tried to detach it from where it was hanging, and perhaps steal it, as well as the Titian."

"What?" Du Sommerard seemed perplexed at the change of subject. "The tapestry?" He shook his head. "It is badly in need of repair, but still, there is no putting a price on it, or the others in Boussac—they are an inestimable treasure, a national treasure one might say—but I do not think, I would not imagine"—he paused to marshall his thoughts—"I would find it hard to think that anyone who wanted to steal the Titian would find the tapestry desirable."

We all stared at one another for a few moments. Du Sommerard's opinion sounded, to me, like the honest truth. I suddenly remembered a question I'd had from the very first, and spoke again.

"And the arrows, *monsieur?* What can you tell us about the arrows? Were they part of the *musée's* collection?" I suddenly recalled the corner in the workshop that held a pile of medieval armaments, among them a wooden crossbow, and a quiver of arrows.

I could have sworn a guilty flush suffused du Sommerard's already florid features, but he answered quietly enough.

"I do not know what you are talking about, *mademoiselle* Paget. I know nothing about any arrows."

We gazed at each other for a few moments with mutual hostility.

Charles broke the silence by rising from his chair.

"If we might speak a little to *mademoiselle* Berthold?" he asked, and du Sommerard nodded briefly. He stood, but allowed us to walk to the door of his office unaccompanied. Charles opened the door for me, and closed it behind us. There was no one in the outer room, but he walked a few steps out and whispered to me.

"He is lying about something," he said. "Actually, several things. I can feel it."

I nodded mutely, thinking the same, then whispered back, "Did du Sommerard see Sébastien's body? I mean before the *gendarmerie* came?"

Charles shook his head. "I cannot say, but I believe he did not come to the scene until later in the morning." He looked at me, a question on his lips, but just then a door opened in the opposite wall, and Claire Berthold appeared. She strode toward us with a quiet, determined look, and I could see at once that we would get little out of her beyond what du Sommerard had told us. The three of us stood in the center of the room, and Charles spoke first, asking about visitors to the workshop to view the Titian.

"*Non, monsieur,*" she said. "I am aware of everyone who enters and leaves the *musée* during business hours, and I can tell you that no one was allowed to enter the workshop without permission, and not without supervision either."

"And were you aware of my presence, and the Sargent family, yesterday, in that workshop?" I asked, trying not to sound accusatory.

"*Oui, mademoiselle,*" she said, not without a faint smirk, I thought. "It was my understanding that Sébastien had strict orders to keep the Titian covered at all times when it was not being worked on, and especially when there were visitors."

I remembered Sébastien's uneasiness when John had removed the cloth from the painting of the martyred saint, and his repeated attempts to draw us away from it. I decided I had nothing to lose by asking her what I had asked her employer.

"And the arrows, *madame*? What can you tell me about them? Were they part of the *musée's* collection?"

Claire Berthold held my gaze for some moments, exhibiting an hostility similar to du Sommerard's response to the same question. "I do not know what you are talking about, *mademoiselle*. I know nothing about any arrows."

In my mind I could clearly see the quiver of arrows in the corner of the outer workshop, behind the Titian. I needed to see that room again.

"May we take another look at the workshop, please?" I asked, and when she hesitated, Charles seconded me, in a voice that would brook no opposition.

We filed up the stairwell to the next floor, silently crossed the long room of vitrines with their precious objects, and entered the workshop; the door was open to it, and it was clear from the condition of the room that it hadn't been cleaned up or altered since the police had been there.

"We were told not to touch anything," Claire Berthold said, indignant and angry. She stood with her arms crossed, at the threshold.

I went to the corner where I had seen the medieval armaments—the shield, the crossbow, but no quiver of arrows. Very curious. What to make of it? The quiver had held several arrows, but only five were used on Sébastien's body.

Charles was looking at me quizzically, but I was too uncertain of my thoughts about this matter to reveal them aloud. I indicated I had no further questions, and we took our leave and departed, with much to think about.

Four

July 1788—April 1789 – Boussac, France
The Scene is Set for Revolution.

"*Mon Dieu!* God save us, it is the end of the world!" Cries and shouts reverberated from every corner and tower of Boussac, servants and children all in a fearful state as the worst hailstorm in memory crashed and boomed across the landscape.

"*François, mon fils!* Shall we all die here today?" Louise de Rilhac de Carbonnières, now seventy-three but still agile and active, ran headlong down the grand central staircase, narrowly avoiding a shower of glass from the skylight as hailstones the size of small cannonballs shattered the windows and scattered ice and glass across the entrance hall.

"*Non, maman, calmes-toi,*" came the reassuring voice of her son, ringing loudly from the bottom of the stairs. "It is but a hailstorm, although rather worse than what we saw in May, I think." He had gathered his children to him, and herded them—his son, Louis François, a thin and sickly boy of twelve, and his more hardy daughter Pauline Louise, barely three years of age—into shelter under the curved arch of the massive stone fireplace in the front hall. The hearth, swept and empty for the Summer months, was large enough for François to stand upright, with room for his children and mother, who joined them in a rush from the stairs.

All light seemed blotted out of the midday sky as the hail fell relentlessly upon the land for the next hour—ripping through straw and wood cottages, striking down man and beast alike, destroying the young vines and the tender ears of wheat in the fields. Elm trees lost massive branches, and scores of partridge, rabbits and birds were discovered later, after the storm, dead on the ground, hailstones melting around their lifeless bodies.

Then just as suddenly the sky cleared, the black clouds blew away, and the fierce Summer sun resumed its fiery work.

François, as lord of Boussac, had much to do to direct the restoration of the land, the tenants' properties, the crops, the animals, and his own chateau. After that first day, spent touring his property to assess the damage, he set about organizing teams of peasants to re-plant and tend the broken vines, gather the dead game for cleaning, smoking and preservation of as much meat as possible, and repair shattered roofs and barns.

At first, it seemed a blessing that once the hailstorm had passed, the weather had been warm and dry. But after three weeks, reports began to trickle in from other towns in Berry, and farther afield. He discussed the news, as he always did, with his mother.

"*Maman*," he said, setting down a bowl of tea he had been sipping, and jabbing his finger at a paper before him, "here is a description from Ile-de-France: 'a countryside, erstwhile ravishing, has been reduced to an arid desert.' "

"It is true," Louise said, "there has been no rain since early June—one cannot count the hailstones as rain."

"We must prepare for a drought, then, it appears," François said, thinking over what was to be done. "It will be hard, what with last year's harvest being so small." Lines of worry multiplied on his forehead—how would everyone be fed?

August came and went without a drop of rain, and the heat blazed across the hills and valleys, scorching the very earth beneath what remained of any vegetation. The leaves on the trees turned brown at the beginning of September, and the vines yielded no grapes, the olive trees no fruit, the wheat fields burnt.

Louise did her best to keep her grandchildren's spirits high, and invented games for them in the Gallery of the Tapestries, where they gathered early in the morning when it was coolest. She had been noticing that the tapestries, all eight of them, were beginning to fade in places, and there was a raggedness to the edges, especially along the bottom, that appeared to signal an unravelling due to the threads drying out.

"Tell us again about the Lady and the Unicorn," Pauline would beg, but her brother always differed.

"I want to hear about the Lion and Unicorn—did they not fight each other? Are they not enemies?"

"*Non, non, mon petit*," Louise would tell him. "They two are stalwart defenders and protectors of the Lady, and would never quarrel with or fight each other. They are united in service to her."

"Why does the Unicorn smile at himself in the mirror?" Pauline asked. They were all three standing in front of that particular tapestry, with Pauline pointing up at the gilded and bejeweled mirror, which flashed sparks of light from the golden threads as the sun rose and shone through the gallery windows.

Louise had asked herself this same question all her life, starting from when she was a little girl, like her granddaughter. She smiled as she thought of the wide variety of answers she had come up with over the years—but she thought that now, with age and experience, she might have divined the best one.

"The Unicorn, as you know," she began, "is a mythical beast…"

"What does *mythical* mean?" Pauline interrupted, and her brother broke in before Louise could speak.

"It means it never really existed at all," Louis François said, dismissively. "It's a fairy tale, it's made up—so it really isn't important, anything you say about it." He looked defiantly at his grandmother.

She smiled sadly at him, and shook her head. "First of all," she said, "the Unicorn is a 'he', not an 'it'. He is a spirit, a soul, a real live being all of his own—and he definitely exists—*still* exists, not just one time in the distant past, but now and always." She led the children to a small sofa and sat down with them, one on either side of her, facing the tapestry. "You see, *mes petits,* when people say something is a *myth,* what is meant by that is a very deep and wonderful truth. The truest things in the world, like Love and Goodness, like God Himself, exist or rather, *are alive* in what is called Eternity—a kind of place where everything is perfect, everything is as it can most perfectly be, not like here on earth, where we see only shadows and faults and imperfections, even in the best people or things."

She looked into their faces, realizing of course that Pauline was far too young to understand, although she was listening open-mouthed, looking from her grandmother to the tapestry and back again. Louis François still maintained a faint scowl of resistance, but she could see that he was interested.

"And why is the Unicorn so special?" he asked.

"Because he is one of a kind, he is unique," Louise said. "He follows a different path, he is gentle and pure, and he has the ability to heal wounds through the magic of his spiral horn."

Her grandson nodded slowly. "Do you think that is why he is looking in the mirror with such interest, and why he is smiling? Because he's never seen another one, another Unicorn, like him?"

"*Trés bien, mon petit!*" Louise cried. "I believe you have discovered the truth there! The Lion, of course, sees many of his kind throughout the earth, but there is nothing quite like the Unicorn—and naturally, he would be amazed at his own appearance—wouldn't you, if you thought you were the only one of your kind?"

Louis François nodded vigorously, and jumped up to approach the tapestry for a closer look. It was not hung up very high on the wall, with the ragged edge of the bottom close to the floor, so he could almost, as it were, look into the mirror himself, along with the Unicorn.

"There is only one of *me*," he said after a moment, turning to his grandmother with a look of wonder and a slight smile. "Could I be a Unicorn myself?"

Louise was taken aback by the question, and chose to give him a serious answer, the boy seemed so in earnest. "*Oui,* my dear one, I think that is entirely possible."

Louis François turned back to the tapestry and stood very still, trembling a little, as he stretched out a hand to touch the Unicorn, stroking the white back gently.

Two months later, mere weeks before a harsh, unprecedented Winter descended upon all of France, Louis François de Carbonnières was buried in the sun-baked ground, next to the grave of his mother, who had died giving birth to Pauline. His grandmother commissioned a carving of a Unicorn with a wreath of lilies on his neck to decorate the gravestone. The little family were inconsolable, and François spent long hours at the gravestones of his lost ones, and long nights wandering the countryside, sleepless, until the howling winds and snow drove him indoors.

By the Spring of 1789, the whole country was starving and restless.

"And will you really go to Bourges, my son, for the Assembly of Wrongs?" Louise shook her head and watched her son's face carefully. "I think no good can come of it."

François sighed and rubbed his face with both hands. He and his mother were sitting in the south-facing morning room of the chateau—the early rising sun warmed that room first, making it more habitable than other chambers. There was a shortage of firewood, *mon Dieu,* he thought to himself, *there's a shortage of everything, including common sense, in this land.*

"*Maman,*" he said softly, taking her hand, "you know it is my duty to attend the Assembly—this is a momentous event—what King has ever before asked his people to give him a list of their grievances and complaints?" He shook his head. "I, too, worry about the outcome—once expectations are raised, what will happen when, frankly, *nothing* happens? Do things ever change?"

Louise tightened her grip on her son's hand. "They do change, but it takes a long time," she said. "I fear the haste with which these reformers are proceeding—one hasn't time to think."

"There is little doubt that reform should happen," François said. "We here at Boussac, we've always worked hand in hand with our people, on our land, and shared the good times and the bad, as we are now. But so many others—" He squeezed her hand and made to stand up from the table. "If any of our class are poised to be a citizen among citizens, as they are styling it now, we are certainly at the forefront." He stood, then bent down to kiss her cheek. "Do not worry, *Maman,* the people here know us—they will not storm the chateau and put us in chains."

"*Mon Dieu!*" his mother responded. "Do you think it will come to that, if not here, then anywhere? In Paris? Versailles? They would not dare approach the King and his family as an unruly mob?" She clutched her head. "It is unthinkable!"

But the unthinkable was soon to happen.

℞ FIVE ℘

SATURDAY EVENING – 7 MAY 1881 – PARIS
Discoveries Large and Small

CHARLES AND I AGREED TO PART AND MEET LATER in the evening, but not until he had seen me to the door of my *pension*. We did not, as we walked along the sunny Paris boulevards, converse much upon what we had learned from du Sommerard—but it was as if we could each hear the wheels in each other's heads whirring and clinking as we churned through the mystery.

"If I may presume, Violet," he said to me on the doorstep, "I believe it would be very helpful if you were to write down your thoughts about this whole situation, for me to peruse later—and I shall do the same," he added, and smiled. "Your clarity of expression, and your insights into human nature, are valuable assets of which I wish to take advantage."

Immensely flattering as his statement was, I couldn't help but agree with him. "I look forward to reading your account as well," I said, and we shook hands in the friendliest manner. He promised to call for me just before ten o'clock, which was the time we had agreed to meet at John's lodgings. I turned into my *pension* with a suddenly weary step, and soon found myself wrapped in a warm blanket and asleep for a refreshing nap upon my comfortable bed.

The housemaid woke me for a late tea, or an early supper, and I dedicated the time between then and Charles' expected arrival to writing out my thoughts as he had requested. Looking over several pages at the end of three hours, I was satisfied I had gotten it all down—but still did not feel any closer to determining who might have committed the murder, or stolen the painting—and more importantly, why? I had many other questions as well, but frankly, there were too many unknowns at this point to come to any intelligent conclusions, as well as more than one suspect—this unnamed person of John's acquaintance, for instance; and I could not rule out du Sommerard himself! Or Claire Berthold either, for that matter—her smirk irritated me still. The Revenant, so called, was of course still to be considered. Geneviève, thank goodness, had been with us at the comedy all evening, so she was above suspicion—although I still had the feeling she was not telling the whole truth about…something. Still too many secrets!

Charles called promptly at about fifteen minutes before the hour, and as neither of us had heard otherwise from John in the intervening time, we drove the distance to John's apartment with great anticipation. I asked him again about any results from the autopsy. He shook his head.

"I have great hopes of hearing something this evening," he said. "I gave very explicit instructions that it was to take top priority, *now*." He leaned back in the carriage to look me more directly in the face.

"I did learn one thing of great interest," he said, "which verifies what we were thinking about our *monsieur* du Sommerard."

I leaving forward eagerly. "That he was lying?"

Charles nodded. "I questioned the agent who had introduced the idea to him of using the Titian as a trap for the Revenant, and was told that du Sommerard asked a great deal of questions about the previous thefts—what kinds of art pieces, where, who had owned them—and that the agent, most unprofessionally, told him about the murder at a previous theft, and how the man was found dressed like the woman in the painting."

My eyes widened at this thought. "That he would deny knowing very much at all is indeed, extremely interesting. But perhaps he merely forgot?"

Charles shrugged. "It's possible, I suppose," he said. "The agent said du Sommerard was most insistent about knowing all the details, especially as he felt he was putting himself, or his staff, in some danger in agreeing to the scheme. Which," he continued with a wry smile, "appears to have been somewhat prescient on his part. Still, something to keep in mind."

I nodded, and pressed him with another question. "Were you able to learn whether du Sommerard saw Sébastien's body, with the arrows? Or if perhaps, one of the officers told him about it later?"

"I did ask, indeed," Charles said. "The body had been removed before du Sommerard arrived—and all the *gendarmerie* were under strict orders not to discuss any details of the murder with anyone outside the force." He grimaced. "We are trying to keep it from the press and the public for as long as possible—it will not be long, I dare say."

"Hmmm," I mused, agreeing with him. "Paris is, in many ways, a small town, and evil news travels fast."

We arrived at John's house quickly and stepped out of the carriage onto the well-lighted street, with Charles giving the driver instructions to return in two hours and wait in the street. Our knock at the door was answered by John himself, dressed rather *'to the nines'* I believe it's called, looking very trim and tailored and a little flushed.

"Welcome, do come in," he said, holding the door open with a flourish, and bowing low—which made me think he had been drinking, not that I minded or disapproved, you see, but I knew from of old that it took a great deal of drink indeed for John, who was a large man with an excellent constitution, to exhibit any signs of intoxication. I curtsied to him in reply, a smile on my face, and Charles bowed as well, and we all burst out laughing—a nervous laughter at best, I thought, perhaps even the tiniest bit hysterical.

"Well," I said, as we stood catching our breaths, "shall we find out where we are in this dreadful situation?"

John immediately turned and led us up the stairs, two floors, to his comfortable quarters next to his studio, where we saw to our satisfaction there was a lovely spread of delectables, along with a bottle or two of wine. The sconces with candles were lighted against the pale green-papered walls, and threw a friendly glow up to the ceiling, the space enhanced by a good fire and more candles set about the room. We shed our light outer garments—the nights were becoming warm—and sat down, gathering our thoughts and helping ourselves to a glass of wine and a plate of food.

A few moments of eating and drinking in silence, and then it was time.

"Shall I begin?" Charles said, and when both John and I nodded, he quickly and concisely brought John into the picture of what he and I had learned from our discussion with du Sommerard and Berthold that afternoon, adding at the end the recent knowledge gained from his agent, as he had told me.

Then it was John's turn to report, and after a moment and a steadying gulp of wine, he began.

"I shall refer to the person in question as David," he said, "as I have absolutely no acquaintance of that name." He paused, drank, fetched a deep sigh, and went on. "He is, however, an actor who is beginning to become known, and therefore, there is all the more reason for concealing his identity. As I said previously, David had indicated an interest in becoming a member of *L'Ordre de la Licorne*, was invited to join at dinner and some *soirées* so he could become known to the group, and was, sadly, subsequently rejected as a member."

I schooled myself to sit still and listen, not wanting to interrupt the flow of John's narrative, but it was a hard task, I admit. Nonetheless! I made an heroic effort, and sipped quietly at my burgundy wine.

"By dint of some earnest inquiries and a bit of good luck, I chanced upon David this afternoon at one of the cafés in the *Quartier Latin*, which I was aware he frequented." John took a long swallow of wine. "I sat down at a table, as if unaware of his presence, and it was all made easy by his addressing me first, in the friendliest manner, although I could see after a moment that he was greatly distressed."

Here John glanced at Charles, seeming to be apologetic. "It seems, Charles," he said, "that word has gone about the town, at least, in certain circles, regarding Sébastien's death—not all the horrible details," he hastened to add, seeing Charles' startled look. "But the plain fact that he was indeed dead, had been found at the *Musée de Cluny*, under mysterious circumstances, seemed to be known by some of the artistic community."

Charles waved a hand lightly, as if resigned to the inevitable, but said nothing. John went on.

"I invited him to lunch with me, to which he readily agreed, not being burdened with *trop de francs* at this time—what young actor is?—and as we proceeded through two bottles of wine and an excellent capon, the poor lad opened his heart to me." John drank again from his glass, and continued.

"It seems David had felt himself to be very much in love with Sébastien, from first sight, he said, and had been keen to pursue him since early March." He sighed, and toyed with a piece of bread on his plate. "But Sébastien always put him off, with one excuse and another, to not meet with him, or dine with him, or even walk out with him—and finally, a few weeks ago, David received such a command to stay away from Sébastien as even his obsessed mind had to take seriously."

I considered this behavior with the least amount of severe judgement I could muster—how could a rational person fall prey to such an obsession? But then, lovers are not rational, I said to myself, suddenly aware of a hectic feeling in my own blood, thrilling through my veins, as I thought of my very dear own Mary, with whom I would be spending several weeks in England—as soon as I left Paris. It jolted me to think I had been so absorbed in the events of the last two days that I had not given a single thought to what awaited me in London.

John's solemn voice woke me from my reverie, and I turned my attention back to his story.

"In short, you see," he was saying, "David could not help himself, and he followed Sébastien throughout the days and nights of the last two weeks—watching him leave his *pension*, and walk to the *musée*, lingering outside in the afternoons in the hope of seeing him on his way home, and haunting the cafés and theatres which he knew Sébastien frequented."

Charles and I both leaned forward at this, but my secret agent friend spoke first.

"Are you saying that he saw Sébastien arrive at the *musée* last night?" And, as John nodded, "What else did he see?"

"Sébastien did not arrive alone, he was accompanied by another gentleman, youngish, slender but not tall, with wavy brown hair and a pointed mustache, not wearing a hat. David said they appeared to be quarreling."

"Quarreling? Could he hear anything they said?" I asked.

John shook his head. "He was too far away. But he saw the unknown gentleman grab Sébastien's arm, as if to stay close to him, or accompany him inside, but Sébastien flung him off and pushed him away, then unlocked the gate to the *musée* and let himself in."

"The other man did not attempt to follow him in?" I asked.

"No, he said the man stood at the gate, looking furious, pacing back and forth, and then finally left."

I thought about this. "But that does not necessarily mean he didn't find another way in, yes?" I looked at Charles, who shrugged and shook his head.

The three of us sat silently for a few moments.

"This other gentleman," Charles said, "your friend did not recognize him?" I looked at him keenly.

"Are you thinking," I asked him, "that it could be that gentleman—with brown hair and a mustache, pointed at the ends—whom we met at Miss Bayard's this morning? De Carbonnières?" Charles nodded, and looked at John, waiting for the answer to his question.

"My friend did not know him," John said. "But he said he thought he had seen the man before, in company with Sébastien, about a week ago." He waited a moment. "But that's not all."

"Come, then, John!" I cried, frustrated at this slow unravelling, then I instantly repented. "I'm sorry, all this has gotten to my nerves! But please, tell us everything."

John nodded apologetically. "David said he stayed on where he was, outside the *musée*, hoping that Sébastien would come out again shortly—it was after work hours, after all, and he said he assumed Sébastien had merely gone in to tend to some short task." He sighed, and went on. "David had a small part in a play last evening, but it was one of those *petit theatre* things, you know, that start very late, around ten o'clock, so he thought he had enough time to wait for Sébastien to come out."

"What time was it when Sébastien arrived with the unknown gentleman?" Charles asked.

John frowned. "I believe he said it was around seven. He waited for another hour or so, and was about to give it up to go the theatre to prepare, when a man approached the gate of the *musée*, and let himself in with a key." John looked up at both of us. "It was du Sommerard."

"What!" I exclaimed, looking in amazement first at him, then at Charles. "Is your friend sure of that? Does he know du Sommerard?"

"Yes, it appears he met him on a few occasions, when, early on, he was visiting Sébastien at the *musée*, when they were still friendly, so yes, he says it was definitely him."

"Did he see him leave?" Charles said.

"No," John shook his head. "He waited around a little longer but was obliged to depart to go to his theatre, and he saw nothing more."

John looked at us, thoroughly tired out after his long narrative. "David swears he didn't go back to the *musée* again that night—he was at the theatre until well after midnight, and then he went out to a café to dine with the rest of the cast."

"So unless he's making up this whole story about the unknown gentleman, and du Sommerard," I said, "we have other suspects, and *he* has a good alibi for the night of the murder." I looked over at Charles. "However—has the time of the murder been determined?"

And just as I asked, the door bell rang below, and John jumped up from his chair.

"That could be the autopsy report," Charles said, and nodded for John to go downstairs to retrieve it. "We may very well have our answer to your question in a few moments."

I rose from my chair, eager to move about the room and stretch my limbs, which I realized I had been holding tightly curled as I listened to John's story. We heard his footsteps on the stairs as he hastened to bring us the news, and coming into the room, he instantly placed a large envelope in Charles' hands.

We stood in breathless silence as Charles quickly perused the report, some three pages. He nodded a few times, then suddenly paled, his eyes wide.

"What?" I said, clutching his arm. "What is it?"

"Three things," he said, looking grim but still stunned. "First, the arrows did not even pierce the flesh, and drew no blood therefore—applied but lightly through the garments, *post-mortem*, as you thought, Violet," he said, nodding in my direction. "Second, the time of death was between seven and ten o'clock—which doesn't quite exonerate your friend David." He inclined his head toward John, then took a steadying breath.

"And third, Sébastien Bayard was, however unaccountably, a woman."

Six

AUGUST 1792 – BOUSSAC, FRANCE
Changes come to Chateau Boussac

FRANÇOIS AWOKE JUST AS THE BIRDS BEGAN TO SING in the trees around the small mansion at the edge of Boussac. He lay on his back, with Georgette nestled against him, her soft fair hair wanton across his chest. He felt a deep peace here in her bed, the world quiet and the house dark. If only it could last.

Stifling a sigh, he disengaged from his *paramour*, slipped out from under the featherbed, and began to dress. Georgette stirred but did not wake—she was used to him disappearing in silence. From the first, there had been between them no promises of marriage, no planning for the future—his grief for his dead wife and son was still too great for him to contemplate starting over. Georgette was a young widow, childless, but had been left well off and independent when her much older husband died two years ago—and she had no desire to encumber herself with another husband.

But now, things had changed, at least, in one respect. Georgette was with child—a surprise to them both. And although marriage for the two of them was not entirely out of the question, they were clear with each other that being husband and wife simply would not make them happy—and François was not surprised to hear that there was a young man in the wings—much younger than François' fifty-three years, and much more suitable as a husband for Georgette.

"*Adieu, ma petite,*" he murmured as he leaned over to kiss her cheek. It would be best not to return anymore. He knew she would understand—and accept the gifts he would send her way, for herself, and for their child. *Unacknowledged,* he thought, but not *unwanted.* He thought for a moment about what he had shared with her—more than affection and intimacy, the momentous secret of his true parentage—but he felt sure that it would remain a secret with her. He kissed her again, and left.

"Papa, Papa, look what I have!" Pauline's cries of excitement preceded her entrance to the breakfast room, where François was seated calmly with his bowl of broth and plate of eggs. Even with the shortages, they at least had eggs— *grâce à Dieu* for chickens, he thought, who seemed to survive anything.

"What is it, my love? What do you have to show Papa?" His six-year-old daughter came running into the room with what looked to be a knitted stocking on one hand; closer inspection revealed two button eyes and an embroidered mouth and nose. She used her thumb and fingers to open and close its "mouth" as she poked at her father's nose.

"He's going to eat your nose, Papa, watch out!"

"*Sacrebleu!* Where is my sword?" François pretended alarm, leaning back out of reach of the girl's short arms. She dissolved into giggles.

"Oh, Papa, he won't hurt you! It's just in fun!"

"Ah, I see!" he said, leaning down to scoop her up in his arms and smother her with kisses. He sat her down in the chair next to him. "Have you already had your *petit déjeuner,* my child?"

"*Oui*, Papa," she said. "In the nursery." She made a face. "Eggs again. Why do we always have eggs?"

François smiled ruefully. "Because the chickens just won't stop laying them," he said. "We wouldn't want to waste them, would we?"

"*Non*, Papa," she said. "That would be wrong." She lifted her head proudly. "We must always do what is right, mustn't we?"

"*Oui*, my little one. Even when it's hard," he said, a wash of sorrow constricting his heart. He picked up his newspaper to read—it was dated a week ago, 13 August—as his daughter prattled on happily at his side. He had received reports from the town hall at Boussac about the growing crisis in Paris and Versailles, but had kept his head down, concentrating on getting the land to produce enough food to feed his estate families and tenants. The headline on the front page took his breath away: *Royal Family Imprisoned in the Temple.*

He looked up as his mother entered the room; seeing his face, she immediately came and sat next to him, and read the paper with him. It was a timeline of horror:

10 August: The Tuileries Palace is attacked by the Paris Commune National Guard—the King and his family take refuge in the Assembly building—the Swiss Guards defending the Palace are massacred—the Legislative Assembly suspends the authority of the King.

11 August: The government is replaced by a new "Executive Committee"—municipalities are authorized to arrest suspected enemies of the Revolution, and royalist newspapers and publications are banned.

12 August: The Royal family are taken from the Tuileries and imprisoned in the centuries-old fortress of the Knights Templar.

"*Mon Dieu,*" Louise whispered, her hand at her lips. "The world has gone mad." She had become very pale, and fell back in her chair, her usually fierce strength and energy failing her. "François," she said, her voice very low. "I am not well. Please help me to my bed."

"*Maman,* this is too much for your heart!" He raised her from her seat with great tenderness, and accompanied her up the stairs to her bed, with Pauline trailing behind, thumb in her mouth, and looking worried. Louise's personal maid was airing out the room when they entered; she ran to them with a low cry and assisted François in placing his mother comfortably in her bed.

The vigil of her last days was not a long one. The heat of high Summer seemed to retreat for those few days, with white clouds filling a blue sky, and a fresh breeze that stirred the curtains in the elegant chamber. Louise preferred the windows open and the drapes drawn back, so she could see the countryside from her bed, and pass the time in peace, sleeping more and more often. The evening of her death, as François sat at her bedside, watching every labored breath, Louise seemed to brighten for a bit, and asked her son to help her sit up.

"François, my dearest," she said. "Please fetch for me the large leather *portefeuille* you will find in my wardrobe, in the bottom drawer, way in the back."

Her son pressed her hand in silence, and did as he was bid. He felt carefully through the soft shawls and blankets in the bottom drawer until his fingers touched the leather pouch his mother had asked for. Drawing it forth, he could tell by its weight that there was not much inside it, perhaps only papers.

Louise took it from him with a smile, and leaned back against the pillows. "Long ago," she said, "you asked me if you had been acknowledged by the King, your father."

François nodded, his heart beating faster. "And you told me he held me in his arms, and blessed me."

She nodded, her fingers playing with the leather thong tied around the pouch. "I should have given you this before now," she said, sighing. "And I had planned for you to have it after my death"—she raised a hand to keep him from objecting—"which I know is very near, dearest, but I can't help wanting to see it again."

"See what again, dear *Maman?*" François asked. In response, she untied the leather thong, and drew forth a small velvet bag from inside the pouch, and placed it in his hands. Whatever was in it felt small, and oval-shaped. Louise gave him an encouraging nod, and he loosened the strings of the little bag, and shook out its contents—a bejeweled brooch, decorated in enamel with a Lion and a Unicorn, with the royal seal of Louis XV—his father's emblem.

"This is yours, now," she said, and touched the leather bag with a tender hand. "Inside there are letters, from the King, both before and after you were born, which verify the truth of your parentage." Her hand dropped away, as if this last effort had robbed her of all her remaining strength, and she fell into a deep sleep from which she did not awaken.

Louise de Rilhac de Carbonnières was laid to rest in the estate cemetery on the twenty-second of August, 1792—just in time to escape the edict sent out from the Paris Commune that henceforth all persons in France were to be addressed as *"Citoyen"*—no longer even *Monsieur* or *Madame*, to say nothing of more exalted titles. And, in light of the news of the first "royalist traitor" having been executed by the Revolutionary Tribunal the day before, François wisely decided to return the royal brooch to its hiding place with the letters, and say nothing to anyone about them for the time being. One never knew how events would play out—he would wait and see.

One morning, a few days after his mother's funeral, which all the town of Boussac had attended, Georgette drove up to the chateau in a new carriage, and hopped out lightly, looking around with a smile. François, who was witnessing her arrival from an upper window, felt himself smile as well—he always enjoyed her company—but then his smile faded as he wondered why she was here.

"My dear, dear François," she said as she was led into the library by one of the footmen, holding out her hand to be kissed.

"Dear Georgette," he replied, and kissed her hand with due gallantry. "You are looking very well indeed," he added, leading her to a high-backed chair, and sitting in one close to her. "I hope your spirits are high for a good reason?"

She smiled, showing her even white teeth and the dimple he had come to love. "The best reason ever, for I am to be married soon!" She watched him carefully, but kept talking. "I wanted to be the one to let you know as soon as I did, *mon amour,* and hope that you would give me your blessing."

François let both his surprise and his approval show clearly in his face. "Georgette, nothing could make me happier than to see you wedded and happy yourself." He reached over and taking her hand, kissed it again.

"Oh, *mon Dieu,* but I am a beast," she said, her smile disappearing to be replaced with a most sympathetic look. "Your dear mother—I cannot presume to express condolences that would be of any help to you, my dear, in your great grief. Please excuse my insufferable selfishness by intruding so thoughtlessly with my own happiness." She seemed truly stricken at her lack of sensitivity, and François forgave her on the spot. He nodded graciously and changed the subject back to her.

"And all is well with the young gentleman in question?" he asked, looking at her meaningfully.

She laughed, a low, sensual sound that thrilled him even now. "You know me," she said. "I will speak frankly to you, and tell you that as of a few days ago, our marriage is already consummated, even before the banns are read. The gentleman was, shall we say, most cooperative and willing." She tossed her head, and waved a hand. "There will be no trouble about the child." She glanced a little sideways at him. "But there is one thing I must ask you," she said.

"Anything," François replied.

"I have no parent living," she said simply. "Would you be so kind as to give me away at my wedding?"

François stared at her for a few moments—was she serious? He knew her to be a forthright, thinking woman, perhaps one might say, even calculating. What would she gain by this?

As if reading his thoughts, she spoke again. "If there have been any rumours—about us, you see—and there are always rumours—your acting in this guardian-like capacity for me would make everything proper! As if you had always been like a well-loved uncle to me, providing advice and comfort"—here she broke off with a mischievous smile—"only not the kind of comfort that we know really occurred, *n'est-ce pas?"*

He smiled slowly then, seeing the justice of it, and admiring her insight.

"I shall be delighted to escort you at the church, and see you married, *Citoyenne* Georgette," he said.

She laughed at this. "Ah, *bien sûr, Citoyen* François! How funny that there are no longer any titles—all are equal!" She laughed again, and shook her head. "As if simply taking away a title makes a lord the equal of a peasant!"

"Equal before the law," François said, growing serious. "That is the most important thing—the individual, in his or her own person, is protected and respected before the law, by the law, as long as he or she adheres to the principles of integrity, justice, and freedom."

Georgette looked slyly at him. "I see you are preparing speeches for the Assembly, to prove you are not a royalist—anymore," she added, looking thoughtful. "You are a wise man."

"*Merci,* my dear one," François said, and turned to the bureau in his library that held his brandy. "Let us toast to your marriage, and to Liberty, Equality and Fraternity!"

℞ SEVEN ℘

SUNDAY – 8 MAY 1881 – PARIS
Another Conversation with Geneviève

THE DISCOVERY THAT SÉBASTIEN WAS A WOMAN left us speechless for some moments. Dazed, I felt behind me for my chair and sat in it heavily. John walked about the room, running his hand through his thick hair, as if to coerce his brain into accepting this new fact. Charles still stood, the autopsy report in his hands, looking it over yet again.

I glanced at the clock on the mantle—it was bearing on one o'clock—and although this incredible news had given me an initial burst of energy, I suddenly felt throughout my whole being how long a day it had been. I imagined that my companions must feel the same; Charles, indeed, looked exhausted. He had probably risen even earlier than I this morning.

"I can no longer think with any possibility of clarity," I announced abruptly, and stood up. "It seems to me our best course is to retire as soon as possible, and regroup in the morning—and then make with all haste to Miss Bayard's lodgings to discuss this astonishing revelation with her." I eyed my friends with some dismay. "She told me, earlier today, that she and Sébastien were twins, and they are older than you and I, John, by some four years. I should have realized…I should have known…."

John just shook his head. "I'm ready to believe myself deceived in every possible respect." He walked over to Charles, and put a hand on his arm.

"Charles, you are very welcome to a bed here in my house for tonight, should that be of assistance to you." He looked over at me apologetically. "I'm afraid, Vi, that there isn't another room available here for you, but we can get you a cab to take you home."

"No need for that," Charles interposed. "Although I thank you most sincerely. I instructed my driver to wait outside this house until I should come down; I'm more than happy to escort Violet to her door, and make my way back to my own hotel."

Exhaustion and silence seemed the order of the time remaining to us, and we gathered our things and walked down to the front door. John accompanied us, and at the very bottom of the stairs, as he opened the door, a sad smile flitted over his face. "Well," he said, "at least my friend will be better able to understand 'Sébastien's' rejection of him, in light of this."

"Yes," said Charles, "but please, John, do not tell him this until after we have caught the murderer. I want to keep this fact very quiet, if that is even possible, given the chatty propensities of the local police." John agreed, and we took our leave, promising to meet him again before noon.

As the carriage travelled through the empty streets, a thought that had struggled to make itself known to me suddenly became clear. "Charles," I said, turning to my friend, "how do you think your Revenant fits into all this now— with both du Sommerard and this unknown gentleman— possibly de Carbonnières—in the picture?"

Charles leaned his head back against the fabric of the carriage wall behind us, closing his eyes a moment. Although the light was uneven, I could see he was beyond exhaustion, and his usually calm, amused look was replaced by tense and anxious lines around his eyes and his mouth.

I started re-thinking my interest in becoming an international policing agent.

"I'm not at all sure," he said finally, opening his eyes and leaning a bit forward. "It doesn't count him out, and yet, there seem to be other issues, other motives, perhaps, at work here."

"My thinking exactly," I said. "And yet, the Titian—the purported Titian—is truly missing, so there's *that* in support of your art thief." I suddenly yawned quite hugely, my hand at my mouth to cover it up, but it set Charles to yawning as well, which made us both smile wanly.

The carriage stopped in front of my *pension*, and Charles alighted to help me out and see me to the door. I had my key ready (I had told the *concierge* I would be *very* late), unlocked and opened the door, and turned to bid him good night. To my great surprise, he leaned forward and kissed me on the cheek.

"Sleep well, dear Violet," he said softly, and trod lightly back down the steps and into the carriage.

We three assembled at John's house at noon, and Charles having sent a request for a visit to Geneviève Bayard earlier, we took our fate in our hands and drove to her lodgings assuming she would be there and would see us. We were correct.

I had settled it beforehand that I should open the discussion, as I felt Miss Bayard might feel less intimidated by a female interlocutor—but nonetheless, despite her current grieving state, we needed some answers, and I intended to be as direct as possible, whilst staying within the bounds of sympathy. We were ushered into the sitting room, where Miss Bayard awaited us—there were no refreshments, no coffee or tea, just a plain table and chairs to sit upon and face her as she sat calmly on the sofa. She still looked pale, but there was a strength and resolution in her demeanour that had been lacking before.

But she was not really calm, as I noticed as soon as murmured greetings on all sides had passed. I opened my mouth to speak, but Miss Bayard, as they say, took the bull by the horns and spoke first, in her perfect, unaccented English.

"I dare say that you have come to me in all this state to tell me you have seen the results of the autopsy," she said, not without a slight tremour at the word *autopsy*. She held her head a little higher. "What would you like to know about me…and my twin sister?"

I admired her spirit! I should have realized that she would guess she had only a very short time after the death of her sibling before the truth came out, and was prepared to meet our questions head on.

"May we know her name?" I asked gently.

"Aurore," she said.

"*Merci,*" I said, and sat quietly for a moment, waiting for her to speak again.

"My sister was always high-spirited and adventurous," Geneviève began the tale slowly, and with a sigh. "Unlike me," she said, smiling a little. "She liked boys' games, and being outdoors, although she was an excellent student and loved to read—but she adored acting and dressing up." She looked at me expressively. "Do you remember, Miss Paget, I told you about the Baronesse, whose wardrobes filled with clothes we would plunder for our juvenile theatricals?"

"Yes, I do," I said, recalling with amazement that it was only some thirty-six hours ago that we had sat in the theatre and chatted. "George Sand—you said she wrote little plays for you and her own children to act out."

"*Oui,* George Sand," Geneviève repeated, with what sounded like a touch of bitterness. She put a hand to her forehead, only for a moment, and then brushed away some tears. "Aurore was named for her, my parents were so devoted to the Baronesse, especially my mother." She paused. "I believe it was in part their devotion to the Baronesse that led Aurore to want to imitate her in every way—but especially in the kind of defiance of all constraint, all convention, that *George Sand* showed to the world—taking lovers openly, divorcing her husband, earning her own money—and dressing up in men's garments so she could walk about with freedom and ease in the streets of Paris."

I ventured a quick glance at John, to see how he was taking this in, but other than a slightly heightened color, he was calm and thoughtful. There was no knowing what Charles was thinking, however, when he put on his "official" face.

"Who knew about this…*charade?"* I said. "Was it something that Aurore did all the time, or only for certain occasions? Surely members of your household, people in the town…did it not cause a scandal?"

Geneviève shook her head, but then shrugged her shoulders, less decisive. "Aurore was just Aurore, from the moment she could talk and walk. We all adored her charms and eccentricities." Here she looked up at me, then over at John, with a very sad smile. "I believe she found her true spirit in being Sébastien. Her intent was not to deceive for any bad reason—she just became more—*herself*—when she was him. You found her charming as Sébastien, did you not, *monsieur* John?"

John had a little trouble answering at first, then said, clearly enough, "Yes, I did, we all did—he was delightful to be with, he was funny and knowledgeable and witty—he will be much missed." He closed his lips firmly, as if he were determined to say no more. I waited, then spoke again.

"So you don't think there was anyone who would—I'm sorry to say this, but I must—*harm* her for her eccentricities?

"Everyone adored her, whether she was Aurore or Sébastien," Geneviève said. A sudden wild grief shadowed her lovely face, and she looked at Charles beseechingly.

"When may I have her back?" she said, her voice breaking. "When may I take her home, and place her with our parents, and our little brother?" At this, she broke down completely and began weeping. John immediately rose and went to her, enfolding her in his arms as he sat next to her on the sofa.

I glanced over at Charles, whose stern look had softened only a little, and raised my brows for an answer to the poor woman's question. He nodded his head and extended a hand as if to say, *whenever she likes, we're done with the body.* I showed my approval of this, and impulsively, turned back to Geneviève and spoke.

"My dear Miss Bayard," I said, "is there anything we can do to help you with this sorrowful task? Is there anyone who can assist you in getting your sister to Nohant?" I had a sudden thought, and—proving to myself that I actually did have a rather chill heart and a calculating brain worthy of a detective—asked another question. "What about *monsieur de* Carbonnières, whom we met here just yesterday morning? I believe you said he was an old friend from your village, or nearby? Is he able to assist you?"

John's ministrations and the lady's own efforts brought her back to a semblance of calm, and she answered with a shake of her head. "François sent a note, late last night, saying he was obliged to return to Boussac." She sighed, a slight look of anger crossing her face. "How he could leave me at such a time…! But it is what it is." She gratefully accepted John's offered handkerchief, and began to wipe her eyes.

"That was a very short visit of his, was it not, all the way from Boussac to Paris, and now back again, not even one night?" I said, impressing myself with my cunning. "I received the impression yesterday that he had just arrived in town that morning."

Geneviève nodded, "Yes, that is what he told me, and it is odd that he has gone away so soon." She shrugged. "He did not tell me the reason for his going, but then, he is an odd man."

I was preparing to ask more about this odd man, but John spoke then, in a low voice, glancing over at me as he did so. "*Mademoiselle* Bayard, may we accompany you and your sister to Nohant, I and Miss Paget? I cannot bear to think of you shouldering this sad burden all on your own."

I stifled my surprise, but quickly added my entreaties to John's. "Yes, yes indeed, we would consider it an honour to go on this journey with you." I did not add that it would allow the possibility of tracking down the mysterious François de Carbonnières and finding out more about him. I looked at Charles, who nodded his acquiescence.

Geneviève started to protest, but I could see her heart was not in it.

"It is settled then," I said, rising from my chair. "My dear, we will take it upon ourselves to deal with the *gendarmerie,* with the help of Mr. Wilkinson here, to procure the release of your sister's body, and John, I trust you can make the arrangements to travel to Nohant?" I looked at my two friends, who nodded readily, then I turned back to Geneviève. "Is that agreeable to you, Miss Bayard?"

She rose and grasped my hand in gratitude, then leaned in and gave me a tight hug. Surprised, I hesitated at first, then folded my arms around her thin form, feeling her shaking like a little bird in a storm. Poor thing! I was indeed glad to help.

And glad to get a further chance to investigate a possible murderer.

EIGHT

21 JANUARY 1793
In the Shadow of the Terror

EVIL NEWS FLIES ON THE DEVIL'S WINGS, and the horror of the King's execution in Paris spread across the land with the swiftness of a plague of locusts. In Boussac, the tenants of the ancient fortress estate gathered in the cobblestoned courtyard, the cold, early dusk of Winter shadowing them, to talk and lament, and hear what François de Carbonnières had to say.

There were no cheers or even murmurs of satisfaction—their King was a chosen vessel of the Divine Will—they had heard this all their lives, for centuries, through scores of generations, and it was not a belief that was lightly held, or easily given up. They stood about, warming their hands by the fires that François had ordered to be built and lighted in the courtyard—he knew his people would arrive by the end of the day—and gratefully accepting the warm possets of wine and ale, along with as much bread as could be gathered in these hard times, that the chateau's servants handed around.

"Mes amis, citoyennes de France." François' voice rang over the courtyard, and the people hushed to hear him. He stood

at the top of the great stone stairway that led to the front entrance of the chateau; seven-year-old Pauline stood by his side, bundled against the cold. "Louis XVI, known of late as *Citoyen Louis Capet*, has been executed by order of the National Convention, by guillotine, this morning at the *Place de la Révolution*." He paused, maintaining his composure, and heard restrained sobbing and muttered curses. "Let us pray to a merciful God that he is at peace, and will be received into the ranks of the angels in heaven this very day."

The local priest, although dressed in civilian clothes for safety, began to say the rosary, and the people responded in kind. When they had done, François spoke again.

"I do not know, nor can I attempt to guess, what changes lie ahead for us, here in Boussac, and for all our countrymen throughout France. We are fortunate in being far from the seat of power, and because we have little to offer beyond what sustains us who live here, we have little of interest to those who might take it from us." He looked around in the deepening gloom, lighted here and there by the fires and the torches along the walls, and tried to sound reassuring even though he did not feel it himself. "I entreat you all to act in every matter as upright, Christian citizens, following the divine laws of prudence, justice, fortitude and temperance, as well as Our Lord's injunction to love God and one's neighbor as one's self. If we follow this path, we cannot be wrong—and if others choose to think that we do, and punish us for it, well, then we must look to God's own justice to set right any wrongs done to us."

"God bless you, François de Carbonnières!" A woman's voice called out, followed by several vehement *Amen's.*

A quavering voice rose above the crowd, chanting a prayer from the requiem Mass. "*Accorde-lui le repos éternel, Ô*

Seigneur"—*Eternal rest grant unto him, O Lord*—and the people responded: *"Puisse la lumière perpétuelle briller sur lui."*—*And let perpetual light shine upon him.*

François and Pauline crossed themselves along with all their tenants and servants and neighbors, and then retreated to the chateau as the people made their way to their homes with heavy hearts and fear for their future.

Boussac was in truth far enough removed from the seat of power—even the smaller power at Bourges, the central city of the Berry region—that the Revolution of the Citizens did not disrupt daily life there—except for the shortages of everything. The government was in disarray, the previously omnipotent bureaucracy barely functioning, and most of the nobles and upper-class merchants and professionals, the lawyers and doctors, were all in Paris, hammering out a new constitution—and falling victim to *Madame Guillotine* if they fell out of favor with the seemingly ever-changing and increasingly arbitrary rulers of the Convention.

No one was safe.

François de Carbonnières knew in his heart that if his mother's letters from the late King's grandfather—and the bejeweled token he had given her—ever became known, it would be a death sentence for him, and probably his daughter as well. For the last three years, he had played a waiting game, resolute and circumspect, always the loyal *citoyen* of the new regime—not that he didn't agree with many of the much-needed changes and ideas for a new France. Far from it, as evidenced by the way he managed his estate, fairly, justly, and with compassion for the poor and respect for the hard-working.

One morning, about four months after the execution of Louis XVI, he sat at his desk in his library, facing a pleasant Spring landscape bursting into white flowers and tender green leaves. The letters and the brooch lay on the table before him. What was he to do with them? It seemed to him the most prudent decision would be to destroy them all—there would be no good to come from keeping them, and there was probable danger in their discovery.

A carriage making its way up the long road to the chateau caught his eye—it was Georgette. He frowned, thinking that perhaps something had happened to the child—the son that had been born about six weeks earlier—their child, his son. *My son,* he thought, and caught himself feeling more than a little regret. Perhaps he should have married her after all? There would be a son for Boussac now. But that was unfair to Pauline. She was bright and gay and delicately pretty—she would find a good husband, in time, and be a good mistress for the chateau. He watched as Georgette alighted from her carriage, and was surprised to see her maid also, handing her a little carefully wrapped bundle—she was bringing their son to him!

He hastened from his room to meet her downstairs, not stopping to put away the letters and the brooch; he pulled on his coat and ran his fingers through his hair, attempting to make himself presentable—he had grown rather lax in his grooming, after his mother's death, and the King's execution—it didn't seem to matter anymore.

There was a bustle in the entrance hall as Georgette arrived with the child and the nursemaid; she looked up as François hurried down the stairs, and smiled brilliantly. She took the child from the arms of its nurse, and dismissed the woman abruptly.

"Go back to the carriage and wait for me," she said, and as the woman left, Georgette walked forward to greet her former lover at the foot of the stairs.

"See, I have brought you the child, Jean François desRosiers," she said, holding the baby close to her. She glanced around. "Can we go to your library, where we may speak more privately?"

Caught off guard, François simply nodded and led the way back upstairs. When they entered the library, he closed the door, and invited her to sit on the upholstered sofa near the fireplace. It was a man's room, there was no doubt, with papers and books in stacks on various tables and chairs, and dust clinging to the surfaces, but the furniture was well-made and comfortable.

"You do not allow the servants in here to clean?" Georgette said, amused and glancing around the room. "How like an unmarried man, careless of the state of his house." She smiled up at him again, and did not take a seat. "I will not stay long." She studied his face, but did not remark on what she saw there. "I thought you would want, at least, to see the boy—our son," she said, her voice dropping to a whisper for the last two words." She pulled back the blanket that was draped over the infant, and held him out a little for François to see.

His face softened as he looked at the child. "All is well with him?" he said, holding out a finger for the boy to touch, which he did, grasping with a strong grip, and a laughing look in his tiny face, his dark eyes large and shining.

Georgette laughed lightly. "He is a very healthy boy, he'll be walking by harvest time, I'd wager on it."

François stifled a sigh, and the urge to take the infant in his arms and hold him close. It was dangerous to indulge such feelings.

"*Merci, Georgette,*" he said, and drew back his hand from the baby's grip. But he sensed something else in her, beyond a desire to show off the child, and the two of them stood, face to face. He watched her gather her resolution and strike.

"I want to have some assurance of his true parentage," she said, and continued quickly, although François had made no sign of interrupting her. "And especially as it relates to yours—to the royal blood that flows in your veins, and now in his—I want to know what evidence you have, what proofs, that this is true." She looked at him, defiantly but also, he saw, fearfully.

He smiled faintly and looked away, glancing at the desktop where the proofs of his heritage lay exposed.

"And with the King executed, his family imprisoned, and the nobles of his family in exile or prison, too," he said slowly. "What on earth are you thinking? What possible benefit could such information be, now or in future, for the illegitimate offspring of a deposed and disgraced monarch?"

Georgette caught her breath at his bleak and blunt description; but she had spirit. "Things will change! They always do, you know," she said, shrugging slightly. "I intend to be ready to claim...whatever is to be claimed...when circumstances are right." She lifted her chin and gazed at him, then taking rapid steps over to his desk, seized the brooch in one hand and examined it eagerly. She had seen his glance at the desk.

François walked slowly toward her, and held out his hand. "It will do you no good, nor the child," he said. She continued looking at it—it was clear to him she knew it was a royal token—and she then handed it to him. Her eyes swept the desk quickly, and fastened on the letter that lay on top, her eyes brightening at the royal signature at the bottom of the page.

"You have written evidence as well," she said, but forebore to pick up the papers.

"*Oui*," said François, his voice soft but steely. "But not for long." He reached over and gathered up all the correspondence, holding it close. "I intend to destroy everything."

"You cannot!" Georgette was fierce. "You cannot deprive our son—*your* son—of the inestimable knowledge of his true heritage—it would be a crime!" Her breath came quickly, and the child in her arms began to whimper. "It would be a sin!"

François was not moved, but he allowed her to continue speaking. "Do you not remember," she said, "how you spoke of this to me, two years ago and more?" She gentled her voice, and touched his arm lightly. "You were so full of wonder, and gratitude, for knowing that all the ways you had felt, all your life, *meant* something—that you *were* someone, *because* you were the son of a King—does not our son deserve to know himself in the same way?"

He did indeed remember all that—it was clear in his face. All those boyish feelings of belonging somewhere else, being meant for something greater—yes, when his mother told him the truth, he had felt such a surge of power and delight and joy. But what, after all, had it come to? He shook his head, bewildered.

"Cannot you let our son determine his own fate in his own way?" Georgette spoke, as if reading his mind. "Do not destroy these precious things, I beg you, for Jean François' sake."

François relented; he couldn't deprive his son of the truth that he himself had known. "I will not destroy them," he said at last. "But he cannot know, not for a long time—it is too dangerous now."

Georgette breathed a sigh of relief, but she had one more arrow in her quiver. "But you shall, I pray, bequeath them to your son, in your will, so that one day, he can see these evidences of his heritage?"

François thought about what that meant—anticipating his death, which he had always avoided thinking about—but then nodded his head. "*Oui, ma chérie*," he said in a whisper. "I swear to it."

She leaned toward him, and standing on tiptoe, kissed his cheek, then laid her fingertips on his lips, and turned to go.

"You must swear to say nothing to him until that time," François said suddenly. She turned back at the doorway.

"*Je le jure*," she said, *I swear it.* And she left the house.

❋ PART FOUR ❋

❦ ONE ❦

THE FRENCH, EVEN MORE THAN THE ITALIANS, take train schedules as advisory only, with departures and arrivals attuned to the apparent whim of the stationmaster, or possibly the newsboy on the corner, or the latest divination of chicken entrails that morning. Our own departure was no exception, although the delay was scarcely an hour, so really didn't signify in the annals of travel atrocities.

Charles Wilkinson had made everything easy in regard to the transportation of poor Aurore Bayard's body, leaving nothing for me to do on that score other than procure some suitable clothing from her sister before we left her lodgings on the Sunday. And thank the deities of travel for dear Emily Sargent! Over a hurried but most welcome tea late on Sunday, she proved herself a true friend and a remarkable proficient as *un agent de voyage.*

"You will leave from the *Gare d'Austerlitz,*" she announced, perusing a pad of lined paper on which she had written, in beautifully legible handwriting, instructions for our trip. "Here are the tickets, for which I thank John," she said, nodding at him, "for his trouble in procuring them in person at the station just now." She held up the envelope of *billets* as proof. "A very good second-class cabin, you see, which will just suit the three of you and your luggage, unless some horrid stranger decides to enter and exhaust you with his company." She looked at me with a wry smile. "I advise you, Violet, to speak sharply and cause a fuss, or better, just start weeping hysterically, if such a person should try to join your group—he will shortly decamp!"

I looked at her in amazement. "Emily, wherever do you get such ideas? You should write a Guide to Rail Travel, I'm sure it would be very popular!" I picked up my teacup and added more sugar, and then more tea, meanwhile reviewing the selection of sandwiches crowded onto little plates.

"You must change trains at Bourges," she continued, "and there will be enough time between the two trains to procure a bit of luncheon at the station. It will be a smaller train from there to Nohant," she wound up, folding up the map she was looking at, and handing it to me. "There is just standard seating, but it isn't a long journey, perhaps an hour, so it will be bearable."

Shadows of sadness crossed her face. "And poor Sébastien's coffin—will it be well cared for? Will you know where it is placed?"

John and I exchanged quick glances. We had been commanded by Charles not to tell anyone of the results of the autopsy, not even dear Emily. To be frank, I was glad not to have to give her that astonishing information; it wouldn't hurt anything if she never knew, would it? John answered her question.

"I shall personally oversee the placement and transport of the coffin," he said, reassuringly patting her hand. "We want to relieve Miss Bayard of every possible trouble."

Emily nodded, a tear trickling down her cheek, which she quickly wiped away. "Where will you stay in Nohant?" she asked, turning to the tea tray to refill her cup.

"Miss Bayard insists we stay at their family home," I said. "Apparently they have plenty of room, and she has wired ahead to inform the housekeeper there will be guests."

"And how long do you think you will be gone?"

I paused at this—prominent in my mind was my expected arrival in London on Friday, when I would join my dear friend Mary Robinson—*that* could not be delayed for even the most important reasons—even such as solving a murder—and I was determined to be back in Paris no later than Thursday, earlier if possible.

"I believe," John said, "that Miss Bayard indicated the funeral would be Wednesday morning, so it's possible we might leave Nohant that afternoon, or at the latest, Thursday morning." He looked somewhat apologetic. "I must return for the Salon announcements on Friday." I nodded my agreement.

"Well, I think it is so very, very noble and self-sacrificing of you, both of you," Emily said. "To take such trouble and expense for someone you have barely known."

John smiled sadly. "The two of them, the Bayards, were all the family they had, I believe, their parents having died some years ago—and now poor Geneviève is left alone." He stood up suddenly, and walked to the window, looking out at the dusky evening. His voice was a bit muffled. "I couldn't bear it if she had to return all alone, with her brother in his coffin, and shoulder that awful burden by herself."

I drank my tea, and thought of my own mother and brother and father—as troublesome and often distant as they were, they were my family, and I knew there was love there between us all, however oddly displayed. That was something.

Charles graciously allowed us the use of his official carriage, collecting me and Miss Bayard in turn, and depositing us at the *Gare d'Austerlitz* well before our wayward train was to depart. John had met him much earlier to arrange transport for the coffin, which was already placed in a special compartment of the train by the time we arrived. Miss Bayard was dressed in dark clothing, not exactly black but very dark brown and grey, with a large hat and a thick veil. She had said very little in the carriage, but gratefully accepted a cup of tea that John had procured for her when we arrived.

Charles, of course, was staying in Paris. He wished us well, shook hands all around, then pulled me aside for a moment.

"Violet," he said, sounding stern and official, "I know what you are thinking, going down to Nohant—and probably Boussac." He shook his head at me. "You have an uncanny ability to get yourself into tight spots, my dear, and I just want to warn you not to take chances with your *monsieur* de Carbonnières."

I decided it would be undignified to dissemble or protest—after all, Charles was very well aware of the kind of 'trouble' I had gotten myself into in Venice two years ago—and merely patted his hand and acquiesced.

"I will take your concern under advisement," I said. "I have no notion of putting myself in harm's way just now." The thought of travelling and writing with Mary was enough to keep me fairly sober and determined to keep myself in one piece, and show up in London on Friday.

He bowed over my hand, and giving me a single, serious look, then an affectionate smile, took his leave and left the station.

The ensuing bustle of finding our carriage, and the cabin within it, took all of our attention and time from that moment until we were seated in our snug little cabin, our boxes and bags carefully stowed below the seats and on the shelf above. John obligingly sat by the window facing forward, against which most of the smoke and coal ash would be flung—if we dared to open the window at all; Miss Bayard sat facing him, and I sat next to her.

Thankfully, I was not forced into weeping hysterically, as Emily had advised, in order to keep anyone else from joining us—no one approached our cabin, and we were left in peace. It was to be a nearly three-hour journey—a marvel when you contemplate how long and uncomfortable a journey of one hundred-fifty miles by horse and carriage would be—and for the first hour none of us spoke. Miss Bayard appeared to be asleep, although I surmised she merely closed her eyes and pretended.

John gazed out the window, lost in thought, whilst I attempted to begin reading the formidable first volume of *Histoire de ma Vie*, by George Sand. By great good luck, the inestimable Madame Millefleurs, my landlady, had a copy of it in her library, which I borrowed for the trip. I hoped it would reveal something about Sand's sojourns at the Chateau Boussac, the ancient fortress which still, apparently, was home to the set of tapestries du Sommerard was trying so diligently to acquire for the *Musée de Cluny* in Paris. I was also hoping, probably irrationally, that we would be able to visit Boussac during our short stay at Nohant.

Paging quickly through the illuminating but rather dense paragraphs of philosophical discussion *vis-à-vis* the French Revolution of 1789, my eye fell upon the section about Sand's *grand-mère*, Marie-Aurore de Saxe Dupin de Franceuil, who in 1793 purchased the house at Nohant, the village to which we were now travelling. I present here the first few sentences that I read with great interest, about a woman with noble ancestors on both sides of her family, including a former King of Poland, faced with the up-heaval—and, for many, execution—of the aristocracy in France:

> *"She had adopted the tenets of equality as much as it was possible in her situation. She was abreast of all the advanced ideas of her time. She accepted the social contract along with Rousseau; she hated super-stition along with Voltaire; she even accepted the ideas of the generous utopias; the word 'republic' did not phase her at all. She was by nature loving, helpful, agreeable, and readily saw as her equal every lowly per-son."*

There followed a long, discursive reflection about the nature of revolutions, at the end of which George Sand re-turned to her *grandmère's* story. I read with amazement that despite all her egalitarian tendencies, Marie-Aurore Dupin had been arrested and imprisoned in Paris during the Reign of Terror.

I settled down for a most interesting tale.

Two

THE 5ᵀᴴ OF FRIMAIRE, YEAR II – PARIS
[26 NOVEMBER 1793]
Under the Terror

"SHALL WE TRAVEL DOWN TO NOHANT soon, *Maman*?" Fifteen-year-old Maurice Dupin leaned over his mother as she sat writing a letter in her study. The apartment they rented in Paris was far from luxurious, but it was comfortable and well-lighted. His mother was fiercely thrifty, and complained about her poverty just as fiercely, even though she had recently purchased the chateau in Nohant for some three hundred thousand francs, and still lived well.

"*Oh, mon fils*," she murmured, shaking her head. "Soon enough, soon enough." She held her pen above the paper, sighing. "What is the date, Maurice? I cannot keep it all straight in my poor head."

"*Cinq de Frimaire, Maman*," he said, smiling. He was a quick study, and had easily memorized the new names of the twelve months of the Revolutionary Calendar, each month divided into three periods of ten days—with a 'leftover' time of five days at the end of the year—and each day given a new name of a flower, a seed, a tree, or some other natural element in order to obliterate the now-despised Catholic

Church's endless procession of saints' days and holy days. The month of *Frimaire* was Frost, the onset of Winter, to be followed by Snow, Rain, Wind—all to mark the seasons of the year.

It was Year II of the new Republic. So far Maurice's aristocratic mother had escaped the predatory notice of the Commissions of Robespierre, and they both lived quietly in the second-floor apartment at 12 Rue Nicolas, along with *monsieur* Deschartres, his tutor, a gentleman devoted to Maurice and his mother. She, unlike many in her class, had refused to emigrate, and remained, steadfast, in Paris, hoping for the best.

But she had made one small mistake, which was to prove her undoing in a few short hours.

She finished her letter, and put her cheek up for her son to kiss. "*Alors*," she said, "now we will go for our walk, *mon cher,* will that satisfy you?"

"*Oui, Maman,* I'm dying to be outside before the sun steals away," he replied, and ran to fetch his coat and his mother's cloak. They had few servants in town, just one maid and a manservant who combined the duties of butler, footman, and valet to Maurice. They shared a cook with their landlord, Citizen Amonnin, who was a disbursements official, and had served in that capacity before the revolution—some of the former bureaucracy were needed by the new government, despite their possible monarchist sympathizing.

Before Maurice returned to her little study, which was on a tiny mezzanine floor reached only through a hidden door behind her bedroom wardrobe (the City's old apartments were rife with hidden rooms), she quickly checked the false panel behind which she had hidden various items of value and boxes of papers just a week before. It seemed secure, but she felt uneasy. The Convention had decreed that secreting certain kinds of wealth—jewels and silver among them—as well as documents pertaining to one's heritage and connections—would be punishable by imprisonment and possibly execution, if the circumstances warranted it. Their landlord Amonnin had persuaded her, in urgent whispers, that it behooved both of them to hide their important papers and precious items—so she had given him some silver spoons and forks, along with jewelry and a few papers, which he joined with his own large silver collection, and hid them in a concealed hiding place in the wall of his drawing room. She was grateful she had already sent a number of things down to the house in Nohant.

She did not tell him about the things she had hidden in the mezzanine—the papers of contract for a loan to the brother of the late King Louis XVI—he had needed money to leave the City, and of course, she did not expect the loan would ever be repaid; but they were related, even if through various sidelines and mistresses. If it were to be discovered that she had done this, she would pay with her life.

Maurice returned just as Marie-Aurore was leaving her bedroom, thinking everything was now in order, and they set off for their walk.

"Ouvrez! Ouvrez-nous, au nom de la loi!" The pounding of fists on the street door awakened the entire household. Marie-Aurore leaped out of bed, lighted a candle with shaking hands, and saw the hands of the clock touching half-past ten. Many months of rigidly enforced curfews had trained the population to bed down early and rise early as well. She tried

to quell her rapid heartbeat as Maurice appeared in the doorway, disheveled from sleep.

"*Maman*, what is it? What's happening?" The boy looked so young, his feet bare below his nightshirt, that she felt stronger just thinking she must protect him at all costs.

"*Je ne sais pas, mon cher*," she whispered, pulling him into a fast embrace. "*Monsieur* Amonnin will take care of it."

Further pounding on the door was soon followed by their landlord's brisk steps down the staircase—he lived on the floor above them—and they heard him call out to the officers in the street to have patience, he was coming. By this time, Maurice's tutor, Deschartres, who was hard of hearing, had awakened and came to join them in the hall, silenced by Marie-Aurore's warning hand to her lips.

Heavy boots and low voices passing their door riveted Marie-Aurore, her son and Deschartres, as they stood in their inner hallway, arms around each other, holding their breaths. The officers continued to the third floor, where they could hear the men walking back and forth, furniture being dragged this way and that, and occasional thumps and bangs as items were thrown aside or on the floor. They were directly beneath Citizen Amonnin's drawing room, and before long they heard a cry of discovery. Marie-Aurore nearly fainted with the terror that raced through her heart; Maurice didn't know what she and their landlord had done, what they had hidden or where, but he knew that such things were taking place throughout the city. She felt his warm hand press hers tightly.

"Don't worry, *Maman*," he whispered. "I will keep you safe." She nearly wept at the thought. She looked at Deschartres, who, though she had not told him either of the hidden items, seemed to grasp quite thoroughly what she feared.

The noise from above suddenly ceased, and the ensuing silence was even more frightening. Then came the boots and the voices, back down the stairs. She prayed they would pass by her apartment again, but the dreaded knock sounded, loud and insistent, on the panels of their door.

"Citizeness Dupin!" She heard the voice of her landlord, pleading. "Please open the door."

Gathering her strength and her wits, she and Maurice went to the door, arm in arm, and she opened it. Deschartres stood close behind them.

The sight of three large soldiers of the Republic, standing stiffly behind the officers of the Convention, and the trembling form of her landlord, almost took from her the power of speaking. But she called out to the spirit of her famous father, the *Maréchal* Maurice de Saxe, the greatest hero of France in his day, and she stood her ground.

"What do you require of a poor *Citoyenne* at this time of night, Citizens?"

"We have it on good authority that you, Citizeness, and Citizen Amonnin here, have secreted away various jewels and documents that are of interest to the Republic, and in violation of the promulgated rules against such activities."

"Come in and search, then, if you must," she said, her head high. Gripping her son's arm, she stepped back into the apartment, and led him to a sofa in the drawing room, where they sat, staring straight ahead, while the soldiers went about their work. Deschartres, determining that silence was the better form of valor, came and stood behind them. She could feel her son trembling under her hand, but she whispered to him only once, to stay still, and show no reaction.

The men were swift and efficient. Although her face (she hoped) was serene, internally Marie-Aurore prayed frantically that finding the hidden door to the mezzanine would be beyond their abilities; there was nothing else hidden in the place. After what seemed an eternity but was probably no more than half an hour, the soldiers returned to the drawing room, shaking their heads at the officer who led them.

"You will excuse us then, Citizeness, young Citizen," he said, addressing her and Maurice. "We are in the service of the Republic, and the people."

"Of course," Marie-Aurore managed to say, and nodded her head graciously. She didn't think she could stand up from the sofa to save her life at that moment, but her son was more stalwart than she, and rose, holding her up with his own young strength. They accompanied the soldiers to the door, and closing it after them, the mother and son held each other closely, giving way to tears and sobs of relief.

But it was short-lived. The next morning, the soldiers were back, with a writ of arrest—the things they had found in Amonnin's hiding places had been identified as belonging to Marie-Aurore de Saxe Dupin, and she was taken away to the convent-school of the English Augustinian nuns, which was being used as a prison for females accused of crimes against the State. Maurice was not allowed to accompany her, and was left in sorrow and bewilderment in the company of his tutor Deschartres.

Marie-Aurore had had only time enough to whisper one word to Deschartres, praying with all her might that he would understand.

"Mezzanine."

Nine Months Later – August 1794

With no warning, the women's prison official opened the door to Marie-Aurore's convent cell, and told her she was free to go. It was a bright, sunny, hot Parisian afternoon, and Marie-Aurore was dismissed from the convent school with less ceremony than walking out of a dress shop. The last three months had seen a sharp drop in the number of letters she had been able to send out or receive, so she had to hope and pray that she would be able to find the one place she knew where she might find her son, and his devoted tutor Deschartres—outside the city walls, at Passy, where they had been driven by officers, and forbidden to enter the city without specific permission of the Convention. Marie-Aurore, too, had been told she would not be able to leave the city without proper papers, but her long separation from her beloved son, and the distress of her imprisonment, combined to make her reckless.

She would go to Passy, no matter what she had to do.

As she limped down the stone street that led away from the convent, seeking shade alongside the buildings as the sun beat down on her, she held her head high and looked fearlessly around—and that's when she suddenly caught sight of Deschartres, standing under the eave of a shop door, his eyes trained on the convent. They recognized each other at the same instant, and ran to clasp each other tightly.

"Dear, dear Deschartres," she murmured, trying to keep from breaking down entirely. "How is it that you are here, on this very day?" They parted from their embrace, and he took her arm in his, walking away at a rapid pace.

"I heard that the tribunal was considering your case, about a week ago, and they have been just turning people free wholesale, in large numbers, so with hope in my heart, I have stood here, day after day, knowing they would just simply open the door and tell you to go, without any notice to anyone."

She nodded, happy to keep pace with him and put distance between her and the convent-prison. "That is exactly what happened, just now," she said. "I barely had time to think what to do, but my first object is to see my son—is he well?" Her breath caught in her throat at the thought of seeing him.

"Very well, indeed," Deschartres assured her. "This trial that both you and he have had to endure has strengthened and matured him, you will see, he is a young man now, not a boy anymore."

They went first to her apartment which, thanks to Deschartres, was still leased to her and available for her use. As they stood before the door, about to go in, a sudden thought stopped Marie-Aurore in her tracks.

"The mezzanine?" She whispered it, her eyes darting about. Deschartres gripped her hand, and bent down to whisper back.

"I took care of it all—I knew what you meant," he said. "Fear not, all has been destroyed, and you are safe."

She kissed his cheek fervently, tears springing to her eyes, and he unlocked the door and ushered her inside.

Her desire to see Maurice immediately was so urgent, she convinced Deschartres they could take a boat across the river to Passy, disguised as peasants, not waiting for any official papers for travel for her, and then they could decide what to do, the three of them—although all she wanted was to take her son and leave for Nohant immediately.

Less than an hour later, the two friends, dressed in the humblest of clothing they could find, joined a queue of peasants and farmers returning to their farms at the end of the market day, crossing the Seine on a boat going toward Quai des Invalides; they could walk to Passy from there. But her costume was not enough to hide her class. The boat was filled with working-class people, several of whom observed the two carefully, nudging each other and whispering. Finally, a rough-looking man spoke up.

"There," he said, "is a nice looking little mother who hasn't done much work in her life." He pointed to Marie-Aurore's soft, white hands.

Deschartres immediately took offense. "And what business is it of yours?" At that moment, a woman sitting next to him put her hand in his pocket, cool as air, and pulling out a small, blue-paper-wrapped package, sniffed at it, and opened it. Inside were a roller of Cologne water, and a few delicate items he had brought along to please Marie-Aurore. The woman held them up to the crowd.

"Look at this!" she said. "They're aristocrats on the run! If they were the likes of us, they wouldn't be toting perfume!"

Deschartres, incensed and heedless of danger, stood up in the middle of the boat, shouting at the top of his voice and brandishing his fists, threatening to throw anyone overboard who might continue to insult his woman. The men only laughed at his bravado, and the boatman merely said, calmly enough, "We'll clear this matter up at the landing."

Marie-Aurore decided it was time for her to act. Leaning forward to two women who sat near her, she took their hands and said, "Aristocrat or not, I am a mother who has not seen her son for more than six months, who believed she would never see him again, and who is travelling to embrace him at the risk of her life." The women all fell silent, looking at her with pity. "Do you wish to destroy me?" Marie-Aurore continued. "Well then, denounce me, kill me, if you wish, on the return trip, but do not prevent me from seeing my son today." Tears filled her eyes. "I put my fate in your hands."

"There, there, Citizeness," the women responded immediately, pressing her hands. "We don't wish you any harm. You can trust us, we have children and we love them, too."

When the boat landed on the farther shore, some of the crew members, who had taken against Deschartres for his posturing, tried to keep him from going with Marie-Aurore, but the women protested and shamed them. "None of that!" they said. "Respect for the female sex! Don't upset this poor Citizeness. As for her valet, let him go with her. He makes a big fuss, but he's as harmless as you are." Marie-Aurore thanked them with all her heart.

The reunion with Maurice was beyond joyful, and the three companions made plans quickly to gain the proper certificates of travel, and leave for Nohant as soon as possible. A week later, they were in a carriage and on their way south.

໐ Three ໐

MONDAY – 9 MAY 1881 – NOHANT
We arrive in Nohant.

A TEDIOUS STOP AT BOURGES at least allowed us to procure a light luncheon, and stretch our legs a bit, and then it had been merely an hour or so on a rather smaller train to the very small station at Nohant. It was late afternoon by the time the family's carriage, which was waiting for us, brought us down the short gravel drive to the stucco and wood-framed Bayard mansion at the edge of the village. A separate wagon had followed us there also, conveying poor Sébastien's—that is, Aurore's—body to the house.

Alighting under the portico at the front door, I was delighted by the freshness of the whole place, the soft Spring light on the hedges and flowers, beautifully mixed and riotous, *so not-English* in its colors and wildness. But the black wreath on the door reminded me it was a house in mourning, and I subdued my enjoyment.

John was assisting Geneviève down from the carriage, but I could see he was observant, as was I, of the beauty and peace of this small estate.

The door opened, and a well-dressed woman, perhaps in her fifties, came quickly down the steps to greet us, and embrace Geneviève with what could only be described as a mother's kindness and care.

"I am Eugenie Bayard," she said, holding out a hand to me, then to John. "Geneviève's aunt, her dear father's sister." She spoke briskly, with a confident friendliness and a generous smile. "You must be Violet and John." Although I was surprised by the familiarity of her address, it didn't bother me in the least, she did it so naturally. She kept her arm around her niece's shoulders, and turned back to her to kiss her cheek, murmuring endearments and support.

"Aurore…" Geneviève barely spoke her sister's name, but her aunt was alert to her meaning.

"All is arranged," she said, then glancing at me and John, "It is the custom here in the country to have the beloved dead in the house, for prayers and honor, in the night hours before the funeral." She lifted her head and signalled to the servant in charge of the wagon with the coffin in it. "To the ice house, if you please, Jules." He nodded and clicked at the old brown horse to move on.

"Please, do come in," she said, turning with Geneviève toward the house. A young maid stood at the door, and curtseyed when we came close. We entered a beautiful, open room with two staircase wings, of some pleasing chestnut-tinted wood, on either side of the tile floors. Fresh flowers stood on tables, mirrors reflecting behind them, bringing the outdoors into the room.

"Celine here will show you to your rooms, my dears," she said to me and John, gesturing to the staircase on our left. "Please take all the time you need to refresh yourselves, I believe we will be having dinner at seven." She walked with Geneviève toward the other staircase, and called back to us over her shoulder. "If you're hungry in the meantime, just go to the kitchen and help yourselves."

The maid Celine showed us up the staircase, and I couldn't help muttering to John, "Extraordinary person, eh?"

He nodded, smiling faintly. "But I rather like her manners," he said, then smiled a bit more. "Very American, I assure you, however odd that may be in a Frenchwoman."

I was shown to a small but well-appointed room, overlooking the back gardens, which faced east. There were toiletries set out on the wash basin stand, which was of marble and wood, sturdily made but with elegance. The room was painted a pale yellow, and the curtains were a delicate green, with embroidered leaves of a darker green scattered across the fabric. The bed looked inviting, and a wardrobe with a full-length mirror stood against a wall by one corner. A comfortable upholstered chair and footstool completed the furnishings, and I regretted that we would be staying at most two nights in this lovely place.

I thanked Celine for her help, and quickly made myself mistress of the room, placing my few things in drawers and on hangers—I have become quite used to 'doing for' myself, independent of servants as I have been for most of my life. I splashed some water on my face and hands to freshen up.

Standing quietly at the window for a few moments, I organized my thoughts. It was a relief that Geneviève had so capable and caring a person as her *tante* Eugenie; she would be the best restorative for the poor woman in her grief. She'd made it rather clear that we would not see either of them until dinner, so I thought about what John and I might do of a productive nature in the interim.

1I2 g2.20420210a e.

I stepped out into the hallway, walked to the chamber door where I supposed John to be lodged, and tapped discreetly. I was correct. He opened the door and invited me in. When we turned to each other to speak, we started at the same moment.

"I believe we should try…." I said.

"I think we must begin…." said John. We smiled at each other. "You first," he said.

"We need to find out all we can about François desRosier de Carbonnières, yes?" I said, and was pleased by his response.

"Absolutely," he said. "Just exactly what I was going to say."

"And how," I put it to him, "do you think we might go about it?" I frowned. "He doesn't actually live here, in Nohant, does he? Didn't Geneviève say he lived in Boussac?"

"Ah, right! Well, then," John said, shoving his hands in his pockets and walking about the room, which was very handsomely done up, with dark wood and leather furnishings, and a strong pattern of striped wallpaper in yellow and burgundy that was vibrant but tasteful. A masculine sort of room; I approved.

"I think we should at least walk about the village and get a sense of the people here," he said. "See what they think of the Bayards, in any case."

I was skeptical. "We are strangers," I said. "No one will talk to us, they may not even deign to greet us—just curious stares and whispers after we pass by."

John smiled, shaking his head. "A true enough picture of country village customs…and city and town and everywhere there are human beings." I laughed, and agreed with him.

THE UNICORN IN THE MIRROR

We alerted the housemaid, Celine, that we were going out for a walk; she pleasantly pointed the way to turn at the end of the drive, so that we could visit the center of town life just a few hundred yards down the road. It was not a street, it was barely a road, made of packed dirt with a few bricks and flat stones embedded here and there—I was quite sure it would be impassable during heavy rains. But today the weather smiled at us, with soft breezes and leafy trees shading our walk into town.

We passed a very ancient church, deeming it to be 11th or 12th century, saw by a plaque on a pillar that it was Sainte-Anne's church, and walked on without stopping inside. The church was centered in a large swath of green, across from which, to the north, was what looked to be the center of town—there were four or five shops of various kinds, a café and bistro, a stables, and a fountain in the center of a small, flat square; its musical plashing and rippling was the liveliest action in the entire scene. Tall trees provided welcome shade, and we strolled along the walkway, peeping into windows and realizing that most of the shops were already closed for the day, including the café, although it had a sign indicating it would be open later in the evening.

"So much for encountering the townspeople," I said.

John merely shrugged, and seemed content to walk about in the open air, his senses keen to the picturesque aspects of the town, which he could not forebear pointing out to me. We followed the curve of the main street, which I guessed would take us back around to Sainte-Anne's, and came to a stop before a massive arched gateway, directly across from the church, that was the portal to a large and lovely mansion set back some way from the road. The wrought iron gates stood open, and we looked through the archway with great interest.

"I wonder," I said, "if this could possibly be the house of George Sand?" I took a step closer, under the shadow of the arch, and was startled by a man suddenly appearing from out of the bushes to the side of the arch, a long and lethal pair of gardening shears in his hands. I stepped back with a little sound of surprise.

"*Excusez-moi, mademoiselle,*" said the man, dropping the shears and doffing his hat, of soft, shapeless cotton with a drooping brim. He briskly eyed both of us up and down. "I did not mean to startle you." He spoke this time in heavily accented English. He was slightly built, with a somewhat military bearing, belying the old trousers and worn cotton shirt he wore, standing straight, shoulders back; his dark hair was flecked with a fair amount of grey, his short beard and mustache almost completely grey—a good-looking man, I would say, somewhere in his later fifties. Clearly not just a gardener.

"*Bien sûr, monsieur,*" I responded in French. (I might look very English, apparently, but I wanted him to know I spoke his own language.) "We do not mean to trespass, but this lovely house is so beautiful, we were tempted beyond politeness to have a closer look." I glanced up at John, hoping for his support, which he immediately gave, in French even more fluent than mine.

"Allow me to introduce myself, and my friend," he said, giving a short bow, and proceeded to mention our names, including my *nom de plume*, Vernon Lee.

"*Ah, bien sûr!*" cried the man. "The famous painter!" He bowed in return, then smiled at me, holding out his hand. "And the equally famous writer!" He did not seem surprised that I was a woman—I guessed it had been long enough now that I had been published, that my masculine disguise was quite seen through. I took his hand and he bowed over it.

"I am Maurice Dupin Dudevant," he said. "But I am also known as Maurice Sand."

I smiled with glee and triumph. "You are the son of the late George Sand," I said, and watched in dismay as his face took on a look of almost unbearable pain. "Although it is some years since her passing," I added quickly, quenching my smile, "I offer my condolences for such a great and heavy loss."

Maurice nodded, shaking away a few tears, and attempted to smile once more. "She is greatly missed still, by me, and by all the town." He had a faraway look in his eye, and then seemed to suddenly return to the present.

"But of course, you must forgive me!" he cried, pressing my hand again, and tears once more springing to his eyes. "You have come here with our dear Geneviève, helping her to bear the sorrow and the burden of bringing her sister back home to her final rest. I knew she was expected today. Bless you both," he added, taking John's hand as well, and bowing low. Such an emotional man! I was rather at a loss for what to say. But he continued on, holding both our hands, and walking backwards towards the house.

"You must come in, I beg you," he said, finally letting go and turning to lead us to the house. "Refresh yourselves, and if you can, please be so kind as to tell me of our poor, dear Aurore and what happened to her, and how Geneviève is faring."

"Of course, *monsieur,*" I said, glancing at John to see if he agreed, which he did, smiling at our host.

"You must call me Maurice, *mademoiselle*," he said. "No-hant is too small a village for us to stand on ceremony, especially under these sad circumstances."

"*Oui, Maurice*," I said, "and to you we are Violet and John." I looked up in awe at the handsome mansion we were about to enter—the abode of George Sand, that tempestuous, passionate writer and independent voice for adventurous women of all times! John and I had passed by the church of Sainte-Anne without going in, but now I felt as if I were entering a temple of a faith I might happily call my own.

We were escorted to a charming, small sitting room, facing west—the lowering sun's warm beams, however, were screened by the tall chestnuts planted behind the house—where a housemaid promptly brought coffee and cake. Once settled, with Maurice doing the honors of pouring and serving, he begged us to tell him all we felt appropriate about Aurore's demise.

"Word has, of course, reached us that her death was sudden, and unlooked for," he said, shaking his head. "There are rumors, naturally, of foul play—but how could that be possible? Aurore was a delightful child." He added a spoonful of sugar to his coffee, and smiled sadly. "I have known the girls from the day they were born," he said.

This was too inviting an opening to resist asking the question that pressed on my mind.

"I hope you will forgive the seeming impertinence," I began, making my way cautiously, "but while in Paris, and becoming acquainted with the Bayards, we actually encountered Aurore as…in a different guise, it would seem…." I deliberately trailed off to see if Maurice would catch me up.

He smiled, like an indulgent parent at a child's whimsy. "Ah, yes, our Sébastien," he said without hesitation. "Yes, we all know of Aurore's other *persona,* here in Nohant." He shook his head, thinking. "I was long accustomed, as a child myself, to my mother's dressing in men's clothes—although she never at any point intended anyone to actually take her for a man, no, no," he continued, a serious smile on his face, "she was always feminine, always a lovely woman—she simply wanted to be able to move about with the freedom that so many men take for granted, especially in a large city." He smiled more amply. "Of course, flouting convention and being talked about were additional benefits, for my dear mama."

"How did people hereabouts look upon Aurore's *persona,* as you say?" John asked, reaching for his cup of coffee.

Maurice shrugged. "Having grown up here, both of the girls were well-known and well-loved, too, by all the populace, especially after their parents died—everyone seemed to adopt them and care for them as their own." He waved his hand in dismissal. "In a small village, we are used to accepting each other's eccentricities and oddities, especially if they do no harm."

I decided to ask my second important question, trying to sound calm and unconcerned; I didn't want to raise any possibly unfounded alarms.

"And are you acquainted with a close friend of theirs, one François desRosiers—sometimes known as François de Carbonnières?"

Maurice frowned, and put down his coffee cup. "Yes, I know him," he said. He looked sharply from me to John, and back again. "He is a most troubled and unbalanced young man," he said slowly. He paused.

"And quite possibly dangerous," he added after a moment. "Why do you inquire about him?"

FOUR

THE MONTH OF FLOREAL, YEAR IX
[APRIL-MAY 1801]
At Home in Nohant and Boussac

"HE IS COMING HOME! AT LAST!" Marie-Aurore pressed the letter to her lips, then hugged it to her chest. Her own boy, a hero of the great battle at Marengo only the year before, had been granted leave. She began to read again the short letter, but was interrupted by a footman opening the door and ushering in a set of visitors.

"Madame, I mean, Citizeness, I hope we are not disturbing you?" By this time, Marie-Aurore was on her feet, and coming forward with a brilliant smile, impulsively threw her arms around her visitor.

"Oh, Citizen de Carbonnières!" she cried. "My Maurice, my son is coming home!" She felt his arms tighten around her frame, and belatedly remembered François' poor young son. She stepped away and opened her mouth to apologize, but François smiled at her and quickly spoke his pleasure at the news.

"What a delightful, joyful thing to hear as soon as I walk in the door," he said, and turned to Pauline, who had accompanied him but was hanging back a little. "My dear," he said, "you will remember Maurice, even though he went off to the army when you were still very young?"

"Papa," she said, mocking a reproach, "of course I remember Maurice! Although I was only nine or so when he left, I have a very clear memory of him."

Marie-Aurore leaned forward and kissed the young woman on both cheeks.

"And now you are a lovely young *mademoiselle,* and I do believe that my own darling has changed as much as you have, these seven years now, *ma chérie.*" She looked happily at her visitors, and linking arms with Pauline, led them further into the room. Her friends were glad to hear her cheerful report of all Maurice's latest honors and promotions in service, and her hopes that he would at last literally lay down his arms and return to her for good. "This house needs his presence, his spirit, his music," she said, looking around rather wistfully.

"We must have a dinner for you," Pauline said suddenly, then glanced at her father. "Is that all right, Papa?"

"We would be delighted," he said instantly, reassuring his daughter. "We must provide a fitting tribute to the hero of Marengo," he said, smiling at the proud look on Marie-Aurore's face. "Perhaps after he is home a little while, you both may be enticed to spend some days at Chateau Boussac, where we will plan our official home-coming dinner."

"You are too, too kind, François," said Marie-Aurore. "I shall be delighted to be a guest at Boussac, and see again those lovely, indescribable tapestries you have there." She looked over at Pauline, and spoke gently. "I know they are very dear to you, *ma chérie,* and I would love to hear how the last few years may have changed, or enlarged, your thinking about them."

Pauline's face lighted up in response to this kindness. "*Oui, madame,*" she said. "And I would dearly love to tell you all my thinking."

The remaining visit was calm and quiet, with each person's thoughts remaining close inside, and their interactions were on the surface, like Autumn leaves on an old pond.

Pauline paced the long gallery slowly, her hands clasped behind her back, her neck arched slightly as she looked up at the tapestries. It was chilly on this side of the chateau in the mornings, and she drew her wool shawl closer around her. She felt a little shiver of excitement as she faced the thoughts and feelings she was experiencing. She turned, as she always did, to the image that had enthralled her from her earliest years—the Unicorn gazing into the mirror held up for him by the Lady.

She had sharp memories of sitting with her grandmother and her brother—both gone from this earth so many years, it seemed a century ago; indeed, even at the age of fifteen now, Pauline felt old, felt that the horrors and privations and insecurity at the end of the last century had aged her beyond her own consciousness of it, that she had lost her childhood to the Revolution and the Terror—but she remembered clearly sitting before this tapestry and hearing her grandmother describe the uniqueness of the Unicorn— his spirit, his soul, his courage, his gentleness, unlike any other being except the Christ, of whom he was a magical symbol, she had said.

Particularly fascinating to Pauline was the mirror in which the Unicorn could see his visage gleaming back at him, both animal and image smiling slightly, shyly. Her father had showed her, in secret, the holy golden monstrance that was kept locked up in a special place in the former chapel of the chateau—it looked just like the mirror in the tapestry, except there was plain glass in the circle where the Sacréd Host, the Body of Christ, would be set on display for days of adoration and penance—in the old days, of course. On the stem of the monstrance, just like the tapestry mirror, was a golden rose studded with jewels. Pauline would look at the tapestry and touch again in her memory the smooth polished gold, the faintly prickly feel of the cut jewels, and see the sparkles and gleams as they reflected the light. It occurred to her she hadn't seen the monstrance for some years now; was it still locked up in safety? She rather imagined that her father had probably been obliged to sell it, in Bourges, for the value of the gold and jewels—so many of their possessions had been sold in the last ten years—furniture, jewelry, paintings. She suppressed a little sigh; it was Necessary, as her father said, and they must learn to live with less.

But never the tapestries, never a thought to trade off those precious heirlooms and symbols of an ancient time, when the Lady ruled a gentler, kinder world, flanked by her two protectors, the Lion and the Unicorn. Never—until now.

Pauline sighed aloud this time, and reached out a hand to touch her favorites, caressing the Lion's mane and the Unicorn's soft hooves as they lay lightly in the Lady's lap. Her father had broached the subject at dinner last night, as the two of them sat in the smaller dining room, eating a simple meal of fish and the first of the late Spring asparagus.

"Only two of them," he had pleaded, over her protests.

"For now," she had shot back. She put down her fork, her appetite quite gone. "All of them will fall to greedy Necessity in time." She felt the blow personally. "Please, Papa, anything but that," she pleaded. "Sell my clothes! Sell this table and these chairs!" She was talking wildly, had risen from her chair and was gesturing around the room. She grabbed two worn velvet cushions from a sofa near the window. "Here," she had pushed them at him, "Take these, nobody uses them! Perhaps some lucky *citoyenne* will have a few sous to buy them at the next market day—she can secretly pretend she is noble!" She threw the pillows on the floor and stood still, shaking with rage.

"My dear, my daughter, this is wild talk," François spoke soothingly. "The material things of this world are not what give our lives value." But he heaved a great sigh, and put his head in his heads. "You, more than anyone, must know how precious those tapestries are to me—the memory of my mother…" His voice broke, and Pauline's heart was softened in an instant. She flew to his side, embracing him and kissing his balding head.

"Forgive me, Papa, forgive me, please," she whispered. "I am a selfish, ignorant girl, and I do not mean to make you unhappy. I know you are only trying to do what is best for us and for Boussac." With more such murmurs and endearments, the two calmed each other down, and after a few moments, attempted to eat a little more of the dinner, and lighten each other's spirits.

But today, in the presence of the tapestries, Pauline's anger and sorrow rose again—how could they even choose which two of the eight tapestries should be sacrificed to the market? She walked back and forth, trying to imagine what it would be like to enter this room and see two gaping spaces on the wall which color and beauty and magic used to fill? The only thing she was sure of was that the tapestry of the Unicorn gazing into the Mirror would never, ever leave Boussac, not while she was alive herself.

Thus determined, she pulled herself together, straightened her shoulders, and took a deep breath. Today was the day they expected Madame Marie-Aurore Dupin de Francueil and her son, Maurice—the grandson of the legendary Marshall of France, and cousin (at some remove) to the last three kings—and by all accounts, a handsome, personable young man of marriageable age. She knew his mother looked on her kindly, and had recently made some veiled references to her son and Pauline as kindred spirits—but it would remain to be seen, in person. Pauline was not in a hurry to be married; she felt that she and her father were content together, and wanted no one else to come between them.

Dinner, though not grand, was plentiful, and François had invited several families from Boussac and Nohant to gather at his table and honor their own local "hero of Marengo" upon his return, including his former mistress Georgette desRosiers and her son Jean-François who, though only nine years old, was a well-behaved, cheerful lad. Her husband had died some four years before, and Georgette seemed perfectly comfortable going on without another husband.

Pauline was seated at her father's right hand, with Marie-Aurore on his left, and Maurice next to his mother. Little Jean-François sat to Pauline's right, next to his mother, which suited Pauline—she loved the boy dearly, but was wary and distant with his mother—there was something about her...she seemed always to act more familiarly than their acquaintance justified, with an air somehow of knowing a good deal more than she was wont to say. Pauline watched the woman's interactions with François, and saw that her father, though not equally as disconcerted as Pauline herself felt, seemed a good deal on his guard when the two conversed.

The table was laid quite simply, with very few flowers and no candelabra, just low, short candles in dishes, so it was easy to converse with the people sitting across the table.

"Citizeness Pauline?" She heard her name being spoken in a low voice, and looked up from whispering to Jean-François to see Maurice Dupin smiling across at her. She felt a little thrill as she took in the appreciative look in his blue eyes, and felt herself surrender to the spell cast by his curling brown locks of hair, a bit long for a soldier, and his military air of rectitude and self-control. Here was a man who might interest her!

"Yes, Lieutenant?" she said, smiling brightly.

"Please," he admonished, "I'm simply Maurice when I am at home. And we have known each other since we were children playing together."

"Then you must address me as Pauline," she said, blushing a little.

He nodded in agreement. "My dear Pauline," he went on, "I so long to see the tapestries in the great gallery again, it's been so many years! May I ask the great favor of your company after dinner to show them to me?"

She saw her father and Marie-Aurore exchange glances, and blushed even more. From the first moment she had greeted him, earlier this afternoon, she had felt the tight hold on her heart slipping away.

"*Bien sûr, citoyen*," she said, then added shyly, "Maurice."

Dinner was soon over, and her father led some of the guests out onto the twilit terrace, while Marie-Aurore and Georgette, and one or two other women, moved off to sofas and chairs near the fireplace to have some quiet talk among themselves of domestic matters, children and goings-on in the town. Maurice presented himself before Pauline, his arm held out to escort her, and they walked down the hallway toward the great gallery. They didn't speak as they walked, but Pauline was desperately searching for something to break the silence.

"I hardly knew you, Maurice, when you arrived today," she said in a rush of words, and kept on. "It's been seven years, you know, since we last saw you, and of course, that is quite enough time for a young boy to turn into a man, especially one who has seen so much danger and fighting, and foreign places." She was almost out of breath as she finished, but was soothed by Maurice patting her hand on his arm in a friendly way.

"Yes, it is true," he said, pausing at the threshold of the gallery, and looking down at her. "I am not that young boy who romped with you in the stables in that long-ago time." He placed a kiss on her smooth forehead. "And you are now a grown-up woman who will soon be wanting a husband, I trust?"

Although taken back a bit by the directness of the question, she answered him in a light-hearted way. "Oh," she said, stepping forward into the room, and looking away from him. "I am in no hurry to marry," she said. "I am happy as I am."

He shook his head. "All you women who don't need husbands!" He laughed charmingly. "My mother, and that friend of your father's, Georgette desRosiers? I wonder she did not marry again—she's still attractive, though older."

Pauline felt a little ruffled by his mention of Georgette, but also bristled at his general comment. "Women don't always need to have a husband," she said with some force. "We get on quite well without you, you know, especially now that the laws support our independence in financial matters, and in owning property."

"Ah," he said, "I see we have a *citoyenne* here who is well-informed of her rights, and stoutly defends the female sex." He patted her hand again. "I admire that."

Pauline felt her heart skip, and a sudden weakness invaded her knees. *Is this what falling in love is like?*

The Dupins stayed at Boussac for a week, with Maurice and Pauline delighting in daily walks around the grounds and studying the tapestries. Maurice was quite a good artist, and made drawings of sections of the tapestries, with Pauline's face in the face of the Lady—she had attempted to protest this as a sacrilege of sorts, in her mind, but the flattery of his attention was too great. By the fourth day of their visit, she was deeply, irrevocably in love.

The night before they were to leave, she and Maurice were walking back and forth in the garden, watched over by their respective parents, who sat on the terrace in the gathering twilight. Pauline had noted the approving looks from

Marie-Aurore, but also the puzzled, slightly sad eyes of her father as he kissed her good-night.

"I beg your pardon, my dear little Pauline," Maurice said suddenly, when they were well out of earshot of their parents. "But I must ask your forgiveness, and tell you a secret that must be kept at all costs."

Startled, Pauline glanced at him first to see if he were joking with her, but the serious look on his face told her otherwise. Her heart began to thump. Maurice cleared his throat, looked away from her, and spoke again.

"I fear that my behavior may have given your father a false impression, in regard to my feelings for you," he began, and hurried on. "Not that I think *you* have imbibed any such notion—indeed, after you assured me in our first conversation, that you have no interest in marrying, I felt confident that you saw through me from the start." He glanced at her when he said this, but her face, frozen into polite attention, apparently satisfied him that she felt as he had assumed. He went on.

"I have been desperate to convince my mother that I no longer care for a woman—whom I have long loved, and do love still—of whom she does not approve. I am, you see, buying myself, and my dear Victoire, some time in which I hope to bring my mother around to my choice." He hesitated, and looking back at François and Marie-Aurore on the terrace, nodded and waved a hand in greeting.

Pauline made herself keep walking, one foot after another, mechanically, trying with all her might to conceal her distress, and the absolute destruction of her heart. She must not let him see her true feelings! Luckily, Maurice was so involved with his own feelings and drama, he was not really paying attention to her. He kept on talking—how she wished he would stop talking, so she could flee or sink into the ground or throw herself into the lake!

"Victoire is even now in the inn at La Châtre, waiting for me to bring this issue to a close, and to return with her to Paris, or perhaps, bring her home to Nohant."

Pauline made a great effort, and spoke, her voice a soft whisper.

"And what do you think is the likelihood of success, with your mother?" she asked. "If she thinks you have become interested…in me…how will that reconcile her to the truth that your affections still lie with…" She could not bring herself to speak the woman's name; she was filled with grief and shame and hatred all at the same time.

"I do not know, truly," Maurice confessed. He fetched a deep sigh. "Perhaps it was an irrational scheme. If only my mother would agree to meet Victoire! I know she would love her, despite her being a commoner!" He shook his head. "I would not have thought that my mother was so proud, so tightly bound to her noble ancestry, that this would make a difference to her, now, in these enlightened times!"

Pauline, with the strictest self-control, made herself speak again. "I shall keep your secret, of course, Maurice, and I wish you well." She glanced up at him, then at the terrace, where she saw her father had risen, and was looking out at her. It was almost as if he had overheard their conversation, and was anxious to be with her and console her. She gestured toward him.

"We will return to the house now," she said, her head high. Maurice gave a little bow, and escorted her as they walked back through the garden.

Pauline never spoke of this to anyone, including her father, but from that day he noted that a certain light that had kindled in her for a while had gone out, and he watched with sorrow as his once lively girl faded and became a greying shadow who haunted the Gallery of the Tapestries.

ॐ Five ॐ

MAURICE SAND QUICKLY APPREHENDED OUR INTEREST in François de Carbonnières. "You think he had something to do with the death of Aurore?" He looked deeply troubled, and waited for one of us to respond.

"We know nothing of his part in it for certain," I said at last, glancing John's way. "But you are correct in speculating that Aurore was a victim of foul play—she was, indeed, murdered—and there is a witness who saw a man of Carbonnières' description arguing with her a short time before her death."

Maurice rose from his chair abruptly, running his hand through his thick hair, stifling a gasp of horror. "It is his obsession!" he said, turning back to us. "His is a soul tormented by vaporous thoughts of an illusory past and an impossible future!"

"You must tell us what you mean by that," John urged, leaning forward in his chair. He and I exchanged worried looks.

Maurice was standing before the French doors that were open to the back garden, one hand on the door frame, the other rubbing his face fiercely.

"Does it have anything to do with the Lady and the Unicorn tapestries?" My sudden question caused Maurice to again turn to face us; the look on his face made both me and John stand up and go to him in the doorway.

"You are clearly a most intelligent and close observer, Violet," he said, smiling faintly. "Have either of you met the gentleman in question?"

I nodded, but John spoke first. "It was a brief and silent meeting—he was with Geneviève the morning after Aurore's death," John said. "We—Violet and I and another friend were there to offer condolences, and de Carbonnières was there, but left shortly afterwards, having said not a single word to any of us."

"Not entirely silent," I broke in, glancing at him. "When he was introduced, you recall, John, that Geneviève said he was François desRosier, but he corrected her and said his name was de Carbonnières."

"Of course, yes," he said, adding, "and Geneviève seemed irritated by that." We both looked to Maurice, who grimaced.

"She would be, yes," he said. "It is a strange tale, and has caused François—whom I have also known from his childhood—to become rather deranged." He sighed, and gestured for us to be seated again. He rang the bell for the housemaid, who came and cleared away the coffee tray. We sat silently, as it seemed he was composing himself to tell us this strange tale, and waited as he took a decanter of sherry from a sideboard. Pouring out three small glasses of the golden liquid, he handed them to us.

"I believe we need greater fortification than coffee," he said, by way of explanation. I made no objection, nor did John. I glanced out the windows to the garden, and saw that the Spring sun was fading; the clock on the mantle was nearing half-past six, and I was reminded that we were to dine with Geneviève and her aunt at seven.

"Maurice," I said before he could begin. "I am about to suggest something highly improper, and completely lacking in etiquette." Both he and John looked at me, Maurice surprised, John wary. "We are engaged to dine with Miss Bayard and her inestimable aunt Eugenie at seven—do you think it possible you could join us, though unasked—and even more, can this matter be discussed with them over dinner?"

Maurice pondered this for a moment. "The wake will not be until tomorrow," he said slowly. "And I was intending to visit them this evening in any event." He smiled and gestured faintly, his hand waving in the air. "We are good friends, and often join each other for meals on a whim, so that is not an issue." He thought for another moment. "Geneviève and her aunt—inestimable, indeed, Violet, you have seen her truly, a remarkable woman!—are both well acquainted with de Carbonierre's obsession and history, so it may be as well to talk it over with them after all."

"Then we shall do it," I said firmly, and drinking my ounce or two of sherry at one gulp, I stood and indicated to John that we should depart. "We will go now, and pave the way for your appearance at seven, if that is agreeable to you?"

Maurice also rose and coming forward, shook John's hand heartily, and leaned to kiss me on both cheeks.

"Most agreeable," he said, and walked with us to the front door of the house. The twilight birds were beginning their flights and their evening songs, and the shadows thrown by the elms and acacias softened the day's light on the flowers and the lawn. Maurice bowed us out the gate, and we made our way back down the dirt road toward the Bayard residence, retracing our steps from a short time earlier. Both John and I were silent, thinking over what we had heard, and anticipating what further we were to hear in the coming hours.

"Maurice, my dear one!" Eugenie Bayard welcomed her old friend as he entered the dining room where we had just seated ourselves. "Come in, come in, it is so good to see you, so good of you to come over to comfort us." They embraced, tears filling their eyes, and I saw an exchange of heartfelt whispers, in which the name "Aurore" was said more than once.

A simple repast awaited us as the evening darkness fell softly in the gardens and the trees outside the mansion, plump *poulet en crème* with fresh young asparagus and little round potatoes, with early strawberries for dessert. But dinner was not foremost in our minds, as we anticipated the discussion I had suggested. However, before that tale began, I introduced a diversion from the direct interest we had in François de Carbonnières, but as serendipity would have it, there always seems to be something gained in a little "frolic and detour" (as I believe the English law terms it).

I held up the volume of George Sand's autobiography, which I had brought down to dinner with me, and saw Maurice's face light up with pleasure.

"I have been reading about your great-grandmama, Marie-Aurore Dupin de Franceuil, whom your mother mentions in her book with intense affection," I said. "Did you ever have the chance to know her?"

He shook his head. "*Non, ma chère Violet,*" he said. "Although she lived a long and hearty life, she died in 1821, two years before I was born." He fetched a deep sigh. "My dear mother was then but eighteen, and became mistress of the house in Nohant, much to the distress of *her* mother, who had thought to inherit it herself."

Eugenie made a small sound of derision, and we all looked at her expectantly.

"Oh," she said, looking slightly abashed. "Not that I was ever acquainted with the lady—your mother's mother that is—myself, being only a few years older than Maurice here." She paused to take a sip of wine. "But I remember your poor mother, Maurice, when she was lamenting your sister's waywardness and bad behavior, making a direct connection to her own mother's ill manners, and the rows *she* would have with her mother-in-law, the daunting Marie-Aurore."

Maurice grimaced slightly, and waved his hand. "All that is past," he said. "Although it's true, mama and Sophie-Victoire"—he glanced at me and John, and added—"my *grand-mere*—she and mama were always at odds as well—but my *grand-père*, the Maurice after whom I am named, had fallen in love irretrievably with the beautiful Sophie-Victoire, and refused to relinquish her, despite everything his own mother tried to do to dissuade him."

John leaned forward across the table to lift the plate of asparagus and, turning, offered it to Geneviève who, I noted, had barely touched any of her dinner. She shook her head, and he replaced the platter, a look of deep concern on his face. He glanced at Eugenie, who shook her head minutely and smiled, as if to encourage him that all would be well, eventually. Then Eugenie spoke again.

"Did you know, Maurice, that your grandfather was once in a way to marry Pauline de Carbonnières, of Chateau Boussac?"

My attention was caught at the name, and I exchanged quick glances with John. "Really?" I said. "How did they know each other?"

"Oh," said Maurice, "although we are some thirty miles apart, the nobly-born know where to find each other, and make their way into proper company." His slightly sardonic smile showed his feelings about such things—I recalled that his own father styled himself a count, another illegitimate son of a deposed King of somewhere, and that Maurice himself was often referred to as *the Count Dupin* in literary circles.

"Is she, then," I asked, determined now to bring the conversation back to the present day, and our investigation, "any relation to the present-day François desRosier—or de Carbonnières—that we have spoken of?"

"Yes, indeed," said Eugenie, before Maurice could answer. I noticed that Geneviève had looked up on hearing the name, and seemed to come awake to her surroundings. She even reached for her wine and took a sip. "Pauline was the only surviving child of François de Carbonnières, the last lord of Boussac—both of them lived through the Revolution, and the Terror, and poor Pauline came out the worse for it—she was a silent, but strong woman, alone most of her life—she lived to be very old." She and Maurice exchanged sympathetic glances.

"But if she was the last of the de Carbonnières…" I let my query trail off, an expectant look on my face. Maurice took up the tale.

"Her father, it was rumoured, was the natural son of King Louis XV, the 'well-beloved' as they called him." He sighed; he looked as if it had happened yesterday instead of nearly a century past. "It was always rumoured that the King had given his lover, Louise de Rilhac, some proofs of the parentage of their child—some letters, it was said, perhaps even a signet ring or brooch with a royal sign." He looked away, drank some wine, and continued. "The child— François Louis—grew up, married, had two children, but after the early death of his wife—she died giving birth to Pauline—François took as a paramour one Georgette desRosier, a well-placed lady in Boussac, and they had a child, Jean-François, who was, however, raised by Georgette and her husband—who apparently was never the wiser—as his own son."

My head was swimming with all these *liaisons* and illegitimate royal offspring, which seemed to occur so regularly and so casually in France—but then, I guessed it was the same in Italy—and England, too, for that matter. I shook my head.

"And the current François desRosier de Carbonnières?" I pressed.

"He is my cousin."

We all started at the sound of Geneviève's voice for the first time since we had sat down to dinner. Eugenie reached over and patted her hand, then looked at me.

"More third cousin or thereabouts," she said. "He is the grandson of the boy born to Georgette desRosier and François de Carbonnières, lord of Boussac. Georgette and her actual husband Jean had a daughter, Marie, who moved here to Nohant when she married Raymond Simon—and *their* daughter Julia married my uncle, Michel Bayard, whose son Jules was Geneviève and Aurore's father."

I nodded slowly. French family histories might possibly be the most complicated in the world. I decided to ask the most relevant question, despite the tangle of relations.

"And what exactly is it that makes our present-day François de Carbonnières such a dangerous man,"—I nodded at Maurice—"and how might that be related to the death of Sébastien—of Aurore?" I watched the faces around me carefully, but I was not prepared for Geneviève's reaction.

She shoved her chair back and stood up, shaking from head to toe. "His family has madness in it, and he is obsessed!" she cried, hitting the table with her fist. "But that is all! He is not a murderer, he could not be the one who killed my poor Aurore! His father filled his head with tales, handed down from that Georgette. He only wants to find the brooch and the letters."

She sat down again heavily, and began weeping.

Eugenie turned to her niece and wrapped her arms around her, murmuring to her in soothing tones. John, too had risen when Geneviève did, and now paced about the room, as if not knowing what to do. Maurice and I exchanged a long glance, and he, after filling his glass of wine, handed the bottle to me. I took it gratefully and poured a little more into my own glass, then held it up questioningly toward John. He seemed to hesitate, then walked over to me and, thanking me in a low voice, took the bottle of wine back to his own place, filled his glass and sat down.

By this time, Geneviève had recovered herself, and we all sat in silence, waiting for her to speak again.

"It is because of the tapestries," she said in a low, wretched voice. She had been staring at her hands in her lap, but now looked up, a fierce light in her eyes. "He thinks somehow they hold the secret—the proof—of his royal heritage. His obsession got worse after…after *madame* Pauline died."

I could have crowed in my delight—I knew it, I knew the tapestries had something to do with all this—but I kept a serious mien and only said, "And do they?"

Geneviève threw up her hands in frustration and grief. "I don't know! I *think* Aurore thought she knew…something…but …. we used to look at them for hours, but…." Here the poor woman broke down again, and her aunt took hold of her and the situation and led her gently from the room.

The three of us remained at the table for a few more moments, pushing what was left of our dinners around on our plates, and drinking the rest of the wine.

"I should like to go to Boussac tomorrow," I announced, causing both John and Maurice to look up in surprise.

"Vi, really, I don't think…," John started to say, but I cut him off with a severe look. I turned to Maurice.

"Is it possible?" I asked him. "Can we go to Boussac and back in the course of one day? And more importantly, can we get inside the chateau and see the remaining tapestries?" Personally, I felt sure that the Lady and the Unicorn looking in the mirror was the one tapestry that was central to this mystery, but I didn't want to overlook the possible importance of the others.

Maurice showed his military training with a splendid flourish, taking charge of our expedition. "Yes, Violet, all of this can be done, especially as I will accompany you myself! I have constant access to Boussac, and my carriage can take us there and back, as long as…." He hesitated, with a small smile on his face.

"As long as…what?" I said.

"As long as you are willing to leave at first light."

I held out my hand to shake his in cordial agreement, and looked at John. He shook his head at my audacity, then nodded his acquiescence.

We were going to travel to the dark heart of this murder at last, and I prayed—yes, I actually prayed—that whatever Light still shone in France would guide our way to justice and truth.

Six

September 1808 – Boussac, France
The End of an Era at Chateau Boussac

François de Rilhac de Carbonierres died at peace in his bed, at the age of sixty-nine, his faithful daughter Pauline by his side. His fatal illness had been brief, but he had been able to leave instructions for his daughter about a great many things still to be done on the estate, from the westernmost fields of grain which wanted turning, to the apple orchards in the south, which needed pruning.

"You are now mistress of Boussac, *ma chérie,*" he had whispered as Pauline clung to his arm, her tears falling freely.

"I would gladly give that up to have you here with me," she whispered back, and kissed his forehead as he closed his eyes.

And now she was truly alone.

She had reached her twenty-second birthday during the Summer, and the only emotion she had felt was an immense fatigue, if that can be called an emotion. At least, she thought as she drifted through the house, ghost-like, on the day following her father's death, at least the Emperor is holding the country together, and there are no longer the shortages, and the soldiers over-running the land, taking the very food from our mouths. Her father had provided well for all his tenants, in any event, and she anticipated that many people would come to his funeral from far and wide.

She found herself in the Gallery of the Tapestries; it had always been a place of refuge in trouble or distress. She touched the fraying, fading edges of each of the eight hangings in turn—the Lady playing the virginal, a kind of small organ, while her handmaiden worked the bellows; the Lady composing a floret of blossoms taken from a dish held out by the handmaiden; the Lady alone with the Unicorn and the Lion, holding a standard and one hand lightly touching the horn of the holy beast; the fourth tapestry showed her feeding a small bird from her hand, her handmaiden holding up the dish of sweetmeats, with the Lion seemingly roaring his displeasure through an open mouth of sharp teeth, his yellow eye wide and fierce, while on the other side, the Unicorn gazed calmly straight out into the face of the observer; the fifth tapestry depicted the Lady carefully laying aside an exquisite necklace into a gem-studded box, as she and her handmaid, and a small lap dog sitting on a cushion, looked prepared to step into a resplendent blue and gold tent behind them, across which was hung a banner with the words "A Mon Seul Desir."

The sixth and seventh tapestries—which her father had once threatened to sell when the family was in dire need—showed the Lady as a royal queen, crowned with a gold and ruby crown, the one a procession through a small grove of trees, and the other of her taking her seat on a gilded throne.

And finally, which Pauline had always thought of as the "last" tapestry, her favorite, there was the Lady seated, melancholy, with the Unicorn's front hooves in her lap, as he gazes at his own image in a small oval mirror, encrusted with gold and jewels, while the Lion looks away discreetly. This

Lady seemed different from the others, older, less pretty in her face, to the point of plainness—very much as Pauline saw herself.

She paused before this last work of woven art. "What am I to do now?" she asked it, murmuring the words. "Who am I, that anyone wants to befriend, or love? A sad and sorry woman, no longer young, not even pretty."

A sob caught in her throat, but as she looked up at the tapestry, she seemed to see a fierce gleam in the eye of the Unicorn reflected in the mirror. "Stop feeling sorry for yourself!" he seemed to be saying to Pauline. "You are a lady, a descendant of ancient nobility, you have an estate and people who depend on you! Do your duty, my child." These last words were softer, almost loving, as they fell upon Pauline's heart, and she felt at once strong and refreshed.

"I will," she said aloud. "I will do my duty, to Boussac and my father." With that, she turned and walked swiftly back down the gallery, intent upon making her life whole in the service of the land. And in the meantime, there was a funeral to be got through.

The funeral was simple and attended by more than a hundred people from all over Boussac and the surrounding counties, as Pauline had expected. Privately, she was glad that Napoleon's more liberal views of the practice of religion allowed for a priest to preside over the funeral ceremony, and lead the prayers over the grave, but she indicated nothing by word or demeanour—the harsh lessons instilled in her by the Terror, while she was still a child, were part of who she was, and could not be gainsaid.

The hardest part, however, was the reception afterwards, which was held at the chateau. She found herself required, again and again, to accept condolences—real or rote—and hear her father's name and praises without breaking down.

And then there was Georgette desRosiers.

Pauline had seen her at the graveside with her son Jean François, now a strapping young lad of fifteen. She had always felt a fondness for the boy, but not his mother, whose sharp eyes seemed frequently to regard Pauline with hostility and amusement, an odd combination, and her vague, sarcastic remarks were perplexing. She had heard there was a daughter as well, but she had been sent off to a convent boarding school, and was rarely seen; odd, to send a daughter away and keep the son at home, she'd always thought.

"So, *ma chère* Pauline, you are now the mistress of Chateau Boussac," she said, after leaning forward to kiss Pauline on both cheeks, a gesture to which Pauline instinctively responded with frozen stiffness. It was not unnoticed by Georgette, who failed to hide a little smile as she stepped back. They were standing near the long table on which the mourners' repast was laid, simple food from the farms. Georgette glanced around, saw that there was no one near, and spoke again, in a near whisper.

"And has your father left you everything in his will?" she said, looking intently at Pauline.

"Madame," Pauline said, feeling a surge of anger and strength—and remembering the fortifying gaze of the Unicorn from the day before. "I can't imagine why you would think that is any of your business, and I find it unconscionable in any case, that you would ask such a question at such a time." With a proud lift of her head, she turned away from the detestable woman, but Georgette caught her arm in a tight grip.

"Oh, we shall see whose business it is, *ma chérie*," she said. Her face showed a pleasant smile, but her eyes were hard.

"*Maman*, please," Jean François suddenly appeared next to Pauline, clearly distressed by his mother's behavior and words. He took her hand away from Pauline's arm and, with an apologetic look of sympathy to Pauline, led his mother away.

The day after her father's burial, Pauline sat at her father's old desk in his library, *her* desk now—and steeled herself to look over the sheaf of legal papers—including his will—that her father had left for her. The memory of Georgette's stinging words had swirled in her brain until she had fallen into an exhausted sleep, but they returned immediately upon her waking this morning. She needed to know the worst, if worst there should be.

She found the will without much trouble and read it through. It was as she expected—as her father had told her—she was the sole heir to Chateau Boussac and all its domains and property. Having assisted her father in the last several years in managing the estate, there were no surprises here.

Until she came to the final paragraphs.

When I am dead and buried, I direct my daughter Pauline de Rilhac de Carbonnières to the locked top drawer of my bureau in which she shall find a leather pouch that contains the following items: letters from His Majesty King Louis XV, now long deceased, to my mother Louise de Rilhac de Carbonnières, also long deceased, regarding their son, François Louis de Carbonnières, meaning myself. These letters bear the King's own signature.

There is also a brooch, decorated with jewels and bearing the images of a Lion and a Unicorn, which the King gave to my mother in Paris three months after my birth, when the King held me in his arms, blessed me, and charged my mother and her husband to care for me and keep me safe, in the event the kingdom should have need of an heir— which, thanks be to God, did not occur.

Only one other person is aware of my true heritage, Georgette desRosier, whose son Jean François is my natural son, born of a liaison between Georgette and myself which at the time gave us mutual comfort and affection. She requested that upon my death, these items should be bequeathed to her son Jean François so that he would know, as I *did, the true nature of his heritage, and the royal blood that flows through his veins.*

However, times and politics being what they are, if my executrix, Pauline de Carbonnières, deems it imprudent to relinquish this information at the time of my death, I leave it to her good judgement and wisdom to make the decision to either reveal or withhold this information, for as long as she thinks necessary.

By my hand,

François Louis de Rilhac de Carbonnières
Dated the Fifth of June, Anno Domini 1799

Pauline sat, stunned and unbelieving. That her father had taken a lover was not so surprising, but that it was the detestable Georgette! The woman's remarks at the funeral reception now became clear—she expected that Pauline would read the will, and obediently hand her the precious evidence of her son's heritage. And more, Pauline thought, her heart hardening and her mind gaining clarity—she might very well claim that her son has an interest in Chateau Boussac and all its estate, or at the least, demand some compensation in lieu of his rights.

She read again the final paragraph and smiled—her canny father had placed the decision in her own hands, and she would take full advantage of that. The times were still uncertain, were they not? The Emperor's endless wars had led to other nations becoming allies to fight against the French, and it was rumoured he was failing on many fronts—who knew what would happen? Perhaps even the return of the Terror! Pauline shuddered at the very thought, but it allowed her to rationalize the decision she knew she had already made.

She found the key to the locked drawer sitting in a covered dish on top of the desk, and opening it, withdrew the leather pouch. The letters she handled with great care, as the paper was getting old and fragile, and she put them aside for the greater interest she felt in seeing the brooch. The gems and gold sparkled and gleamed as she held the inestimably precious jewel in her hand; holding it nearer, she smiled at the familiar Lion and Unicorn painted in the center.

She, too, then, had royal blood flowing in her veins. She, too, was a descendant of the Sun King, and Louis the Beloved, and centuries of royalty stretching back to ancient days. She contemplated this with a small smile, and then looked around at her life. It meant nothing; it was as dust, as ash, as smoke in the wind. She felt a deep, comforting bitterness suffuse her being, and she let it take her heart.

She vowed that day that Georgette would never have the satisfaction of even an acknowledgement that these cherished bits of evidence still existed; they would never be hers.

⚡ SEVEN ⚡

TUESDAY – 10 MAY 1881 – BOUSSAC
An Expedition to Chateau Boussac

THE DAWN'S LIGHT STILL HID BEHIND THE TREES as John and I stepped into Maurice's comfortable carriage. I was pleased to note that four horses were to take us there, promising a swift journey over the thirty miles of what turned out to be very good road, and silently blessed Maurice's forethought. I eagerly watched the sun rise over the meadows and fields as we made our way south from Nohant to the more rugged hills, rocks and streams of Boussac.

Eugenie had provided us with a hamperful of good things to eat, bread and jam, thick slices of smoked pork, with a few bottles of lemonade and water, of which we partook halfway through our journey, stopping at a wayside travellers' inn to rest, stretch and renew ourselves for the remaining journey. Three hours brought us to the quiet village of Boussac, just beginning to awake—merchants removing the wooden planks over the windows, revealing their stands of fruit and other wares; housewives or maids chatting in small groups before moving off to buy the day's produce and goods.

Maurice had informed us that he had no need to retrieve any key or seek permission to enter the Chateau Boussac, so our carriage hurried us through the village and up to the enormous ninth-century castle which crowned a high precipice, with the *Petite Creuse* river far below. I looked up in awe as we swept through the ancient iron gates into a cobblestone courtyard, where we alighted, facing a magnificent though somewhat crumbling staircase to the main entrance.

"Ah," sighed Maurice in nostalgic satisfaction, "I cannot help but see my dear mother ascending those steps, and calling to me from the top to run up to her!" He smiled. "I was more entranced with exploring the passageways and towers"—he pointed to a length of arched stone doorways along the courtyard's north side—"than going to sit sedately in the drawing room with my mother's friends."

"She had friends who lived here?" I asked.

"One in particular," Maurice said, gesturing to us to walk up the stone steps. "Pierre Henri Leroux, perhaps you've heard of him?" John and I both shook our heads to the negative, and our guide continued. "He was the son of a bartender, and became a famous—or infamous—socialist in the forties. He and my mother started a newspaper, *La Revue Indépendente*, which flourished for some years. The chateau housed his printing press, and we often visited him here."

We had reached the front door, which was surprisingly unlocked; Maurice simply turned the great brass knob and opened it, though not without an extra shove from his shoulder. We stepped inside and immediately were assaulted by stale, dank air and the sounds of mice scurrying hither and yon.

"It appears the town fathers are not overly concerned about the state of the chateau," Maurice said, frowning in apology. "I hope the tapestries aren't suffering from their continued neglect."

"Wouldn't the interest in selling them to the *Musée de Cluny* prompt the town to protect their investment?" John asked, looking around the vast, dim space. It must have been truly magnificent once, I thought, as I took tentative steps on the cracked tiles underfoot, and touched with a gloved hand the faintly mildewed wood panelling along the walls.

"One would hope so," Maurice said.

We heard a door open and close at the far end of the foyer, and through the dim light of the sun's feeble rays that reached in from windows high above the staircase, we perceived a short figure making its way toward us.

"Ah, Antoine!" Maurice called, and led us to walk a little further into the interior. The man approached with a quick, light step; his face had the timeless look of the French country man, neither old nor young—he could have been anywhere between forty and sixty; his clothes were homespun and drab, but well-made.

"*Bonjour, monsieur le Comte*," said Antoine, giving a quick nod of greeting, and eyeing me and John curiously. "You have come to see the Lady?" I marvelled once again about the manner in which these folk referred to the tapestries.

"*Oui, Antoine, merci*," Maurice said, and presented us to Antoine, who bowed a greeting.

"Are the tapestries still in the ballroom, Antoine?" Maurice asked.

"Non, *monsieur le Comte*," the man said. "I have taken the liberty of hanging them again in the Gallery, where they belong." He nodded with satisfaction, and gestured for us to follow him down the hall. "We couldn't bear to see them lying crumpled on the floor, and felt it would be easier to brush the dust and dirt from them if they were hanging."

"Well, then," Maurice said, turning to us, "you shall have the singular opportunity, my friends, of seeing the tapestries as they were originally displayed."

We walked into a long gallery with tall, clear windows on the north side, with the tapestries hung across from them. Even with their ragged edges and dirt-stained colors, they were magnificent.

I began to scrutinize each tapestry. "So there are five here," I said, "plus the one that is now in Paris."

"There used to be eight," Maurice said with a sigh. "My mother and Prosper Mérimée, around 1840, originally discovered the tapestries, all rolled up and deteriorating, in an attic of the Chateau." He and Antoine exchanged rueful glances.

"Two of them had been damaged beyond saving," Antoine said sadly. "When we tried to move them, they fell into dust and threads."

I was caught by his use of the plural pronoun. "Surely you were not here personally at the time, *monsieur*," I said. "You seem much too young to have been present here forty years ago?"

"*Merci, mademoiselle*," he said, a twinkle in his eye. "I have seen sixty summers come and go, and then some, so *bien sûr*, I was here at the discovery of the Lady and her court by the mother of *monsieur le Comte*."

We continued to gaze and stroll back and forth before the tapestries, admiring the woven flowers and animals, and the glory, undimmed, of the royal Lion and the mythical Unicorn. But my mind was working fast on our murder investigation, and I thought Antoine might be a source of further information.

"Did you, then, know the lady who used to be the mistress of Chateau Boussac, Pauline de Carbonnières?" I asked our guide.

Antoine nodded. "I grew up here, working on the estate, helping my papa and *maman*—there were very few of us for the whole place, but Madame Pauline did not require much." He glanced up at the tapestries with a sad smile. "She used to walk here, sit here, every day, sometimes for hours, not speaking or moving." He shrugged. "I believe they were the only consolation in her life, after all the trials she had lived through."

"The Revolution," I said, and he nodded.

"I have heard she lived to be very old," I said. "Did she live here until she died?"

He shook his head. "She was born in 1786, so that would make her only about fifty at the time she left the Chateau—but she always seemed much, much older than that— frail, and without any spark of life in her. She had been married, for a while," he added after a moment. "De Ribeyreis, her husband was, but he died." He seemed sad at another thought, and said simply, "No children."

John, who had wandered off to gaze out the windows, came back to my side, and had heard the last of our exchange. "Why did she decide to leave the Chateau," he asked, "and where did she go?"

Antoine sighed. "She passed on in 1876, the same year Madame La Baronesse Aurore died"—he glanced quickly at Maurice at this, then went on. "We were all surprised she lived so long after leaving the Chateau, to tell you the truth. She lived in the town, a little house near the church of St. Anne, and seemed quite content."

"Perhaps," Maurice said, "she couldn't bear to live with the memories and ghosts of the past that inhabited the Chateau, and found comfort in more neutral surroundings?" He looked, to my eye, as if he knew very well how that felt.

"And what about François desRosier?" I asked. "The man who claims some relationship to the de Carbonnières family?"

Antoine's face darkened and he looked both startled and troubled. "Why do you ask about him, *mademoiselle*? Do you know him?" He looked from me to Maurice, questioning.

"We met, briefly, in Paris," I said, hoping to forestall either Maurice or John saying anything about our suspicions regarding the murder.

"Strange you should mention him, because I saw him just today," Antoine said slowly, walking over to the windows that overlooked the gardens and an abundance of trees. We followed him, stopping when he pointed to a dry fountain in the lawn below. "Early this morning. He was walking toward the Chateau, but looking around as if he didn't want to be discovered."

"Did he come inside?" John asked, his brow furrowed as he looked at me.

"I do not know, *monsieur*," Antoine answered. "I didn't hear anything that would indicate he had entered, but shortly afterwards I was called outside to attend to some deliveries, and was detained for some time." He shrugged, and turned to look back at the tapestries. "Every time he has come here, he has stood right there"—he pointed across the room—"and stared and stared at the tapestries for hours on end."

"He never goes anywhere else in the chateau?" I asked.

Antoine appeared to think about this for a moment. "When he was much younger, and would be accompanied by the other children—the twins, you know"—nodding at Maurice—"and you, *monsieur le Comte*, and your esteemed mama, you would all range about the house, from the cellars to the attics and the towers, looking for treasures." He smiled at the memory, and Maurice smiled as well.

"And did he—or any of you—find any treasures?" I asked.

Maurice answered, shrugging. "What is treasure to a child might be anything or nothing in an adult's eyes," he said. He paused a moment. "I remember, though, that Aurore—our little Sébastien even then—claimed she had found 'important things' during her ramblings, but I never learned what they were." He looked around the room, sorrow in his eyes. "We cannot ask her now."

Antoine did not appear to have heard this last remark, as he made no sign of surprise; or perhaps he already knew of Aurore's death. I hastened to pursue the information I sought, and addressed Antoine again.

"And did you—did anyone—know that François thought himself related to *madame* Pauline's family? And to the heritage that entailed?" I was answered by an outpouring of scorn from Antoine.

"Bah! He thinks himself the heir to the French throne, whatever *that* is in this day and age!" He smacked his hand against the wall. "Every other son of a *bourgeois* boasts he is a by-blow from some royal *infidèle* in the past, claiming the blood of the Bourbons, as if one drop of blood isn't just the same as another."

"You think there is no credibility to his claim?" I asked.

He shrugged, calming down some. "Those who have lived in Boussac for generations have always said that Louis the Well-Beloved was the father of our last lord of the Chateau, François, who was *madame* Pauline's father, and I have no reason to doubt it."

He had turned away as he spoke, back toward the door leading out of the Gallery, and we followed him. "And it was known, even at the time, that François had *une affaire de coeur* with that Georgette, who—though may she rest in peace—hounded our madame Pauline to make her acknowledge that her son was also the son of Pauline's father, and therefore had the royal blood of the Bourbons in him."

My head was reeling from the complications. But two things were clear—our suspect had been seen at the Chateau this very morning, and I felt certain that *something* about the tapestries would provide the clue we needed to unravel this mystery. I turned to John and Maurice.

"Let us make with all speed back to Nohant," I enjoined them. They looked surprised, but being gentlemen, they agreed to do as I wished. I gave them a wisp of a rationale.

"I believe the only tapestry that is significant to our investigation is the one presently at the *Musée de Cluny*," I said, feeling so certain that I couldn't help myself from feeling a bit smug. But a second thought sobered me up quickly, and I hesitated only a second before I spoke it aloud.

"And it's just possible that Miss Geneviève Bayard is in mortal danger."

EIGHT

AUGUST 1830
Another Revolution, and Matters Domestique

"WHO IS OUR KING? DO WE EVEN HAVE A KING?" Pauline de Carbonnières looked up from her breakfast to see her husband, Henri Arnaud, *comte* de Ribeyreis, slap his newspaper with one hand and then throw it to the table in disgust.

"What has happened now, *mon cher?*" she said, sudden fear striking her heart—was it starting again? She tried hard to remain ignorant of the news coming out of Paris; it had lately been riots and protests and insurrection, but seemed to be confined mainly to that city, the heart of government.

"Charles, that scurrilous dog," her husband said in a calmer tone, "fled the city three days ago, after naming his grandson as the next King—but now *he* has been removed and the regent—that Orleanist Louis Philippe—has been given the crown by the government."

"Orleans isn't so bad," Pauline said, sniffing. "Better than the current crop of Bourbons." She smiled secretly, savoring her own connection to the "old" Bourbons, the truly royal ones, as she thought of them.

"Peu importe!" Her husband, who was given to sudden mood swings, quickly stood up from the table. "Nothing matters, nothing makes much difference, down here in Boussac, eh, *ma chérie?"* He leaned over to kiss her cheek, and left the room hurriedly, calling back over his shoulder, "I'm going riding, up toward La Châtre, I'll be back late in the day!" The room settled down to an intenser quiet when the whirlwind that was Henri departed.

Pauline stifled a sigh. They had been married fourteen years, and she still couldn't quite figure out how it had even happened. She had been thirty years of age, far past the time of marrying, one would have thought. Perhaps, in her stupor and depression after her father's death, she had just let herself be led along by the first person to show any real interest in her. Henri de Ribeyreis was the last son of a noble line, his family seat in La Châtre partitioned and sold off during the Revolution, leaving him and his mother nearly penniless. He and Pauline were of an age, and upon the death of his mother, he had moved to Boussac, and came to Pauline's attention when he, nearly desperate to find any means to live, applied for work as a manager for the estate, the old man Pauline had always relied on having died of pneumonia. Henri was given lodging at the Chateau; they were much thrown together and found it easy in each other's company. One thing led to another, and it just made sense.

"It just made sense," Pauline said aloud, although there was no one in the room. She sighed again, feeling anew the awkward fumblings of their early intimacy, and the relief that seemed to satisfy them both when they decided that was not something they needed to do. Pauline had not conceived and, secretly, she was terrified of becoming pregnant, so the relief was manyfold. Henri found his pleasures elsewhere, it seemed—Pauline never asked—and they lived more like companionable brother and sister than husband and wife. She was content.

And one other major benefit was gained by Henri's presence at the Chateau—he kept the horrid Georgette desRosier away from the door, had told her in no uncertain terms to never approach the mansion or its environs again, on pain of arrest for harassment—and it had worked. She was grateful for that, and for his respectful treatment of herself; he saw her as the head of the Chateau, and although a helpful and prudent advisor, deferred to her judgement in serious matters.

Yes, she was content.

Pauline had forgotten that she had invited guests to lunch with her at the chateau that day, and spend the night as well, Madame Marie Simon and her daughter Julia. Pauline was aware that Madame Simon was the legitimate daughter of Georgette des Rosiers and her husband Jean, but Marie clearly did not know of her mother's *liaison* with Pauline's father. Marie was an interesting, progressive-minded woman, who had moved to Nohant from Boussac upon her early marriage; Pauline had met her at an agricultural lecture one summer, and they shared a warm sympathy that gave them pleasure in their half-dozen or so visits every year. She was completely unlike her mother in both looks and temperament, for which Pauline was grateful, and Marie, in moving to Nohant, had effectively cut herself off from her mother, especially after her own father died.

Marie was also an inveterate gossip.

Pauline rose from her desk, thinking to consult with the cook and inquire into the luncheon, but just then there was a knock at the door, and her housekeeper let herself in.

"Good morning, Madame, do you wish to see the menu Cook has prepared?" She held out a carefully handwritten menu.

Pauline took the paper from her and glanced at it briefly. Handing it back, she smiled at the woman, who had been with her household for many years. "Greta, please tell Cook this is just delightful. I'm sure my guests will be pleased."

Greta smiled as well. "The blue and the yellow rooms are prepared for them, madame. Their girl can share Anne's room, of course."

"*Merci, donc*," Pauline said. What a relief it was to have a well-run household.

"*Bonjour, ma chère* Pauline, such a scandal, I must tell you all about it!" Marie Simon paused for breath as she ran up the stairs, calling out to her hostess who stood at the top. Julia, her daughter, who was fifteen, ascended more sedately, and the three ladies embraced and moved to walk inside the house.

"Yes, my dear, do tell me," Pauline said, smiling; she glanced at Julia, who rolled her eyes, then smiled too.

Marie drew Pauline to her side as she sat on the blue satin sofa, its threads splitting and the once-sparkling pattern faded to grey. "It's the Countess Dudevant, Amantine, yes? She's left her husband, and the children! She's in Paris, they say, living openly with her lover, some novelist, it is said!"

"*Non! C'est impossible!*" Pauline put her hand to her lips. Aurore? Calm, lovely, amusing, charming little Aurore? She looked at Marie, doubting. "Aurore would never leave her little Maurice, nor Solange! You must be mistaken," she insisted. "She has only gone away to have fun in Paris, that I can see her doing, but not—."

Marie shook her head. "We all know how dreary the Countess finds her life with that old man—." She broke off at her daughter's hand on hers.

"*Maman*, really now," Julia said. "He can't help that he's old—and besides, he has money."

Her mother just stared at her. "Wealth does not turn a man's character from bad to good, Julia—the rich man simply has the means to be bad to everyone, everywhere. Besides," she added with a frown, "it's really her money anyway—the husband always owns everything these days."

"But is it really true?" Pauline asked again. "Is she such a deep romantic that she would give up everything—for a man?" Pauline blushed a little as she realized what this implied about herself, but Marie didn't seem to attach any significance to the words, and she continued relaying the gossip with great relish.

Pauline had seen that Aurore was unhappy, was restless, the last time they met, what was it, she thought, six months now? As dreadful as the choice to flee was, Pauline wasn't really surprised that Aurore would take such a risk—the young countess was a woman who wanted everything that life would give her; not like me, Pauline reflected, I who always choose the path of least resistance.

After the ladies had lunched and the guests gone up to their rooms to rest, Pauline's thoughts turned to her husband's absence. She had expected him home by now.

Late afternoon brought no Henri thundering home on his black horse, Champion, nor late evening. Marie and Julia endeavoured to soothe Pauline's worries, and nearly convinced her that Henri was probably lodged in a good room in the inn at La Châtre—he had done this before. Reluctantly, Pauline at last agreed to try to sleep, and the three ladies made their way up the stairs, kissing each other affectionately good night.

In the early hours past midnight, Champion limped into the courtyard, neighing softly and awakening the stableboy. Within minutes, servants and tenants streamed out from the chateau with torches and hounds, as Pauline kept anxious watch from the Gallery windows. The calm demeanour of the Lady, especially, served to quiet her fears.

They found his body some three miles from the Chateau; it appeared he had been thrown from his horse, and fell, striking his head on a rock. The doctor said that death would have been instantaneous; he had likely felt no pain beyond the first strike. Marie and Julia did their best to comfort Pauline, and wanted to stay with her, but she bid them depart the next morning—she would fare best on her own, she told them, and they could not oppose such a wish.

Pauline passed the next days and weeks in a stoic trance, submitting to the ministrations of her maid, eating when she was told, sleeping when administered a draught of some ill-smelling liquid. She spent her days standing before her beloved tapestries, walking to and fro endlessly, sometimes close to them, sometimes across the room by the windows. She longed to be inside the world of the tapestries herself, where she would always be young, always single, independent, and secure—and where nothing ever changed.

At first, a few weeks after Henri's death, the woman dressed in lurid purples and greens stood only in the archway of the entrance to the chateau, glaring up at the windows of the Gallery, which partly overlooked the courtyard, and smiling in triumph when Pauline would appear, though it was unclear if the mistress of Boussac even saw Georgette looking up at her. This went on each day for a week, and then one day she stepped forward and climbed the stairs, and rang the bell by its worn rope hanging next to the great carved door.

Having been given no orders to the contrary, a new housemaid let Georgette in, and showed her to the Gallery, as she had asked to see Madame Pauline. Once inside the room, Georgette exhibited not the slightest pretense of politeness. The fifteen or so years that had passed since her last appearance at the Chateau had not been kind to her once-charming face and figure—she was heavy in every sense of the word, from her thickened waistline to the dark shadows under her eyes to her plump, beringed fingers.

"There you are, you thief!" she said, coming near Pauline, who stood gazing at the tapestry of the Lady holding the mirror for the Unicorn to see his image. Pauline neither moved, nor turned to look, nor spoke—she was wrapped in another world entirely.

"I am speaking to you, *madame*," Georgette insisted, stepping between Pauline and the tapestry. "You owe me, you owe my son—and *his* son—the proofs of their heritage." She scowled fiercely, her face reddening as Pauline continued in motionless silence. She peered closely into Pauline's face, but as she began to see that her enemy truly did not even seem aware of her presence, her self-possession faltered a little, and she fell back a step, confused.

"It is true," she said, speaking half to herself, "my son, my Jean, does not care one tiny bit about the royal blood that flows through him—he is a *citoyen* through and through, but be assured, my fine lady," her voice growing louder as she addressed Pauline again, "my grandson hears from me daily about who he is and what place he could take in the world, if only you would be honest and fulfill your father's wishes!"

She began to pace back and forth, throwing cautious, anxious glances at Pauline now and then. There was a furtive fearfulness in her dark eyes, but she spoke with aggression. "Yes, you know, I know you do, that your father promised me—do you hear?—*promised* me the things would come to my son—the brooch and the letters!"

Pauline still had not moved; her glazed eyes seemed to encompass worlds beyond the present time. Georgette stopped and confronted her again, but found her words dying away before she could speak them.

Pauline had closed her eyes, then opened them again. Georgette was gaping at her, and seemed about to draw breath to start talking again. Pauline raised her hand, a finger pointing to the tapestry in front of her. Georgette whirled around, bewildered, and the mistress of Boussac finally spoke.

"Nothing is as it seems," she said. Her shoulders drooped and she looked at Georgette, but with a look that seemed not to see the woman before her. "We are both mad."

She turned away from her tormentor, and walked slowly to the door and out of the room.

Georgette did not follow her; she stood gazing up at the tapestry of the Lady and the Unicorn in the mirror for some minutes, then muttered something that sounded very much like a curse, if anyone had been listening.

She saw herself out.

PART FIVE

⟨ ONE ⟩

TUESDAY NIGHT – 10 MAY 1881 – NOHANT
The Vigil before the Funeral

RETURNING POST-HASTE FROM BOUSSAC, my companions and I arrived to a hurried repast in the smaller dining room of the Bayard mansion, the larger one being given over to refreshments for the people of Nohant who would be coming to the vigil in the evening. Our discussions on the way, at first lively, had failed to yield any further ideas or clues than we had already gone over several times, and at the last we merely sat silently, each with his own thoughts.

Those of you who know me, are aware that I am not the least little bit religious, but I do have a healthy respect for ceremony, and the solace of the sound of prayers and hymns, how little else I regard their efficacy in entreating a Deity who seems to care so little for a suffering world.

The vigil for Aurore, as I was beginning to think of her, was in the Roman Catholic style, with an open casket past which people would walk and gaze upon the poor face, her hair beautifully arranged, her fingers entwined with a rosary of pearls. I smiled, a sad smile, when I saw that her sister and her aunt had dressed her in a man's shirt and bowtie, with a dark jacket, and I glanced at John who was standing next to me, sorrow suffusing his brown eyes. I think he was particularly affected by the way that Aurore looked once more so like Sébastien, that he felt it a double sorrow. I linked my arm in his and he patted my hand absently; then we moved on.

There was a rosary said—I nearly fell asleep from the repetitious droning of the Latin syllables—followed by a short set of prayers for the dead; and then a litany, which, I believe, was a catalogue of nearly every saint in the Roman Catholic heaven; then a hymn or two; and finally people rose to gather in the dining room for a little refreshment. Aurore was left to the peace of the quiet room, a large candle having been placed at each of the four corners of the table on which she, in her casket, lay in state. An antique *prie-dieu* was placed nearby, for any family member who wished to keep vigil throughout the night and pray for the repose of her soul. I found it very moving that such attention would be paid to the poor deceased one.

I walked into the dining room with distinctly morbid and sentimental feelings, which I strenuously fought to shake off, remembering the task before me. John and I had agreed beforehand that we would gently query the townspeople about whether anyone had seen François des Rosier de Carbonnières around the village this evening.

John was already engaged with a likely looking prospect for gossip, an older lady with a sharp eye and a pursed mouth just brimming with tales and village chatter. I gave him a brief nod and turned to the youngish man I found myself next to in the group gathered round the table. He smiled at me affably; he was only a bit taller than I—therefore short, especially for a man—but he looked well-fed and strong. He had wavy brown hair, a small, neat moustache, and an intelligent look, and seemed to be some sort of prosperous professional—possibly an advocate or a medical person.

He turned out to be the town's chief of police.

"Jean-Davide Montserrat, *à votre service*," he said in French, with the accent of Paris, a gentle nod of the head showing his good manners. "And you are Miss Violet Paget, also known as Vernon Lee, the esteemed author," he added in English, an impish look in his eye.

"I say, you country police don't waste any time finding out about strangers in your town, do you?" I was amused, and showed it; besides, he seemed an excellent person of whom to ask questions about de Carbonnières. His smile was pleasant and sincere as he added, a quick glance at John across the room, "And your companion, the famous American artist, he is already asking questions of the townspeople."

I nearly gaped in amazement, then did a quick accounting in my brain—Paris accent, chief of police, well-dressed and professional-looking—"You are a friend of Charles Wilkinson!" I accused him with mock-indignant glee, and he started to laugh, then remembering the occasion, stifled his amusement and nodded somberly.

"You are as astute and lightning-quick as Charles said you would be," he said. Our lively exchange had garnered more than a few stares, so we quickly helped ourselves to a plate of food and a glass of wine, and moved away to some chairs by a little table in a quiet corner. I immediately pursued my attack.

"Did Charles give you instructions to keep an eye on us?" I said, before I began to devour the little sandwiches on my plate. "Make sure we didn't 'get into trouble' to use a favorite phrase of his?"

Montserrat grimaced and denied it, but I imagined I had hit the spot. The proof was in his next question.

"Did you learn anything useful at Boussac today?" he said, trying not to smile, and glancing around the room, checking that no one was near enough to hear.

I shrugged. "Only that de Carbonnières has spent a great deal of time over the years at the Chateau, staring at the tapestries," I said, then added, "and that everyone knows he thinks he can find evidence that he is a descendant of Louis XV."

Montserrat nodded; he knew this already too.

"Nothing else?" His piercing eyes fixed me with that look that only certain kinds of very successful policemen have. I immediately felt guilty.

"As children, the Bayard twins, and de Carbonnières, used to search throughout the Chateau for hidden treasures," I said, mustering a supercilious glare back at him. "Maurice said he remembers Aurore always saying she had found something 'important' but never said what it was."

He shrugged. "Something or nothing." I nodded.

"If he *is* the murderer," Montserrat said, and directed another sharp glance at me, "and we're a long way from knowing if that's true or not—does he have any reason to strike again? And who would be his victim?" He nodded in the direction of Geneviève's rigid, exhausted frame, seemingly held up by strength of will, and the tireless ministrations of her *tante* Eugenie.

"Possibly," I said slowly. "He was seen at the Chateau early this morning, by the estate manager," I continued.

"Has he been seen here, in Nohant? Either today or recently?"

"Not that I know of," Montserrat admitted. He looked around the room again; people were beginning to take their leave, as it was getting late. "He certainly didn't show up here, which is odd, considering he is a friend, and a relation, of the Bayards."

I nodded, thinking some things through. "Why are you here, in Nohant? You're much too young and urbane, if you'll forgive my impertinence, to be in this out-of-the-way place." I regarded him carefully. "You are—or have recently been—one of those international agents, like Charles, haven't you? But now you are here."

He slapped his hand against his thigh and looked at me narrowly. "Charles said there was no getting anything past you!" He lowered his voice. "Yes, I am in the same agency as Charles, and have been working on the same cases as he, until recently."

I decided to take up the 'why' of this at another point. "And does Charles imagine that de Carbonnières is his Revenant? His art thief?" At his surprised look, I smiled and pursued my thought. "Is there anything that argues against his being *both* the art thief and the murderer?"

He considered that for a moment. "That would make things very tidy," he said at last, then shook his head. "Too tidy. I wouldn't trust it." He shrugged. "But it shouldn't be dismissed out of hand." His eyes seemed to warm with a hint of admiration in them. "A formidable thinker indeed," he said.

Grateful that the darkness of our corner hid my blushes, I gave him no answer, but rose from my chair—we were practically the last ones still sitting down, and I thought it best to join the family where they were saying final farewells to neighbors and friends.

Geneviève disappeared as soon as the last neighbor left the room, accompanied by her aunt, who threw me an apologetic look as she hurried after her. I tried to indicate acceptance and reassurance in my smile—we would manage just fine on our own. I turned back to see that John had walked over to where Montserrat stood by the chairs we had vacated, and was introducing himself. I joined them to hear what John might have picked up from questioning the mourners.

"How did you guess who I am?" Montserrat was saying, much to my amusement, looking askance at my artist friend, who towered over both of us.

"Oh, not a guess," John said, smiling. "One of the ladies I spoke with, a *madame* Grossard? She told me your name, your position, what your house looks like, even…" he smiled more broadly, "that you and your lovely wife are currently expecting a 'blessed event', is I believe how she phrased it."

Montserrat chuckled ruefully. "You chanced upon the village gossip, with a vengeance," he said.

"And that is the reason why you are currently stationed in Nohant, then," I said, not concealing my satisfaction.

"Yes," he agreed. "But nonetheless, I *am* actually the chief of police for this district, and as such, you'll have to deal with me if anything 'troublesome' happens."

John looked a little confused, and I hastened to explain briefly that Montserrat was linked to Charles' organization, and therefore we could speak openly of our activities.

"Good, then," John said, and looking around, invited us to sit down (where, I assumed, he thoughtfully realized we would not have to strain our necks looking up at him to talk). "Madame Grossard has indeed been quite helpful, be-yond what she even imagined, I suspect—in short, she her-self saw François de Carbonnières, or someone very like him, ride into town on a big chestnut horse about mid-after-noon."

"Does he have a usual abode here in Nohant, when he comes to visit?" I asked eagerly. "Or do you suppose he has taken a room at the inn?" John shook his head.

"I'll have my men check right away," Montserrat said, alert and decisive. "If he's in town, we'll find him, and keep our eyes on him." He turned to me with a quiet air of defer-ence, but included John in his question.

"Do you intend to keep watch over Miss Bayard?" he asked. "Or would you prefer I send over my sergeant? In fact," he said, before we could answer, "I will have a man posted at this house, just to make sure no one enters it in the night."

We nodded our agreement, and suddenly realizing, with the clock sounding in the hallway, that it was very late, near-ing midnight, we parted the best of acquaintances and col-leagues. John and I decided he would take the first 'watch' by staying awake in his room, with the door slightly open, to listen for any untoward sounds. Geneviève's room was at the end of the hall. He agreed to wake me in two hours for me to take my turn.

Sleep eluded me, however, and I decided to refresh my weary brain with a little light reading, flipping through some pages of George Sand's *Story of My Life* again, and stopped when an interesting sentence caught my eye—Sand was speaking of the need to economize in Paris, where she had moved in late 1830, temporarily (at least) abandoning her husband and children in Nohant, to live a more fulfilling life as a novelist, and she remembered her mother telling her this:

When I was young and your father was short of money, he got the idea to dress me like a boy. My sister did likewise, and we went everywhere on foot with our husbands—the theater, all sorts of places. Our cost of living was reduced by half.

I was struck by this, and remembered what Geneviève Bayard had said about her twin Aurore being influenced by Sand's predilection for male attire. I continued reading with great interest, not the least because, I admit, I was drawn to attempt the practice myself. Sand continued about herself:

"At first this idea seemed amusing to me, and then very ingenious. Having been dressed like a boy during my childhood, I did not find it at all shocking again to put on a costume which was not new to me…. My clothing made me fearless. I was on the go in all kinds of weather, I came in at all hours, I sat in the pit in every theater. No one paid attention to me, no one suspected my disguise. Aside from the fact that I wore it with ease, the absence of coquettishness in costume and facial expression warded off any suspicion… Women understand very little about wearing a disguise, even on the stage. They do not want to give up the slenderness of their figure, the smallness of their feet, the gracefulness of their movements, the sparkle in their eyes; and yet all these things—especially their way of glancing—make it easy to guess who they are. There is a way of stealing about, everywhere, without turning a head, and of speaking in a low and muted pitch which does not resound like a flute in the ears of those who may hear you. Further, to avoid being noticed as a man, you must already have not been noticed as a woman."

"You must already have not been noticed as a woman," I repeated softly. This sentence, this *truth* resonated to a very deep ache inside my heart. I have never been thought pretty, or even minimally attractive, in the conventional sense. The attentive male gaze rarely shone upon me, and when it did, I was realistic enough to know it was the strength of my mind and not the beauty of my face that drew that gaze—a much more satisfying principle, to be sure, but not one given to romanticizing about. It had been some time now since the attentive *female* gaze had struck a more responsive chord—and I thought again of my dear Mary, waiting for me in London.

I started as a gentle tap on my door caught my attention—glancing at the clock, I saw the two hours had swiftly passed. I threw back the rug I had drawn across my legs—I had not changed into nightclothes, given the watch—and softly stepped to the door. It was John, and without a word but with a great yawn, he consigned the next two hours over to me.

Returning to the bed, I closed Sand's book with care. Her words, so insightfully and so wisely expressed, had given me much to think about.

TWO

MARCH 1836

Chateau Boussac is Abandoned

IT IS EASIER TO LEAVE WHEN IT LOOKS LIKE THIS, Pauline de Carbonnières de Ribeyreis thought to herself, walking through the dark, long-unused rooms of Chateau Boussac. After her husband's death, her interest in keeping up appearances had dwindled to nothing, and large sections of the house were shuttered, closed off, left to harbor insects and vermin, mold and dust. Servants were dismissed to find other employment, the stables were emptied, revenue from the farms was paid directly to the lawyers.

Only the tapestries in the Gallery remained on the walls, and with only Pauline to see or care for them, they too deteriorated along with the draperies, the furniture, the linens and the bed hangings. Her world had shrunk to her small bed chamber, the kitchen, and the Gallery.

But there was the occasional visitor.

"My dear Pauline," Julia Simon Bayard said during the most recent of these visits, in October. She had looked around the Gallery in dismay. "You really must make an effort, don't you think? Your health is at stake."

Pauline had shrugged and smiled dimly at her young friend. She was so like her mother, Marie, who had unexpectedly passed away two years ago, and like Marie, had become a good friend to Pauline. Julia had married and was a mother now, and had brought her three-year-old son Jules along with her from Nohant for the day. The boy wandered quietly around the Gallery, accompanied by his nurse, examining the tapestries and looking out the windows. Well-behaved, Pauline thought idly.

"Why don't you move into the village?" Julia had pressed her. "I know you own property there, and the nicest one, you know, across from St. Anne's? The Maupassants who live there are moving away, I heard it just the other day, so you could easily move in without displacing anyone—and Elise has kept the place up marvelously, there would be very little for you to do." Pauline let her chatter on, extolling the benefits of living in a smaller, more comfortable place, closer to other people, and on and on, but hadn't taken the idea at all seriously.

But the seed had been planted, and now, in the cold wet Spring of the new year, Pauline had made her decision.

She would leave Boussac. She would say farewell to all the ghosts who haunted it—her mother and brother, so long dead they were as legends or myths; her beloved father more than anyone, even than Henri, whose hearty voice and rapid movements she could still hear from time to time, in the stairwells and from distant rooms.

One other reason allowed her to think of a new life in the village—Georgette desRosiers had died in January, fat and apoplectic, a harridan whose ill temper verged on insanity. Without the fear of Georgette showing up on her doorstep in town, it even began to seem a pleasant change to be among people again, and activity—she might even go to church. She looked around the Gallery again, swept clean and kept tidy by Antoine's efforts.

The young manager was barely twenty, but mature enough to have taken charge for some time now, and she thought with satisfaction that he would do well under the new owners: the town of Boussac. He had been shocked when she first broke the news to him.

"But *madame!* You cannot sell Boussac! What are you thinking!" His eyes wide, Antoine had looked at her, unbelieving, thoroughly dismayed. She had explained, patiently, that with the lack of any family to inherit the Chateau, she felt that the village would be the best caretaker of its heritage—the village was inextricably linked with centuries of history, legend, and protection that the Chateau had afforded—it was part of its glory that Jeanne d'Arc had inhabited it for a time, during the wars with the English.

"But the tapestries, *madame*," Antoine had protested, looking up at them, for they had met in the Gallery. "How can you leave them?"

Pauline had sighed. "It is in the contract of sale that the Gallery and its tapestries will remain as they are, and that I will have access to them without obstruction, until my death." She sighed again. "After that, who knows?" She smiled sadly at the young man. "Even these beauties," she said, "are, after all, only things of this earth, and as one grows old, one's thoughts begin to turn elsewhere." She did not speak about the ache in her heart that looking at these tapestries brought on—it was getting too difficult for her to even look at them without weeping.

Antoine had only stared at her, reproachful yet respectful. Pauline noted that he had not asked about himself, or the fate of any of the remaining servants of the Chateau. She smiled again.

"And it is also part of the contract that you, and any other of the Chateau folk who wish to stay here and work for its maintenance and upkeep, will be allowed to do so," she said, and saw the flush of consciousness that showed his relief.

"*Merci, madame*, you are most kind," he said. "But where will you go? Will we not see you anymore?"

She shook her head. "I will only go so far as the village, dear Antoine, where I hope you will come visit me often, and tell me the goings-on here in the Chateau."

"*Oui, madame*," he said, bowing to her. "You may be assured of it."

And so now here she was, taking leave of her whole life. She would be fifty-one in Summer, older by far than she had, as a girl during the Terror, ever imagined she would be. But not so old, she thought, smiling at herself, that one cannot begin again. Somehow, somewhere in the depths of her broken and tired heart, there was a little spark that started a flame— to leave the past behind, though only to go so far as the village of Boussac; to escape the nightly visits of ghosts and spirits and trials of her childhood—this was something to look forward to. Irrational, she knew it was, to think so, to hope for change, but it had entered her heart, and she found her step a little lighter, her view of the world more sun-infused.

It was Spring, and she was ready to grow a little.

September 1837 – Boussac

"Aurore has been victorious!" Julia Bayard exclaimed as she walked through Pauline's wide-open doorway of the house in the village. "Pauline! I must tell you all about it!"

Pauline laughed and shook her head at her gossipy friend as they embraced. Julia pulled back to take a good look at the older woman. "You are transformed!" she cried. "Truly, you look more and more each time I see you as if you have drunk a tonic from the fountain of youth!" She leaned in again to kiss her cheek. "Soon you will look younger than I!"

Pauline only smiled fondly at her friend, and looked beyond her to the open door. "And *mon cher Jules*, is he with you today?"

"*Non, hélas!*" Julia said, setting her reticule on the table, and unpinning her hat. She handed her small travelling bag to the maid who had accompanied Pauline to the door, and who now curtsied as she disappeared upstairs to the bed-chamber Julia always used when she came to visit. "He is a big boy now, he says," she sighed, "and no longer wants to go about with mama on all her visits." She glanced at Pauline, as if assessing whether she should say something particular, then spoke carefully. "I rather think that he prefers visiting the Chateau over anywhere else, and when I told him that was not the point of my journey today, he declined to accompany me."

"Ah," Pauline said, feeling a little tug at her heart—both for the Chateau and for the boy, whom she loved. "Then you must assure him, the next time you visit, that we will make an expedition there, just for him."

Julia kissed her friend again. "You are too kind."

"So," Pauline continued, leading her friend upstairs to her comfortable, light and airy drawing room, "tell me all the latest news about our dear Aurore." They seated themselves side by side on a pretty little sofa of yellow satin, with embroidered pillows. Julia looked admiringly at the sheer drapes fluttering at the open window, letting in the sunlight on a large vase of sunflowers in the center of a round table.

"Oh!" she said, turning her attention to Pauline again. "Of course, she has become known far and wide by her *nom de plume*—George Sand—so I wonder if we'll be obliged to call her that? How odd that would be!" Julia laughed at the thought, and continued. "Well, you know that she had been fighting the Count for a divorce forever," she said, settling herself while Pauline leaned forward to pour some tea. "He had stubbornly refused to leave the house at Nohant, even though it is hers by rights, an inheritance from her grandmother—you knew her, did you not? The great Marie-Aurore de Saxe de Franceuil, once the Countess of Horn?" Julia gratefully accepted a cup of tea and looked inquiringly at Pauline.

"Yes, yes, I knew her," said Pauline, thoughtfully stirring a spoonful of sugar into her tea. "She was a…monument of individuality! There never was anyone like her, in all my acquaintance," she mused, then smiled. "Except Aurore now—she is her grandmother's heiress in many ways—the same stubborn independence, the flouting of convention, the drama." She sipped her tea. "So what has happened?"

"The divorce has been adjudicated, and, although Aurore must pay dearly, she will have the house—and more importantly, the children—legally restored to her, and the Count will go to live in Paris. She is coming back to No-hant!"

"And has she been separated from the children all this time?" Pauline inquired.

Julia shook her head. "Not at all, in fact, she has just come back from Majorca, where she"—Julia lowered her voice, al-though there was no one else to hear—"she and her latest lover, Frederic Chopin, you know, the pianist and composer? Polish I believe but he is very Parisian, they say, anyway, they and the two children were actually all living to-gether on the island, in some abandoned old monastery—imagine that!" Julia shook her head and sipped her tea.

"It *is* rather unorthodox, even for Aurore," Pauline said.

"But then," Julia continued, "she's actually been rather more a nursemaid than a lover, I had it from her in the course of a few letters over the past months, the poor man is consumptive! Although despite his illness, apparently he composed several new *Préludes,* she calls them, at first even without the aid of a piano!"

Pauline was able, in the midst of Julia's news and gossip, to track her own thoughts about this unusual woman in their circle, whose scandals and successes were scrutinized daily by them all, and generally severely judged. But Pauline felt a kinship with Aurore—George Sand—in her need for inde-pendence, and further, a strong admiration of the active, per-sistent spirit who could accomplish so much on her own! She was a testament to the strength of women—a true daughter of the Revolution.

✠

A week passed after this visit from Julia, and Pauline was idly looking out the window, enjoying watching the occasional passerby—she lived near the town square, but not in the thick of it—and contemplating going for a walk. Movement at the gate from the road caught her eye, and she watched in growing interest as a young man, perhaps fifteen or so years of age, and unknown to her, opened the gate and stood just inside, closing it firmly behind him. He was fair-haired and somewhat attractive, but for a certain dull heaviness that seemed to lay across his features like a shadow. He wore a knitted scarf of purple and green around his neck, though it was the height of the Summer's heat. The colors threw light on Pauline's searching memory, and, with a little *frisson* of alarm, she remembered who used to wear those colors.

Her first instinct was to turn from the window and disappear, but then she felt as if a firm hand had taken hold of her shoulder, and counseled strength. She should face this young man, this grandson of Georgette's, and not hide cowering indoors—these were the thoughts and encouragements she heard, and she quickly ran to the front door, opened it, and walked briskly down the path to the garden gate.

The young man started at first, and flushed as if caught out, but then he recovered his pride, and stood stalwart.

"*Bonjour, monsieur,*" Pauline called out when she was nearer. "May I help you?" She tried to form a pleasant smile, but her heart misgave her when she saw the young man's face—it was haughty, disdainful, and simmering with anger. He pointed his finger at her, and said in a low voice, "You are the one who has stolen my heritage. You alone have the means to prove that I am descended from a King!" His red face had drained of color now, and he looked pale and ill, although his dark eyes were lit with a point of fire.

Pauline's fears dissolved into a kind of pity—so like his grandmother, she thought, angry to the point of madness—Georgette must have imbued him with her sense of wrong, her rage for justice, her irrational accusations. The boy's father, Jean, had never seemed interested in the connection, as far as she knew. The thought of Jean, who was her own half-brother, although completely unacknowledged, softened her yet more. She had seen him from time to time, after the death of her father (*their* father!), but had not spoken to him from that date.

"You are François Louis desRosiers, are you not?" she said, addressing him softly. He looked affronted by her saying his name.

"You know very well who I am," he said, drawing himself up to a fuller height, which was a little above average. His dark blond hair was pulled back in a ponytail and tied with a black ribbon. He wore a white linen shirt, open at the neck, and fawn-colored linen trousers. The anomaly of the woolen scarf around his neck was alternately ridiculous and unsettling. She had opened her mouth to speak again when another person, the boy's father she instantly saw, came to an abrupt halt at her garden gate. She stepped forward, holding out her hand.

"Jean François," she said, and dipped her head in greeting. "I have not seen you for…you look well, it is good to see you."

The man looked at her with soft eyes and a sad smile, so like her father's that she nearly gasped, putting her hand to her heart. He nodded as he spoke to her.

"*Madame* Pauline," he said, deferentially.

He then turned to his son, and putting a firm hand on the boy's shoulder, he shook him slightly and leaned forward to whisper to him. The lad jerked away after a moment, and throwing a contemptuous look at Pauline, slammed through the gate and walked away.

Jean-François took a step or two closer. His smile was even sadder, and he lifted a hand in apology.

"My son," he said, his voice gentle, "listened far too much to his grandmother's tales, God bless her soul, and with a youth's intemperance, he feels himself on a crusade of sorts." He lifted his shoulders as if to say, *this will probably pass, he'll grow out of it.* Pauline wasn't so sure.

She just stood there, looking silently and long into her brother's eyes, he and she exchanging unspoken thoughts with each other, thoughts that would remain forever unspoken, she knew—and wondered if she'd been wrong to withhold the precious items of evidence. He nodded farewell, and turned back to the road to follow his son, leaving Pauline to stand alone, suddenly caught up and whirled into the past with all its sorrows and drama.

She herself hadn't thought about those things—the brooch and the letters—in a very long time, and as she searched her memory, she realized she wasn't quite sure where they actually were. In her madness and grief after Henri's death, in her stupor and lassitude, she did something...she took them and.... Pauline dug at her mind, trying to find the link that would reveal whatever rash action she had taken—she knew with certainty that it was rash, somehow—the smell of burning paper assaulted her, in her mind's eye she beheld fire curling and crisping the sheets of ink with their red wax seals—she had burned the letters, she knew that now.

But what of the brooch? Her memory yielded nothing, try as she might. Perhaps she threw it from the tower, down into the *Petite Creuse* far below the ancient walls of the Chateau; perhaps it lay, tarnishing and moldering in some hiding place in the floor. It wearied and saddened her to think about it, after all these years.

Personally, she didn't care for proofs or evidence of such a relationship, and she didn't think Jean François cared either; perhaps he never had even believed in their existence, although clearly his son did.

But at the very least, she began to feel that her decision, all those long years ago, had set something in motion that she rather thought would have been better left unleashed.

❧ Three ☙

Wednesday Very Early Morning
11 May 1881 – Nohant

A Special Mourner at the Vigil – Return to Paris

After John had turned over the night watch to me, I tiptoed to the window and peeked around the edge of the drapery. After a moment, my eyes adjusted to the dark, and I saw a large lumpish figure, a nightstick swinging in his hand, walking slowly to and fro across the drive that approached the house, nearer the road. Montserrat's man, then. Feeling that all was well, I nonetheless decided I would more easily stay awake if I crept downstairs and checked that all was as it should be, especially in the room where Aurore's body was laid out. Would anyone be keeping vigil there?

The Spring evening had turned quite cool, and the house was far from warm. As I stepped quietly down the stairs, wrapped in a woolen shawl, I felt a desperate need for a cup of hot tea, and wondered if I could find my way to the kitchen.

I held a small candle with a shield on one side of the holder, which helped to both reflect the light forward and to keep the glow from being too visible. As I passed through the hallway toward what I hoped was the door to the kitchen downstairs, I caught the glimmer of light from the partly opened door to the vigil room, and then, catching my breath, I heard the sound of voices, soft but urgent.

I blew out my candle, waited for my eyes to adjust to the darkness, and cautiously crept to the door—it was open wide enough for me to slip through without a betraying creak, and there being a large Japanese screen immediately to the right of the door, I stepped behind it soundlessly. The two persons—there seemed to be only two—in conversation, were at the farther side of the room, near Aurore's coffin. Applying my eye to the division between the panels of the screen, I made out the two—Geneviève, and François desRosier de Carbonnières! Questions abounded! How could Geneviève have come downstairs without John hearing her? How long had she been in the room? And more importantly, how did de Carbonnières get past the policeman in the front yard?

The scene appeared to me to reveal that Geneviève had been disturbed by her cousin as she knelt in prayer before her sister's bier, and she had just risen to speak with him. He was agitated, wringing his hands and grasping his forehead, but it seemed to me that he wasn't acting in a threatening manner. I was about thirty feet away, and the gleaming candles in the room showed that tears streaked his face. I strained to hear what they were saying—they spoke in French of course—and caught most of their words.

"...*tu dois savoir quelque chose!*" de Carbonnières was saying. *You must know something.* Geneviève denied it, insisting that *Aurore was very secretive as a child, she was full of nonsense.*

"But she always taunted me," the man lamented, twisting his hands, "once she knew that I...that there was...the son...the King... my own grandfather..." His words came to me brokenly as he turned back and forth. "She always…there was a *secretiveness* about her…not like you, not so good and kind…" He broke off, weeping, and Geneviève leaned toward him, putting her hands on his shoulders. What she said to him was too low to hear, but the result was powerful. François pulled away from her, stunned and stammering.

"She, she, *said* that? She told you that?" A look of crazed delight suffused his face, and Geneviève looked at him with alarm. "Then I must go at once!" he cried, and looked around him as if to find his hat or coat.

I had to act, or our chief suspect would dash out the door and disappear again. I stepped from behind the Japanese screen and into the open. The candles threw a steady light on the scene, which was still quite dim, and I believe both of the cousins at the other end of the room thought that a ghost had suddenly appeared. I and my candle approached them slowly, wary of sudden movements.

"I beg you not to leave so suddenly, *monsieur* de Carbonnières," I said, in my more than passable French. "There are a number of questions many people would like to ask you," I continued, then almost froze as I realized no one but I stood between this man and the door—and if he had gotten in past the police guard, he would certainly be capable of getting out, possibly not hesitating to use violence. I really hadn't thought this through.

Geneviève let out a little cry, and turned to her cousin. "Is she saying that you know something, François, something about how my poor sister died? Were you involved in her death?"

He looked sincerely shocked, and shook his head. "*Mais, non,* how can you possibly think such a thing? I loved

Aurore, you know that! I loved her." And the poor man wept again into his hands. They both seem to have forgotten I was in the room; I had to move quickly.

I turned into the hall and called out in the loudest voice I could muster, "John! John! Come at once!" and had to hope that would wake my trusted friend—or someone who could help me subdue and retain desRosiers.

I turned back into the room to see Geneviève earnestly endeavouring to calm her cousin, but at the sight of me again, he bolted out the other door to the parlor, farthest from me. I ran out of the room, heard the sound of John flying down the stairs, and shouted to him, pointing down the hall, "That way! He will probably try to find an outside door in the back of the house!" He ran past me in a blur, and I re-entered the parlor and joined Geneviève, who was weeping quietly into her handkerchief, leaning against the fireplace mantle.

"Why do you suspect François?" she managed to ask. "He would have done anything for Aurore. He could never hurt her." I realized she didn't really want an answer, so I just nodded and led her to the sofa to sit down.

It was agony waiting to hear what had happened outside; I heard a few shouts, and saw lights swinging as men ran past.

After nearly half an hour, John returned, grim and winded. "We lost him—he had a horse waiting—he galloped off, into the darkness."

"Where do you think he will have gone?" I asked, although I was sure I knew. I had risen to greet him, and placed a tentative hand on his arm.

A small voice turned us toward the sofa—Geneviève looked at us with remorseful eyes. "He will go to Paris," she said dully. "I told him he must be the Unicorn, and look into the Lady's mirror. It is what Aurore told me."

Before the funeral was held the next morning, John and I had a half-hour of Montserrat's time; he had been on the scene quickly in the night, but beyond telling what we could, there wasn't much to be said then, and we left him to sort out what his men could do, and to contact the Paris authorities. He now caught us up on what had been done.

"Charles, of course, is aware of de Carbonnières' movements, and what occurred last night, and will be watching the Paris train stations today for his arrival," he said, sounding optimistic.

"But he could easily get off at an earlier station and make his way in by carriage, or on foot," I said glumly, and he nodded in agreement.

"We know where he is headed," said Montserrat, "and Charles will have men posted at the *Musée de Cluny* as well. He won't slip past us again." He looked rather fierce as he said this.

John, who had been silent, spoke up. "Do you think any of this has anything to do with the missing Titian, and the art thief that you chaps have been hunting?"

Montserrat shrugged. "Who knows? We have been thinking that the simple fact of it being missing, along with the dramatic staging of the death scene, points to our thief— but that and whatever it is de Carbonnières is after could be completely separate—or he could be both thief and murderer—or he could just be a murderer with a flair for the dramatic and someone else entirely took the painting!" He threw up his hands. "At this point, I must leave it to Charles, in Paris, and hope for the best."

His words burrowed into the back of my mind, and I let them sit there quietly, knowing that in time something would be revealed, from my subconscious self, as they were calling it these days, that might make sense of this chaos.

We said our good-byes, wished Monserrat well, and to convey to his wife our wishes for good health and happiness, and prepared to accompany the Bayard family in the procession to the cemetery. John obligingly walked beside Geneviève, with her aunt Eugenie on her other side; both women were arrayed in black, with long veils covering their faces. Maurice Sand honored me with his presence as we walked in the procession, which swelled to sizeable numbers as the townsfolk joined in behind the hearse carrying the coffin to the churchyard—not a long journey, but a slow one.

I admit I preferred to look at the sky and the trees above us as we stood at the gravesite, the priest solemnly intoning prayers in Latin and French, rather than at the flower-strewn coffin that sat waiting to be lowered to the depths of the earth. When the last prayer was said, and the last clod of earth thrown down into the grave, the family received the condolences of the townspeople, and everyone moved off to their homes.

Maurice Sand accompanied us—John and me—with the Bayards walking ahead of us, as we began the short walk to the Bayards' home. "It has been the greatest pleasure to me," he said, taking me familiarly by the hand, "to have met both of you. It seems astounding to me that we have never met before, in Paris at the least, especially you, dear John." He smiled sadly at him. "If it were not for these sorrowful circumstances, I would be grateful for the occasion that has led us to become acquainted. I shall look forward to seeing your wonderful portraits, which already acclaim your talent and good fortune, for many years to come."

Still retaining my hand, he raised it to his lips for a gallant kiss. "And you, dear Violet, I have already ordered your latest work—you know, perhaps, that I too am an *aficionado* of the Italian *Commedia dell'Arte?*" He smiled. "We shall have much to talk about when we next meet."

At the gate to the Bayards' mansion, he bowed to both of us, and continued walking back to his own house. I felt a great affection for this interesting man, and hoped that we would indeed meet again.

John and I had reserved our seats on the noon train to Bourges, and we had about forty-five minutes to say our farewells and be taken to the station, just time enough.

Eugenie, that admirable, efficient woman, already had the servant waiting at the door, with the trap loaded with our bags, when we arrived at the house. She and Geneviève turned to us as we entered the house for a few minutes' farewell.

"John, Violet," said Geneviève, throwing her arms around first me, then John. "I can never thank you enough for all the kindness and goodness you have shown me." She was quite overcome, and clung to John, who held her tenderly and kissed the top of her head.

"We will never forget dear Sébastien," he murmured, eliciting a small hiccup and a sad smile from Geneviève. "We shall find who did this, Geneviève, I swear it."

I shook hands heartily with Eugenie. "Please do look me up," I said, "if you're ever in Florence, which is my home. I would be delighted to see you there, both of you," I said, smiling at Geneviève.

"Perhaps we shall," Eugenie said. "A little travel might be just what we need, one of these days."

We climbed into the trap, started off, and made it to the train station with ten minutes to spare. Seated without delay in our cabin, John took out his watch and calculated the time.

"It is noon, we will be in Bourges in an hour," he said. "The train to Paris leaves at two, which means we will be at the Gare d'Austerlitz around five o'clock." He sighed, and looked at me, weary and sad.

"I say, Vi, this has been a rum go, hasn't it?" he said.

I smiled ruefully, and took a deep breath.

"It's not over yet, my friend," I said. "It's not over yet."

On that train journey, especially from Bourges to Paris, I found myself drawn to read again from George Sand's *Histoire de ma Vie*. I had been in her house, I had made friends with her son, I had spoken to people who knew her, loved her, were scandalized by her. I had seen the tapestries of which she had written and of which she had recognized the inestimable value. What an astounding byway on this investigative path I had taken! What benefits, what friends and new relationships might have sprung from the first act of kindness, prompted by John—I give him all the credit—toward relative strangers.

As before, I found a particular passage which struck to the very heart of me, especially as my thoughts turned more and more to my dear friend Mary Robinson, whom I would see at the end of the next two days in London, Fates willing! Sand was writing about Friendship.

"So, do not be afraid to be fully affected by surges of benevolence and sympathy, nor to give in to the sweet or painful of the many concerns that make demands on generous spirits. But be no less attentive to the cultivation of special friendship, and do not believe yourself absolved from having a real friend, a perfect friend; that is to say, a person whom you may love enough to want to be perfect for, a person who may be sacréd to you and for whom you may be equally sacréd. The great goal we must all pursue is to kill the great evil that gnaws at us—the cultivation of self-love. You will soon see that when you have succeeded in becoming excellent for someone, you are not long in becoming better for everyone."

A person you may love enough to want to be perfect for. I murmured the words to myself, and my heart swelled as it never had before. It was only what I had ever wanted.

FOUR

OCTOBER 1843

The Tapestries are Discovered Anew

"MADAME PAULINE, YOU MUST SEE THIS!" Antoine barely paused at the threshold to the house in Boussac—the door was open—before bursting into the hallway, calling for his former employer, waving a newspaper. Pauline emerged from the kitchen at the far end of the hall, swathed in an apron, her flour-covered hands evidence of Autumn pie-baking.

"*Mon Dieu, Antoine,*" she said, "what is so important? Have they started yet another revolution?" Pauline deliberately sounded a note of insouciance, but her heart was beating fast. Thank the Lord they lived in this isolated village in the forest, whose craggy hills and valleys made it an unenviable spot to all but those whose lives were bound to it. The roilings of politics and even war seemed to pass over their village, time and again, leaving them, sometimes, a little leaner and a little poorer, but able to get on with their lives. She ushered the man into the kitchen and bade him sit at the big table, at one end of which were strewn the implements and ingredients for her baking—apples from the orchards of the Chateau, flour and sugar and salt, and baking tins that were battered and worn, and turned out perfect pie crusts and tarts.

Antoine fetched a few deep breaths, then spread the paper on the table, pointing to an article titled, *"Un coin du Berry et de la Marche"* by George Sand.

Pauline wiped the flour from her hands and picked up the paper, last month's issue of *L'Illustration*. *"A Corner of Berry and the Marsh,"* she read aloud. She looked at Antoine with amusement.

"Since when have you been subscribing to *haut culture* journals, Antoine? I'm impressed."

"Non, non, madame," he said earnestly, then realized she was joking. *"Mais oui,* I read them diligently, at the café." He

grinned broadly. "You know how much free time I have these days."

Pauline quickly scanned the first few paragraphs, which had begun at the bottom of a right-hand page, then turned the sheet to see the article continue across the whole of the next page, with beautiful illustrations of The Lady of the

Tapestries—drawn by Maurice Sand, Aurore's son. She calculated quickly—he would be almost twenty now, and from the looks of the illustrations, a very competent artist.

"*Formidable,*" Pauline murmured. She read the caption for the illustrations aloud. "*Characters from a tapestry at the Chateau de Boussac, from the drawings of Maurice Sand.*" She looked at Antoine in amazement. "They're very good. How did this come about?"

Antoine looked guilty. "I should have told you, *madame*," he said, pointing to the paper. "*Madame la Baronesse*, that is, *madame* Aurore, when she and that man from the government, Mérimée, came to the Chateau last year, they wanted to see the tapestries."

Pauline nodded encouragingly; she could see he was worried for her feelings. "*Cela n'a plus d'importance*, Antoine. I have done with all those memories," she said, smiling. "They are no longer part of my life, you see," and she gestured around the sunny kitchen. "This is my domain now. So do go on, tell me all about it."

Antoine looked relieved, but still wary. "You will know, of course, that the town decided to house the *prefecture de police* there for a while, after you departed." She nodded, and he continued. "They moved many things between the rooms, and one day—I had been gone for a week or more, you see," he explained, apologetic, "I saw that the tapestries had all been taken down, rolled up, and carried to one of the attics to be stored."

Pauline looked at him for a long moment. "That is very sad," he said. "But you are not to blame, *mon ami*."

He shook his head, and continued his story. "When Madame Aurore came with *monsieur* Mérimée, I took them up to the attic, and because *monsieur* Mérimée is the Inspector-General for historical monuments and all that sort of thing, he had the authority to have them taken back down to the Gallery and unrolled." He gave a deep sigh. "Sadly, two of them were in tatters, the rest somewhat damaged but still intact."

Despite herself, Pauline felt a tug at her heart. "Which two?" she said, turning back to her apples and beginning to peel another one.

"The two that showed the Lady as a Queen, the one where she is processing through the forest, and the one where she is approaching her throne?"

Pauline nodded—*the ones my father thought to sell, a thousand years ago, it seems.*

"And then?" she asked, rousing herself from reveries that would do her no good.

"The two of them talked a great deal about their 'discovery' and how the tapestries were priceless treasures that should be rescued from their obscurity and shown to the whole world."

Pauline nodded, smiling. "I agree with that," she said. "They always were, to me, the most magical, the most wonderful things in the world."

Antoine touched the newspaper. "You know, *madame*, my reading is not very good—I wonder if you would be so kind as to read this for me—perhaps not today," he added hastily, "I don't want to take you from your work, but some day when you have some leisure."

"No time like the present," Pauline assured him. She wiped her hands on her apron, sat down and drew the paper closer and began to read to her friend.

"*A Corner of Berry and The Marsh,*" she began, reading the title of the article. Antoine listened raptly, nodding here and there as she read George Sand's glowing, rapturous story of the marvelous tapestries, presenting her theory that they certainly dated to medieval times, based on the style of clothing worn by the Lady and her handmaiden, as shown in her son's drawings. Sand indicated that the coat of arms depicted on the banners—the diagonal sash of blue against a red field, and three white crescents, like partial moons, running down the blue sash—was unknown and therefore the original owners, or those who commissioned the tapestries, could not be identified. Pauline searched her memory for anything her father, or her grandmother, Louise deRilhac, might have said about the origins of the Lady, but as far as she knew, they had always been at Chateau Boussac.

Reading about them drew Pauline's heart perilously near the borders of the world she had left behind, seen through a dim veil of heartache and suffering that she dared not breach.

She took a deep breath when she finished reading, closed the journal, and handed it back to Antoine. "*Merci, mon cher,*" she said. Then she rose, her hands firmly on the table for support—after all, she thought, she was nearing sixty, and her bones often ached—and she smiled. "Now, I must get back to my pies," she said. "And you must be sure to come by again later and pick up one for you and your good wife."

With that, she turned to the sunlit table, straightened her apron, and put her hands to work. Antoine took the paper and left quietly by the back door.

May 1861

A Visit to Boussac

PAULINE SAT AT THE WINDOW that faced the front garden
and the road to the village, and leaned forward, her elbows
on the wood sill. She would soon be seventy-five years old,
a fact that struck her as both marvelous and tiresome. Why,
after all the illnesses and early deaths, by accidents and child-
birth, war and revolutions and executions, had she been sin-
gled out to live to such a great age? She shook her head at
the perversity of Fate and Chance—she had long ago given
up believing in God, in fact, she didn't believe in Fate or
Chance either.

What *did* she believe in? An answer came swiftly,
straight from her heart—her father's love for her. That was
the one, true thing that still, after long decades of change and
time passing, that still meant something to her. How she
wished she could see him again. *That* would be a reason to
believe in God and heaven, she thought, laughing at herself.
Well, if believing in heaven would result in seeing him again,
then she would believe it. What had she to lose?

"I believe in heaven!" she said aloud, then looked
around to see if there was anyone to hear it. She laughed
again. "*Cher papa,*" she murmured, touching her hand to her
heart, "heaven or not, I hope you are waiting for me somewhere."

A gentle tap on the door drew her attention away, and
her housekeeper came into the room. "It is almost time for
your visitors to arrive, *madame,*" she said. "Is there anything

I can do for you?" She looked pointedly at Pauline's dressing gown, which was not suitable for receiving guests.

"Oh, my dear," Pauline said, laughing. "I am an old woman, no one cares how I am dressed!" But she rose from her chair, not unsteady, but slowly. "However, to please you, I shall put on a day gown, and you may dress my hair, will that do?"

"That will do perfectly, *madame*," said the woman. "I shall lay out your green day dress, and your turquoise shawl, those are good colours for you."

Dressed and seated again in the drawing room, Pauline looked forward to her visitors, whom she saw had arrived and were making their way through the garden, exclaiming over the abundance of Spring flowers and fresh green leaves on the old trees. Julia Bayard was now a grandmother, and had brought her eight-year-old twin granddaughters to visit her dear friend.

"*Bonjour, bonjour, mon amie!*" she cried as she led the twins into the drawing room. She bent and kissed Pauline on both cheeks, insisting that she stay seated, then presented her granddaughters, who curtsied prettily as they were intro- duced. They were dressed in similar style, but with fabrics of differing colors and accessories.

"Geneviève, the eldest by four minutes," said Julia, smiling. "And here is little Aurore, named for our dear friend *La Baronesse*. Girls, this is my most wonderful and important friend, *madame* Pauline de Rilhac de Carbonnières de Ri- beyreis."

"Goodness, that is far too many names!" said Pauline. She held out her hand to the girls. "You may call me madame Pauline, and I am delighted to meet you." They curtsied again and shook hands with her, then seated themselves on the sofa as their grandmother took a seat across from Pauline.

"How delightfully they are dressed," Pauline said. "I am glad to see their mother does not insist they look exactly alike, as one sees with so many sets of twins." She looked at the girls with a smile. "Is that what you would prefer?"

"Oh yes, *madame*," Aurore said promptly, while Geneviève just nodded, a bit more shy than her sister. "But truly, I would prefer to wear trousers and boots, like my papa!" Geneviève *shushed* her quickly, but Aurore tossed her head defiantly. "I would, you know," she insisted.

"Girls," said Julia quietly, and Aurore subsided good-naturedly.

Tea and cakes and coffee were brought in, and the ladies were chatting companionably while the twins sat quietly and whispered and giggled with each other. The warm Spring sun made its way further into the room, then suddenly disappeared behind some ballooning white clouds that drifted overhead. Pauline noticed the girls looking toward the window with longing eyes, and asked Julia if they might not be allowed to go outside into the garden to play. She readily gave her assent, and dismissed the girls with only a mild warning not to pick the flowers or get too dirty.

The two women were exchanging gossip from their respective villages when some change of movement and noise in the garden caught Pauline's attention, and she rose to look out the window. The girls, who had been laughing and calling out to one another, were suddenly silent, and had drawn near the garden gate, where a very young man stood, looking at them. Mildly alarmed, Pauline motioned to Julia to join her at the window to see what was going on. Julia, a little near-sighted, peered out and after a moment, shook her head, smiling.

"It's François, he's a somewhat distant relation, you know, goes all the way back to the legendary Georgette, *ma grand-mere*, whom I never really knew," she said, glancing sideways at her friend. She knew a part, though not all, of the village tales about Pauline's father and Georgette. "He lives here, in Boussac."

"Yes, I know," murmured Pauline, although she had not recognized the boy, who appeared to be in his early teens; he didn't look at all like his father, the scowling young brute in the green and purple scarf who had accosted her at that very gate so many years before—and certainly not like his grandfather, her own half-brother, passed on now some decades, who had reminded her so strongly of her own dear father. She turned to Julia.

"Why don't you invite him in?" she said. "He seems a little lost to me."

Julia nodded. "I think that's an excellent idea. Family is family, after all, and the girls should know their cousin, how-ever many times removed."

She slipped out the door and approached the little group at the garden gate, talking animatedly on the way, and clearly pressing the young François to come into the house. He happened to look up just as Pauline came to stand in the doorway, and their eyes met. Pauline at first feared she would see the same anger and disdain she had experienced from the boy's father some thirty years before, but *this* François was different—he did, indeed, look lost, and, her heart whispered to her, in need of a friend.

"Please," she called, holding out a hand, "please do come in and join us for some refreshments. I do so want to know you, François." The boy acquiesced with a certain grace and, opening the gate carefully, walked toward the house; the twins had each taken one of his hands, and fairly skipped by his side, making him laugh with their antics.

Pauline hadn't any idea what made her want to do this, as she welcomed him into her home. Perhaps, somehow, she was beginning to right a wrong.

❧ Five ❧

MUCH AGAINST MY OWN PREFERENCE, John insisted that we not be driven directly to the *Musée de Cluny*, where I was certain that events were occurring that would unravel the mystery of Sébastien's murder. I was stubborn, however, and insisted just as adamantly, that we at least should go to the *Sûreté* and find Charles to hear the latest developments. Tired as we both were, we felt the urgency of the investigation hounding us, and he at last agreed to do as I wished.

We were surprised and pleased to find Charles Wilkinson was indeed in his office, and he rose to greet us warmly, dismissing the wary officer who had led us to his door.

"Violet! John! It's so good to have you back, I have much to tell you," he started in immediately. Noticing our travel-worn looks, however, he quickly called back the officer, gave him rapid directions to procure food and drink, and then turned back to us.

"You must be weary after your journey," he said, inviting us to be seated. I saw that this new office was much more comfortable, and warmer, than the previous cell in which we had gathered, with a fire in the grate, books on shelves, and gas lights that would be lit when the sun ceased to throw its beams through the large windows, facing west. I wondered if the Paris *gendarmerie* were affording Charles' agency a bit more respect. Whatever the reason, I was grateful for the improvement.

"And we have much to relate to you," I said, settling myself in a large leather chair that smelled faintly of cigar smoke. "Although you know already, of course, about our encounter with François desRosier—de Carbonnières that is—early this morning, last night really. And by the way," I added, before he could respond, "your man in Nohant, Montserrat? Excellent creature, very competent—we became good friends quite quickly." John nodded his agreement; he had taken off his greatcoat and now sat down in the chair next to mine, both of us facing Charles across the wooden desk, upon which were strewn a great many papers.

"I'm glad to hear it," he said, smiling. "Jean-Davide had equally complimentary things to say about you as well." Then he became serious. "He telegraphed the bare details of what occurred, and what he thought we should do here—it is done," he said, looking grim. "We have men stationed—discreetly—around the perimeter of the *musée,* since early this morning. I have heard nothing as of yet." He glanced at the clock on the wall.

"I suspect de Carbonnières is waiting until dark," John offered, and Charles nodded his agreement. A tap on the door brought the very welcome refreshments—the officer set a tray on the desk, saluted, and left the room.

"That appears to be the case," Charles said, responding to John's speculation. He shuffled some papers on his desk into a more orderly stack, and set them aside, leaving more room for the tray; after pouring the coffee, he gave us his full attention. "Now, tell me everything."

⤶

"Very interesting," Charles said when we had related all our adventures, leaning back in his chair for a moment. The coffee urn was empty, the pastries and sandwiches consumed, and we were all the better for it. "And did you ask Miss Bayard *why* she said what she did to de Carbonnières, that odd phrase about the Unicorn and the mirror?"

I sighed. "Yes, we asked," I said, glancing at John. "It seems that her sister—Sébastien, Aurore—I'm sorry, my brain is tired sorting out the various *personae* here—a few years ago, had taken to teasing de Carbonnières, desRosier *then,* about a 'secret' hidden in the tapestries, claiming she'd heard it herself from the previous owner of the Chateau, one Pauline de Carbonnières, before she died—and that the image of the Unicorn held the answer, or something to that effect." I looked at John for corroboration.

"She did say," he added, "that her late sister always was very imaginative, and talked a great deal of nonsense, as a child believed in magic and fairy-tales, that sort of thing." He looked apologetic. "Geneviève said she never took Aurore seriously when she took on in that way."

"But why did Miss Bayard say that to de Carbonnières?" Charles pursued. "If she didn't think there was anything to it?"

"I think she felt sorry for him," I said. "And she was quite worn down, with grief and fatigue, and perhaps she thought it would satisfy him and he would go away."

Charles looked at me sharply. "And what is your judgement of Miss Bayard's belief that her cousin is not the murderer, could never harm her sister?"

I chewed at my lip in frustration. "Frankly, I'm inclined to believe her—but I find myself at a loss then, as to who could have done it!" I had leaned forward to answer, and now fell back in my chair, dissatisfied and scowling. I remembered what Montserrat had said, in Boussac, about all our options in 'choosing' a murderer, and as if he'd read my mind, John spoke up.

"Have you given up the art thief as the murderer?" John asked. "Have you traced the missing Titian?"

Charles shook his head, weary and impatient. "Nothing on that front at all," he said. "Nonetheless, it's still a theory, that we're pursuing." He paused a moment, and looked at the two of us, concerned.

"You both look worn out," he said. "Why don't you go to your lodgings and let us sort this, as we shall be doing?" It seemed like a question, but I could tell he wanted us to remain on the outside of the investigation now.

That did not suit me, and I willed myself to ignore my fatigue and depressed spirits.

A sharp rap at the door brought us all to attention, and an officer stepped into the room.

"Sir?" he said, then looked questioningly at us.

Charles waved him in.

"Tell me," he said.

"There's a ruckus at the *musée*, sir," said the man, who seemed to me very young. He delivered his news in an excited rush. "Some woman let herself in with a key, seems she works there, so the man watching the place thought it was all right, then next you know she comes screaming out the door, yelling about her *patron* dead on the floor, or something like that." He took a breath.

"Du Sommerard!" I said, instantly alert and ready to go. I spoke before Charles could intervene. "You must let us go with you, Charles, you must! I swear we'll stay out of the way," I said, looking at him beseechingly.

He hesitated only a moment, then nodded tersely. "Get the carriage, now!" he told the young officer, and hurried to gather his coat, and then shepherded us out the door. I couldn't help but comment as we walked rapidly down the hall. "You gave in rather quickly, I must say, Charles," I said, and received a playful but sardonic smile in response.

"I knew I would lose the battle if I fought you on this," he said. "And I chose surrender as the better part of valour, Violet." He and John exchanged amused glances over my head—but I saw them.

I smiled, to myself, then turned my mind to the task ahead.

The "ruckus," as the young officer so quaintly put it, that awaited us at the *musée* had calmed down considerably by the time we arrived. We were met at the door by an intelligent-looking, well-dressed young man, who immediately relayed essential facts to Charles, not waiting for him to ask. I assumed (correctly, I learned later), that he was an agent in Charles' organization.

"The woman who let herself in, sir, is a Miss Claire Berthold, who works here." He spoke rapidly in English, but clearly, with only a slight accent. "The men tell me that earlier in the day, around noon, the director of the *musée*, Du Sommerard, let himself in with his own key. They followed orders about not interfering with anyone appropriate entering, and the *musée* is otherwise closed. No one else but those two persons were seen entering the place."

"And Du Sommerard? Is he dead?" Charles asked bluntly, and I was relieved to see the officer shake his head.

"No, sir, he was struck on the head, and is currently unconscious, but alive. The doctor is with him." With this said, he led us into the vestibule where Claire Berthold had her desk, behind which was Du Sommerard's office. There was one officer standing by the desk, but no one else; the agent led us up the stairway to the first floor, then through the gallery with its rows of vitrines and precious objects. I had guessed that the scene we were heading for would be the workshop—again—and I was correct. The hidden door panel was open, and we could hear voices as we approached.

Claire Berthold was seated near a window, looking wretched, her hair falling from its pins, her face tear-streaked. Her eyes were fixed, unwavering, on the prone figure of her *patron,* Edmond Du Sommerard, to whom a doctor was ministering with care, tucking a blanket around the still form, preparatory to him being lifted on a pallet and carried away. The doctor looked up as Charles took a few steps nearer, then stood to address him. John and I moved closer.

"*Monsieur le docteur,*" Charles said, greeting the solidly built professional, who nodded politely. "What can you tell us about the injury *monsieur* Du Sommerard has sustained?"

"A single but severe blow to the head," the doctor replied. "He is unconscious now, probably from a concussion, but I'm hopeful that he will soon wake. His pulse is strong and he is breathing normally." He looked down again at his patient; the orderlies were waiting for his signal to proceed. "We will keep him under observation at the hospital—the most significant concern is internal bleeding, then swelling of the brain." He snapped shut the black bag he was holding, and nodded to the two orderlies to gently pick up the man. "Let us hope it doesn't come to that," he said, grimly.

Charles nodded. "There will be a policeman assigned to his room, to insure no visitors or intruders shall enter."

The doctor nodded curtly, then took his leave, supervising the men carrying Du Sommerard as they made their way down the staircase. We three turned as one to question *mademoiselle* Berthold, who had risen in the meantime, as if to follow the doctor out the door.

"One moment, *mademoiselle,*" Charles said, and motioned for her to be seated again. "I'm afraid we must ask you some questions." He glanced at the doorway, and said reassuringly, "*Monsieur* du Sommerard is in good hands, he will receive the best of care."

Charles pulled a chair from the side and set it a few feet away from the woman, then sat down, turned at a slight angle from her. I watched him carefully, thinking I might pick up some valuable lessons in questioning people—I have found that an inquiring mind and keen observation invariably yield *some* benefits, although often much later in time.

John had stepped away for a few moments and then returned, carrying a cup of tea in a saucer, which he offered to the poor distraught woman. I glanced over and saw there was a carafe and some cups on a side table, probably for the convenience of those who worked on the restoration of paintings. She looked up in surprise, then gratefully accepted the tea. I marvelled once again, as I often have done, at John's sensitivity and thoughtfulness for others, and I gave him an approving smile.

"*Mademoiselle* Berthold," Charles was beginning, in a gentle but firm voice, "can you please relate to us everything that happened since your arrival here today?"

She sipped her tea, then set the cup on the table. She looked calmer. She took out a dainty handkerchief from her sleeve and wiped at the tears on her cheeks. "You will forgive me, *monsieur*, I was so startled, I thought he was...." She cleared her throat, and spoke in a composed tone.

"My usual hour of arriving here was much delayed today," she began. As she spoke, she pulled a piece of paper from a pocket of her dress and, unfolding it, handed it to Charles. I peered a little closer, standing just behind him, but couldn't make out the few handwritten words on the page. "I received this note as I was about to leave my lodgings— and as it was apparently from my mother, who lives in Passy, just across the river, I judged by the words that I must go to her immediately."

Charles had been reading the note intensely, then without a word, handed it up to me. It read: *Claire, you must come to me at once, I must speak with you on an urgent matter. Mother*

"You said 'apparently'?" Charles urged.

We all three looked at Claire Berthold, waiting, and she continued, shaking her head. "When I arrived—and it took almost two hours to get there—my mother was surprised to see me, and absolutely denied having sent any such note, nor knew of any reason why someone would play such a trick."

She sniffed into her handkerchief. "By the time I came back here, I was, of course, very much later than usual—if only I had come on time, if only—" She stopped, collected herself, and began again. "I was concerned to let Edmond—*monsieur* Du Sommerard know that I had finally arrived, and the reason why I was late—it unnerved me, thinking how that note had kept me from the *musée,* and why that could be—so I came up here to the workshop when I saw that he was not in his office, and I found him—there," she said, pointing to the floor behind us, where Du Sommerard had lain.

"Was he conscious at all when you first saw him?" Charles asked—which I had been wondering about, too.

Claire Berthold shook her head. "I knelt down next to him, at first I thought he was indeed dead, and I didn't know what to do," she said, twisting her handkerchief fiercely in her hands. "I just, I just ran outside and starting screaming for help," she said, and glanced at Charles. "I had no idea that there were policemen guarding the *musée*," she said, "but it was the greatest good luck that they were, and were able to come assist me immediately."

Charles gave her a long, assessing look. Impatient, I broke in to ask a question, the answer to which I couldn't wait for any longer. "Is anything missing, *mademoiselle* Berthold?" I said, as Charles started slightly at the sound of my voice.

She raised her eyes to mine; I was shocked by the degree of hostility in them, directed to me. "And who are you, *mademoiselle,* that I should answer your questions?"

"Tell us if anything is missing, *mademoiselle*," Charles repeated, not so gently this time.

She held my gaze for some moments, then turned to look at Charles. "I have not had the opportunity to look," was all she said. I judged she had fully recovered her equilibrium, especially knowing Du Sommerard was not dead after all, and had assumed her usual demeanour of sour superiority.

Charles glanced up at me, and I nodded. "We need to look at the tapestry," I said, and looked expectantly at Claire Berthold. She glared at me for an instant, then rose to lead us to the door to the inner room. We were silent as we approached the sliding panel, and once it was open we stepped inside.

The tapestry was gone.

SIX

SEPTEMBER 1876
Farewell to All This

"MADAME PAULINE, LET US TAKE YOU THERE." Maurice Sand bent his head over Pauline's shaky hand as he said these words. "Consider it a late birthday present, my dear lady."

She waved her other hand, then reached up to pat his cheek. "When one is as old as I am," she said, smiling, "one doesn't want to remember birthdays too precisely." She leaned back, dropping her hand. "But I will allow you to transport me up to the Chateau for a short visit, if you will," she said. "I've had bit of a longing to see it one more time." She caught at his sleeve as he began to turn away.

"Your dear, dear mother, my poor Maurice," she said, and tears filled her eyes as she saw Maurice's stricken look. "How is it possible that she could pass on, and I am still here?"

Maurice found himself unable to speak, and merely patted the old lady's hand for a moment. Collecting himself swiftly, he went to the front door to speak to the other visitors who had gone into the garden.

"Geneviève! Sébastien! François!" He called out to the trio of young people admiring the garden, and his artist's eye took them in as if they were a painting—Genevieve—the twins were what, twenty-three now?—resplendent in a light muslin gown with blue ribbons and a straw hat perfect for the still hot, still sunny September day; her sister, who today was Sébastien, not Aurore, he thought with amused indulgence, dressed as a Summer dandy with ballooning pants, a white shirt and light embroidered vest, and a slouch hat pulled across her cropped curls.

François was somewhat jauntily dressed, for him, in tan trousers and a short jacket over a linen shirt, and seemed to be entertaining the girls with some comic tale. He was nearing thirty now, Maurice mused, why hasn't he married? He looked with keener attention to the young man's interaction with the twins—ever since their parents had died, some years ago now, he had taken a strong paternal interest in the orphaned girls, and anxiously watched their progress and general happiness. They had inherited a good estate and were well on their way into marriageable age, both being quite intelligent as well as attractive girls—another reason to scrutinize their admirers.

"*Oui,* Maurice?" Sébastien looked up and answered. A smile broke on her gamin face, and she called out, "Are we going? Did she say yes?"

Maurice nodded, and Sébastien, in her enthusiasm, leaped into the air and then ran laughing around the garden. The other two just shook their heads and smiled at her.

Maurice turned back into the house and came to stand by Pauline's chair. "It is a very warm day," he said, and gestured to her shawl, which lay on the back of her chair. "Do you think you will be warm enough with this? Or," he said, thinking further, "the Chateau may very well be cold and damp—you remember how it always was of course—may I retrieve a heavier wrap for you?"

Pauline shook her head. "This one will do," she said, and smiled. "I will not go far into the Chateau, nor will I stay there long." She smoothed her skirt over her lap. "These legs are not going to climb any stairs to the chambers above for a last look." She looked up at Maurice. "The entrance hall will have to do."

"*Bien sûr,* Madame Pauline, whatever you like."

The road to the Chateau was lined with trees glinting the first signs of Autumn, tinges of orange and red at the edges of green leaves, and fading ones already scattered on the ground. Pauline looked about her avidly, peering into the bushes and stone walls for signs of birds, flowers, anything she could see. At ninety years of age, she rarely left her house, but she was still clear in her mind and able to look back on a life spent surviving revolutionary tempests with more equanimity than she thought possible as a younger woman.

"Ah, there it is!" The twins and Pauline cried out the words at the same time as the massive walls and great gate came into view. Geneviève turned to her excitedly. "I feel as young as if it were the first time we came here!" she said, and touched her sister's hand. "How long ago, dear? Ten years?"

"Closer to twelve," François answered first. "I remember because I had just come back from school, and was here to visit Madame Pauline, when you two showed up." He laughed. "You were eleven then, such babies."

"You were an old man, then," Sébastien said, sticking out her tongue at him. "Nineteen! Old enough to be my father."

"Don't be ridiculous, silly girl!" Geneviève said, indignant for her cousin. "He just seemed old to us then, because we were so young—now he doesn't seem old at all!" She gave François a brilliant smile.

Sébastien seemed to consider this a moment, then nodded decisively. "Not at all in looks, I'd say, but perhaps...old in the mind? The head?" Her face took on a prim look, and she spoke as if parroting an oft-heard phrase. "It doesn't fare well for one to offend society in such a manner." She started laughing, and poked François, who was looking sullen at her remarks, "You may not have said it that way, you know, but that's what you meant."

"Please, young ones," Pauline intervened. "Let's have no quarrels or harsh words, today, yes? It is a day to celebrate and surround oneself with beauty and friendship."

"*Je suis désolé*, Madame Pauline!" Sébastien was instantly contrite, and leaned in to kiss Pauline and ask forgiveness, which was as promptly given.

The carriage rolled under the arched entranceway and into the cobblestoned courtyard, coming to a halt at the foot of the great staircase. The group stepped out of the carriage and stood looking up and around.

"Oh, my," Pauline said, eyeing the staircase. "I had forgotten how very many stairs there are here."

"Not to worry!" cried Maurice. As he spoke, two large men appeared from under the colonnade, carrying a small sedan chair between them. "*Madame*," he said, turning to Pauline, "your chair awaits. You will enter in the manner befitting such a great lady."

"*Merci, Maurice*," Pauline murmured, accepting his hand to help her into the chair.

She arrived at the top of the stairs without incident, though marvelling to herself at the situation, and stepped forward through the open door, held by the twins, who had run up before her, into the entrance hall of Chateau Boussac.

Her heart lifted when she looked up at the high windows, and around the panelled room which, even devoid of the furnishings she had known, brought back instantly so many memories, good and bad, of war and peace and drought, revolution and hard work. But it began to overwhelm her—she had thought that none of it could even touch her now, that she had come too far for mere feelings to make a mark. But she had mistaken the nature of her heart—it longed fiercely to be at home, and at peace, and the yearning grew in her.

"The Gallery?" she said, looking at Maurice, who had her arm in his.

"*Oui*, Pauline," he whispered.

"Look at François," Sébastien whispered to Geneviève. They were walking arm-in-arm, strolling about the Gallery while Maurice accompanied Pauline from tapestry to tapestry. She pointed to their cousin as he stood, rapt, in front of the tapestry of the Lady holding the gilded mirror, with the Unicorn resting its feet in her lap. "Do you suppose he's thinking about when he will come here as master of the Chateau, as he has informed us is his heritage?" She giggled.

"Shhh, someone will hear you!" Geneviève repressed her sister with a squeeze of her hand. "You don't want to distress *madame* Pauline, do you?"

"No, of course not," Sébastien said impatiently. "But really, don't you think she knows all about it anyway? It all happened so long ago, as Maurice has told us, and *grandmère* Julia too—*her* father and our *great-grandmère*, why, it all happened in a different century, didn't it?—you wouldn't think any of it would affect her now, one way or the other."

"Yes," Geneviève admitted slowly. "You wouldn't think so, but Maurice has always told us…." She trailed off, looking reproachfully at her sister.

Sébastien laughed. "You are such a good girl!" she said. She tossed her head, laughing and defiant. "I'm going to ask her!" Before Geneviève could stop her, her twin strolled rapidly to where Pauline was seated on a chair, alone—Maurice had walked off with François to look out a window—gazing up at the tapestry before her, the very one that had transfixed François some moments earlier. Sébastien came to stand at Pauline's side. The old woman raised a delicately veined hand, and pointed to the Lady holding the mirror.

"This was my grandmother's—and my father's—favorite tapestry of all of them," she said. "Mine, too." She fell silent, and Sébastien leaned down to whisper to her.

"Are you aware that I have been employed, *madame* Pauline, through *monsieur* Edmond Du Sommerard's interest in gaining the tapestries for his *musée* in Paris, in helping to research how to restore these priceless works of art?"

Pauline turned her eyes in wonder at her. "You? That is perfect," she said, squeezing the young woman's hand. "If you are involved, then I need not fear that these beauties will come to any harm." She seemed to be speaking from somewhere far away, another land or time.

Sébastien smiled at her. "I remember," she said, "when I was much younger, and we came here with Maurice and the wonderful Baronesse his mother, that we would scout around the house looking for treasure." She smiled a trifle sadly, and she and Pauline looked back at the tapestry.

"And did you find any, *ma chérie?*" asked Pauline, absent-mindedly, her head tilted a little as she contemplated the weaving before her. When Sébastien didn't answer, Pauline looked up at her and repeated her question. "Any treasures?"

Sébastien hesitated, then put her hand into her trouser pocket, drawing out a very small, dark blue velvet bag with a ribbon as a drawstring. She held it in the palm of her hand.

"One time, when we were in the attics—where the tapestries had been stored for a while, after you left here, and then they were re-discovered by Maurice's mother, and Prosper Mérimeé, of course you remember—one time, I was searching in the cracks in the floor, and found these." She looked at the velvet bag in her hand for a moment. "They seemed like something the fairies would leave behind," she murmured, then looked at Pauline. "I never told anyone about them, except Geneviève."

She opened the drawstring of the bag, and let fall the contents into her hand. A tiny, sparkling blue gem tumbled to a stop, and a slim strand of a tarnished bit of gold joined it. Pauline looked intently at these minuscule items, and sought hard for the memory that was just outside her reach—something she *knew*, but could not see it or name it now. She looked up at Sébastien, concerned. A great weight seemed all at once to press against her heart. She felt suddenly afraid, but then, just as suddenly her fear dissipated. *I am home,* she thought. *All will be well.*

"I do not know, my dear, what these mean, to me or to you," she whispered. "Something tugs at my memory, but I have no way to retrieve it. *Désolée,*" she said, and let her hands fall back to her lap in resignation. The pressure in her chest was increasing, and she began to breathe more heavily.

"Does it have anything to do with your royal heritage?" Sébastien burst out with the question, but in a low voice, and more urgently, as she saw Maurice slowly walking in their direction. "Or François? Isn't he, too, part of that royal line?"

A sudden perception flashed in Pauline's eyes. She saw it; saw what she had done, intertwining the woolen threads of the tapestry, hiding, hiding. Then it went dark, that old memory, just as quickly. She wasn't even sure it had actually happened.

Sébastien's hand was urgent on her shoulder, and she turned to the young woman with a gasp.

"Be the Unicorn, and look into the mirror." Her voice was a harsh whisper, and a wild joy filled her eyes. She slumped in her chair, and Sébastien knelt quickly to hold her up, crying out for Maurice who ran to them. Together they eased the woman onto the floor, with a pillow under her head, and her shawl wrapped around her. François and Geneviève came running, and the four friends knelt around this legendary woman whom they'd known all their lives, held her hands in theirs, and wept when she bade them farewell for the last time.

ℬ SEVEN ℬ

WEDNESDAY NIGHT
11-12 MAY 1881 – PARIS
Things Hidden Everywhere Come to Light

WE STOOD AGHAST WITH SURPRISE AND CHAGRIN as we walked further into the inner room, gazing up at the ropes from which the tapestry had lately hung.

"How could it be gone?" cried Claire Berthold. "I saw it there last night—how could anyone move it?"

"How could anyone have carried it out the door, without my men having seen it?" Charles said, exasperated.

"Maybe no one did," John said, and we turned to look at him. "Carry it out the door, I mean," he said. "What if it's stowed somewhere on the premises?" He looked at me for support. "It's *very* heavy."

"François—or whomever we're chasing—might have hidden it away to retrieve it later?" I said, liking the idea. I nodded, and saw that Charles was coming to the same conclusion. "We must search the *musée*," we said in unison. He turned to Claire Berthold.

"I must ask for your assistance, *mademoiselle*," he said. "You will please show us every hidden room, every closet, every sliding panel in the place." He looked at her, eyes narrowed. "Can you do this?"

I noticed Berthold had turned rather pale, but her voice was strong and defiant. "If I must," she said. I wondered at her reluctance, and was determined to keep a close eye on her.

Charles called additional men into the room and instructed them to search carefully for any clues "about anything" he told them testily, when they asked what they were to look for. Then he motioned for Berthold to lead the way. We were led through several rooms, many filled with remarkable *objets d'art*, paintings, artifacts and relics. In nearly every room, Berthold opened a panel that led to a hidden space, although none of them were large enough to contain the whole missing tapestry.

I began to question our search, after about an hour's going through the first and second floors. We stood at the top of a stairway, irritated and at a loss. A sudden thought struck me.

"Are there any hidden rooms that can be accessed from the room the tapestry was hanging in?" I had turned and addressed Claire Berthold directly. We had just simply left that room to begin our search—its four walls had looked, of course, reassuringly solid and immoveable.

Claire Berthold glared at me again, and bit her lip. But she didn't say anything.

"Let's just go and have a look, then," Charles said, taking her by the arm.

We made our way back down to the first floor, through the workroom and into the tapestry room. Berthold stood defiantly in the center of the room, carefully not looking at any one section of walls.

"What do we have here?" Charles demanded. "Tell us." I could see his instinct, like mine, had penetrated this woman's façade and he was looking at her in a very different light.

I began slowly strolling past each wooden panel in the walls, examining them up and down, pressing my hand here and there. John was doing much the same on a different wall. Claire Berthold stood solidly, unmoving, her arms crossed and her eyes down. She wasn't going to give anything away.

As I knocked on a certain panel that seemed a likely prospect, I pressed my ear against the wood, to discern perhaps the hollowness of a thinner panel, when to my shock, I heard a low moaning from the other side.

"Good Lord, there's someone in there!" I cried, and began quickly running my hands up and down the panel to see if I could find the spring. Recalling at last what I had seen Sébastien do when he had opened a similar door—was it less than a week ago?—I felt in the corner of the panel, at the top right, and found the lever that would do the trick.

I entered the hidden room gingerly, before Charles could stop me; it was rather small, with only two dirty windows high up in the wall to shed any light on the dusty, small enclosure. There was a great lump of something in the middle, but it was too dim to discern it properly.

"John, a light! A light, please!" I called back through the doorway; I had stepped inside a few paces, gingerly.

John and Charles both arrived with lanterns at the same moment; Claire Berthold was right behind them, her eyes wide with surprise. The four of us stepped into the room, the men holding the lights high.

There, lying on top of the rolled and rumpled tapestry, his arms embracing it, was François de Carbonnières. I rushed to him, and knelt down. Looking back, I noticed the astounded look on Berthold's face.

"He is alive and…." I looked carefully at his head and arms, "and unhurt! He has no visible injuries," I said. His eyes were glazed over, as if delirious, and he was mumbling words in French I could not make out, although "la licorne" was repeated several times. *That* I understood.

John knelt down next to me, putting the lantern on the floor. "François," he said, his voice low and soothing. "François, are you all right? François!" Something in the tone or timbre of John's voice seemed to reach the man, and he slowly ceased his mumbling; a clearer light seemed to settle in his eyes, and he at last looked upon us with intelligence.

"What has happened?" he asked us, much to our bewilderment.

"You do not know?" I said.

"He's the one, you all can see it," cried Claire Berthold, pointing to him with a shaking hand, her voice high with passion. "He attacked Edmond, be sure of it—see, he is trying to steal the tapestry too, all because of that stupid, treacherous…" She stopped herself abruptly, and turned away. Charles stood between her and the door, however, and she came to a halt in front of him.

John looked at François, troubled. "Can you stand? Are you injured in any way?" François seemed to be thinking it over, then shook his head. "I am fine," he said. "I am not injured." John helped him, and me, to rise to a standing position, and dusted him off. François looked around himself in wonder. "Where am I? What am I doing here?" He looked down at the tapestry lying crumpled at his feet. "Why is the tapestry here?"

Charles and I and John all exchanged long, puzzled looks. Was the man deceiving us, playing a part? Had he been struck with sudden amnesia—I had heard of it happening—and truly knew nothing of himself or the place?

"He is lying," snapped Berthold, looking at François. "Can't you see, he's the one! He's the murderer! He clearly was after the tapestry, and that little, that cousin of his got in his way, so he committed murder, and he attacked Edmond for the same reason!" She sneered at him. "Perverts, all of you, dressing up and carrying on like children in a Christmas theatrical! And she thought no one could tell!" Berthold looked at me, saw me staring (almost open-mouthed, I'm sorry to say) and drew herself up short, as if she suddenly remembered who was listening, and what she was saying. There was a small, almost triumphant smile on her face, and it made me very suspicious. A sudden thought hit like lightning in my brain.

"We should check *this* room for another hidden panel," I said abruptly, and watched as Berthold's face took on a look of fear, and loathing, directed at me. Her eyes quickly glanced to her right, and she looked back just as quickly.

"There is no hidden space in here," she said, her voice hard, but wary.

"Oh, isn't there?" I said. I walked over to the place near her at which she had inadvertently glanced; I felt around the panel, and my fingers caught at yet another lever.

With a desperate cry, Berthold slammed into me, throwing me against the wall, and attempted to push Charles away from the door to effect her escape, but he was too strong for her, and subdued her in an iron grip. He nodded to me to proceed.

I opened the door to a narrow but long closet, about a foot in depth and six feet across.

Standing directly in front of me was the visage of the youthful St. Sebastian, his painted face an ecstasy of martyrdom, his white flesh gleaming even in the dark of the closet—the missing Titian, and lying on the floor at its foot, a quiver of ancient date, with only two arrows in it.

A low cry was wrung from Berthold's lips as she sank out of Charles' grip, sobbing, onto the floor.

I looked over to see François standing like a lost soul, watching the spectacle of the weeping woman, his hand clenched tightly around a bit of cloth.

It all clicked inside my brain at that moment. François was innocent—of all but a sad, obsessive desire for proof of royal blood, although he did likely attack Du Sommerard. Claire was the murderer of Sébastien—and also the "thief" of the Titian.

I looked at Charles and John, and they both nodded, slowly. An officer appeared, tentatively, at the door to the room, and Charles, with a few words spoken low, had him take Claire Berthold into custody.

Walking over to François, I smiled at him, as one would a slow child, and he offered me what he had in his hand, wrapped in a handkerchief. Curious, I opened it: a tiny red gem, and what looked like a bit of painted enamel; it was too dim and too small to see what had been painted on it.

I looked at him, a question in my eyes, but his were closed, and he was smiling.

Over the next three hours, in Charles' office, in the interrogation rooms, we were able to piece together the shards of this tale of obsession and desire, jealousy and love, chance and fate and just plain bad luck.

Claire Berthold, jealous and angry at what she perceived as a "special" relationship between the man she loved unrequitedly, Edmond Du Sommerard, and Sébastien, who had fooled the older man as to her gender, plotted her revenge against both of them.

"I discovered the truth about that lying wench," she told Charles, who had allowed me and John to sit quietly in the interrogation room.

"I heard them talking, those twins, when they didn't know I was nearby," the woman continued. Her voice was a monotone, and only occasionally flared into indignation or anger. "To think she would try to fool everyone into believing her to be a young man," she said, then shrugged. "Edmond is an old fool, and saw what he wanted to see." Her face twisted with a pitiful mix of disgust and yearning. "But I couldn't see him disgraced and made ridiculous by such a thing."

She looked over at me, pure hatred in her eyes, then looked back down at the table where she sat. John took my hand in his and pressed it reassuringly.

"What happened that night, in the workshop?" Charles asked when she continued to be silent. "How did you know Sébastien would even be there, so late?"

Berthold smirked. "I sent him a note, as from Edmond, demanding he go to the *musée* to check on something in the workroom, and I waited for him there—*her,* I mean," she added spitefully. She took a deep breath, and passed her hand over her face. Despite myself, I was shocked and sorry at her appearance—she seemed to have aged twenty years since earlier in the evening. I glanced at the clock and saw it was past two in the morning—Thursday morning, I thought idly—and tomorrow I go to London. I pulled my attention back to the cold, airless room as Berthold spoke again.

"I confronted *la salope*," she said crudely. "She laughed at me, laughed! And said Edmond deserved to be disgraced—and any number of horrible things," she said, growing angry at the memory. She looked straight at Charles, then at me. "I grabbed her by the neck—she wasn't very strong, really—and just kept squeezing until she was no longer laughing—what else could I have done?" Berthold shrugged, indifferent and uncaring.

Charles was silent a moment, then said, "And the Titian? The staging of the death scene?" I felt John stir at the mention of the painting he had found so interesting, and we exchanged quick looks.

She actually smiled at his question, seemingly proud of her cleverness. "That was, I must say for myself, a brilliant bit of on-the-spot contrivance, don't you think?" She shot a contemptuous look at him. "Edmond had told me what the *gendarmes* told him, about the art thief and the previous murder, how the victim was dressed as in the painting, so I quickly arranged that stupid girl's body as the saint whose name she was dishonoring, may she burn in hell."

John made a sound like a low growl, and he tensed as if about to leap, but I spoke up first; I couldn't help myself. "And it would be an added revenge to have Du Sommerard charged with 'stealing' the painting for his own gain, perhaps, after you would arrange for it to be 'found'?"

She answered calmly enough, at first. "Edmond is a fool, both for ignoring the one who loved him, and drooling after one who held him in contempt—and who deceived him utterly!" Then her anger got the better of her, and she nearly spat at me. "You think you're so clever, miss show-off, with your airs and your pathetic attempt to look important!"

"And yet," Charles interrupted, bringing her back to order, "she is the one who discovered your scheme." He looked over at me, admiration in his shining blue eyes. "Clever, indeed." He looked back at his prisoner. "We shall have this written down, and you shall sign your confession in due time."

He nodded to the sergeant who stood post at the door. "Take her to the women's prison," he said. "We're finished here." He glared at Berthold. "For now."

She rose when the sergeant approached her, tried to shake off his hand on her arm and failed, then gave up, walking submissively out the door.

I let out a long breath, one I hadn't realized I had been keeping back, and rose from my chair, holding on to John's arm, for strength and for friendship. We smiled at each other, and sighed, as Charles also stood up; walking over to me, he took my hand gently in his, and bestowed a kiss on the back of it. He then shook John's hand most heartily, and the two men embraced as brothers.

"Once again, my dear Violet, my dear John," he said, smiling at us both, "I am indebted to your genius and your perseverance in bringing this case to a satisfactory close."

John was grinning, and I tried to laugh off my share of the compliment. "My insatiable, impolitic curiosity, rather, and dogged interference in matters that don't concern me! You are very indulgent and forgiving, Charles."

He regarded me with what I could easily see was true affection. "If only my organization would hire female agents—you would rise to the station of *capitaine* within weeks!"

I shook my head, although delighted at the thought.

John spoke up. "But what about your Revenant, Charles? Are you not discouraged that the Titian—real or fake—was not the object of your art thief this time? What will you do about him now?"

Charles smiled ruefully. "We have word that he has struck again, in New York City!" He looked at us sideways. "Anyone interested in a little sea voyage?"

I laughed. "I have more pressing business to attend to, in London. But I'm sure John would be happy to give you a letter of introduction, as he has friends and relatives there by the dozens." John readily assented.

"And I hope you know," I added more seriously, "that, as John and I have sworn to each other, we will come whenever you call, and do our best to assist you."

We all shook hands, then, and walked out the best of friends.

Thursday, 12 May 1881

The next day, for me, was filled with the bustle of packing and making final arrangements to transport myself from Paris to Calais, then across the Channel to Dover, then to London—at last! Mary Robinson (whose family had a good deal more money than mine) had sent three telegrams in twenty-four hours, anxious for confirmation that I was indeed coming on Friday. It made me wonder if I had exhibited flighty tendencies previously, or if she didn't think I would keep my engagement? But I put it down to simple anticipation on her part, wishing me closer to being there through the telegraphic communications. I answered her three with one: Never Fear. STOP. Arriving 5 pm ChCr. STOP. Much love VP.

I knew she would be waiting at the entrance to Charing Cross station, and smiled to think of the fervent embraces we would exchange.

John had sent a note in the early afternoon, asking if I would come to dinner with him and his family—he had important news. I could easily guess it had to do with the Salon. Thinking of dining with the Sargent family reminded me that Emily was still ignorant of the true nature—that is, gender—of the Sébastien she had begun to have tender feelings for. John and I had previously decided that it might be best for her never to know the truth, but somehow that rang false to me—truth should be seen as a fortifier, not a destroyer; a shield and support, without which one relinquishes control over one's own self, one's character. I believed we ought to trust Emily's maturity and understanding to hear this truth without damage to her mind or her heart.

I had arrived at John's apartment early, and managed to commandeer the library for a short discussion with him. He was in high spirits, but declared he wouldn't tell me the news until we were all gathered at dinner.

"All right, then," I said, pleased for him. We spoke for a few moments about the revelations of the past few days, both agreeing that most of all, we were relieved that it was all settled at last. I had a moment's thought to ask him about his actor friend, "David" and how the gentlemen of *L'Ordre de la Licorne*, were faring, but decided it was, after all, really none of my business.

"I had a note from Charles late this morning," I said. "Edmond Du Sommerard awoke last night, and the doctor said he will be just fine. Charles went to question him, told him about how we found François, and du Sommerard there and then declared he would not press any charges against the younger man—that clearly he was delirious, or something, and Du Sommerard does not want any more scandal to attach to the *musée*." I nearly snorted in disgust. "And he confessed that he had begun to suspect Claire Berthold, especially when we started asking about those arrows, and he realized later they were missing from the workshop—in addition to her increasingly odd behavior about Sébastien in the previous weeks."

John shook his head. "If only he'd said something earlier...." He paused a moment, then, looking away, said softly, "My friend—*David*—and he has become a friend now—I'm not sure how I'll be able to tell him about all this."

I moved closer to John and put a hand on his arm. "Your friendship will be a great comfort to him, I have no doubt," I said. "And you always know the right thing to say, John."

He smiled gratefully, and blinked away a tear. I moved away, to give him time to compose himself.

"But there is one more thing," I said, and saw him look wary.

"There's always one more thing with you, Vi," he said, but with half a smile that took the sting from his words.

I smiled back. "I think Emily deserves to know the truth."

He frowned, but as if thoughtfully rather than disap-provingly. "I've been thinking that myself," he said, and pulled at his beard. "She's been so melancholy, unlike her-self," he said. "Perhaps such knowledge would change her perspective?"

I nodded. "Can we talk to her now, here, before we go into dinner?"

He agreed, and left the room to fetch his sister.

You could have knocked both of us over with a feather, when we heard Emily's response to our revelation.

"Yes, I know," she said, looking down at her hands in her lap, then looking up at us, sad but just a bit mischievous. "But I promised not to tell! And even though I imagined the truth would come out, with the…autopsy, and all that…well, then you both went away, and there was no time to talk about it." She looked up, guiltily. "Should I have said?" She dabbed at her eyes with a handkerchief. "I did so enjoy her company."

"Not if you promised, no," said John quickly, glancing at me. "It didn't make any material difference, I don't think. We found out late the next day."

"Of course you had to keep your word," I said.

We all sat there in the library, silent for a few moments together. Then Emily spoke again.

"Has that friend of yours, that agent, Charles—has he found the murderer?"

I looked at John, a question in my eyes; he nodded, so I proceeded to give Emily a much abbreviated account of the murder and who had done it. She was aghast.

"Miss Berthold? Really? I never would have imagined! And *monsieur* Du Sommerard? Will he be all right? Who is this François person any way?"

I assured her that Du Sommerard would fully recover, and related a brief account of François de Carbonierres.

"But what was it about the tapestry that this François was so obsessed with?" Emily asked, and it gave me pause.

"I've been thinking about that," I said, mulling over how to put it.

John looked at me with a sly smile, and he spoke before I could. "It has to do with the little red gem, and the bits of gold and enamel, doesn't it? That François had in his hand?"

I looked at him in amazement. "I didn't realize you had seen that," I said, smiling. "But you're right."

"I remembered what Maurice Sand told us, the other night in Nohant," he said. He looked at me archly.

"About the proofs of François' royal heritage," I said. "Yes, the possible signet ring or brooch or something."

"And you think the gemstones, the gold shards," he continued, "could be part of a brooch, that somehow, some long time ago, was concealed in the tapestry, and then broke apart when they were moved?"

I nodded slowly. "That's exactly what I'm thinking." I looked at him keenly. "You saw François' smile as he looked at those poor bits of some long-dead past? I hope he will remain satisfied with only that, and go back to Boussac quietly."

John nodded, and glanced at Emily, who sat looking from me to her brother, and back again.

"But the tapestry," she said, "The Lady and the Unicorn, they're all right? They weren't hurt?"

It amused me to hear her speak of them as beings, and not just a woven piece of art.

"They are fine," I assured her. "But whatever secrets they may have held to themselves, we will never know." I sighed deeply, and stood up to go in to dinner; it was time to bring this case to an end. Tomorrow beckoned, but tonight, with friends and family around the dinner table, we could put aside thoughts of murder, obsession, and secrecy, and immerse ourselves in love and friendship—and hear about John's having won a second place at this year's Salon, for his marvelous portrait of Madame Subercaseux, and also now being designated *hors de concours*, which meant he could exhibit automatically, without submitting his paintings first to be accepted.

A celebration indeed!

❉ EPILOGUE ❉

I MADE IT TO LONDON ON THE FRIDAY, but in such a whirl of thoughts and feelings from the events of that week that I confess I was quite abstracted and vague in company for the first few days. Mary noticed my distraction, but forebore with an angelic patience to reproach me, which only made me love her more.

There were gathered in my mind the interesting and unusual individuals whom I had met on this short journey—Geneviève and poor Sébastien, her *tante* Eugenie, Maurice Sand, François de Carbonnières. And above all of them, I seemed to see, as the Testament has it, "clouds of witness" stretching back centuries—two in particular: George Sand, who had clearly marked her son, for good or ill, with her brilliance, her independence, her deep love, and her own remarkable ancestry; and Pauline de Carbonnières, about whom I learned much after the fact, in letters from Eugenie Bayard, who had known her and admired the long-lived woman from an earlier century who had seen and endured so much.

But, as always, the change of place and companions worked their magic upon my reveries, and I was soon busy and happy, writing every day with Mary and comparing our scribbles with joy and insight, and making the rounds of the brilliant and often comically entertaining *salons* of the London *literati* and the celebrated artists and bohemians of the day.

I shall tell you, dear Reader, all about them, in my next recounting of a mystery, one in which my dear friend John Sargent had a prominent role, after his retreat to England following the debacle of the infamous Madame X, you may have heard of that?

I believe I shall title it, "Carnation, Lily, Lily, Rose: A Domestic Mystery" and when you read it, you shall see why.

Violet Paget
Il Palmerino
Fiesole, Italy – 1928

End Notes

Characters Fictional and Real

Of course, John Sargent and Violet Paget are real histor-ical people, as is Edmond du Sommerard, the first direc-tor of the Musée de Cluny. Incidental famous persons—Chopin, Mérimée, all the French kings and queens, etc.—are real, as are Sargent's family members. Charles Wilkinson is a fictional character who first appeared in *The Love for Three Oranges*, the second mystery, set in Venice. All smaller roles are fictional characters. See be-low for more detail on the real people who lived in Cha-teau Boussac.

Tracing the **LesVistes** Family to **de Rilhacs**
to **de Carbonnières** and *Bayards*

BOLD = Real people in history
Italic = Fictional characters/names

1500	**Les Vistes Family** -14-16th centuries – in Lyons, commissioned Unicorn tapestries: 1480-1500
1660	**Geoffroi de la Roche-Aynon** (descendant of Les Vistes) married **Madeleine de Rilhac** 1660 (both were previously married, widowed)
	Their adult children, **Jeanne de la Roche-Aynon** and **François de Rilhac** also married in 1660, moved from Lyons to Boussac, deRilhac family seat, bringing the tapestries with them.
1704-1711	**Jeanne & François** had a **son**, who married, & had a daughter: **Louise de Rilhac,** b. 1704 d. 1792
	King Louis XIV & **Maria Theresa had son: Louis XV,** b. 1711 d. 1774
1738-1739	**Louise** & **Louis XV** *had a son François Georges Louis de Carbonnières, b. March 1739 d. 1808* **Louise** *marries Georges de Carbonnières (a cousin) in 1734, d. 1754*

1775- 1793	*François* **de Carbonnières of Boussac** marries *Marguerite 1775 (she dies 1785 giving birth)* Children: *Louis Francois, b. 1776, d. 1788* **Pauline Marie,** *b. 1785, d. 1876* *François has a liaison w/Georgette, she marries* *Jean des Rosier, has François' son Jean François* *des Rosier in 1793; Georgette & husband Jean* *have a daughter, Marie, who marries Raymond* *Simon, moves to Nohant, has a daughter Julia,* *who marries Michel Bayard; their son Jules mar-* *ries and is the father of the twins Genevieve and* *Aurora/Sébastien (b. 1854)*
1814 -1847	*J-F des Rosier marries in 1814, has a son J-F des* *Rosier II in 1822 (grandson of Georgette)* *J-F desRosier II marries in 1846, has a son* *François des Rosier (de Carbonnières) in 1847—* *he is the "cousin" to the twins.*

George Sand's Family

1748 -
1804

Marie-Aurore de Saxe Dupin (Countess), grandmother of George Sand, b. 1748, d. 1821

- Her son: **Maurice de Saxe Dupin** (George
  Sand's father), b. 1778, d. 1808
- He marries **Sophie-Victoire** (b. 1773, d.
  1837) in 1804 (she has two children al-
  ready)
- Their daughter **Amantine Aurore (George
  Sand)** is born 1804, d. 1876

1804
-1876

Amantine Aurore Dupin (George Sand)
b. 1804, d. 1876
Married **Count Casimir Dudevant** 1822,
divorced 1837

- **Son Maurice Dupin** (later known as Maurice
  Sand), b. 1823, d. 1899
- **Daughter Solange Dupin**, b. 1828, d. 1899

Bibliography

Letters of George Sand, Vol. I. Translated by Raphael Ledos de Beaufort, originally published London, 1886; republished 2009 by Cosimo Classics.

Story of My Life: The Autobiography of George Sand. A Group Translation edited by Thelma Jurgrau, State University of New York Press, 1991.

Colby, Vineta. *Vernon Lee: A Literary Biography*, (Charlottesville and London: University of Virginia Press, 2003)

Gunn, Peter. *Vernon Lee/Violet Paget* (London: Oxford University Press, 1964).

Lyall, Sutherland. *The Lady and the Unicorn,* (London, England: Parkstone Press Limited, 2000).

Internet Resources – I am grateful for all the incredible information to be found on the internet, and would especially like to call out my appreciation for the following:

WIKIPEDIA for everything from the French Revolution timeline, the availability of trains from Paris to Nohant, life of George Sand and her family, to what the weather was like in 1779!
www.jssgallery.org – A complete gallery of Sargent paintings and timelines of his travels.
Visit the **Musée de Cluny** (*Musée du Moyen Âge*) at https://www.musee-moyenage.fr/ and take a look at the tapestries in detail.

If you enjoyed *The Unicorn in the Mirror,* we hope you will review it on Amazon or Goodreads!

Other books by Mary F. Burns

Portraits of an Artist:
A Novel about John Singer Sargent

The Spoils of Avalon – Book One
of the Sargent/Paget Mysteries

The Love for Three Oranges – Book Two
of the Sargent/Paget Mysteries

Isaac and Ishmael: A Novel of Genesis

J-The Woman Who Wrote the Bible

Ember Days

To see book trailers, contact the author, and order these books, please visit the author's website at
www.maryfburns.com